BARBACOA
erik orrantia

Dreamspinner Press

Published by
DREAMSPINNER PRESS

5032 Capital Circle SW, Suite 2, PMB# 279, Tallahassee, FL 32305-7886 USA
http://www.dreamspinnerpress.com/

Barbacoa
© 2014 Erik Orrantia.

Cover Art
© 2014 AngstyG.
www.angstyg.com.
Cover content is for illustrative purposes only and any person depicted on the cover is a model.

ISBN: 978-1-63216-119-2
Digital ISBN: 978-1-63216-120-8
Library of Congress Control Number: 2014945898
First Edition October 2014

Printed in the United States of America
∞
This paper meets the requirements of
ANSI/NISO Z39.48-1992 (Permanence of Paper).

To my husband, Francisco Orrantia, who lends his enthusiastic ear and keeps me young when I forget and take life too seriously.

And a special thank you to my readers, Jerry, Michael, and Alan, whose friendship, encouragement, and hard work made this endeavor possible.

Glossary of Aztec Terms

Atlcaualo	The first month of the Aztec year, meaning stopping of the water
Auianime	A courtesan
Axolotl	A newt, considered a delicacy by the Aztecs
Chinampa	A plot of land, primarily used for agriculture, created in the shallow regions of a lake with landfill
cihuatlanque	A sort of matchmaker or go-between who would help to arrange marriages
Ciuacoatl	The vice-emperor, supreme judge in martial and criminal law; literally woman-serpent, the name of a goddess
Cuepopán	One quarter of Tenochtitlán, the elite district, literally meaning the place of the blossoming flowers
cuicacalco	The house of singing and dancing in which young men were allowed to enjoy and unwind after their duties
Etzalqualiztli	The sixth month of the Aztec calendar, the month of maize and beans
macquauitl	Wooden swords used for combat practice
mecatlan	Musicians school
mestizo	A person of mixed race, typically Mexican indigenous and Spaniard
metzli	The moon
Motecuhzoma	A leader of the Aztec people, sometimes mistakenly written Moctezuma or Montezuma
Moyotlán	One quarter of Tenochtitlán, a poor section, literally meaning the place of the mosquitoes
octli	An alcoholic drink made from cactus, largely forbidden by the Aztec society
patolli	An Aztec game of chance, not unlike craps, played with painted beans

pelota	A game played between two teams in which a leather ball was attempted to be launched through vertical stone rings without the use of hands
piochtli	A man's lock of hair allowed to be cut off after a number of accomplishments in battle
pochteca	Aztec merchant class, a higher echelon of Aztec society
pozole	A water-based soup consisting of hominy, spices, and pork or other meat
quachic	A title bestowed to a warrior who had taken or killed five or more of the enemy; literally, a soldier of the sun
quachtli	Twenty pieces of cotton cloth used as a medium of exchange
Quetzalcoatl	Aztec god of priests
telpolchcalli	The house of the young men, an Aztec school designed for producing ordinary citizens in contrast to the stricter calmecac, tied to a temple, whose pupils were the children of dignitaries
temazcalli	A domed room in the shape of an igloo used for as a steam bath
Tenochtitlán	The heart of the Aztec empire where modern day Mexico City is located
Teopán	One quarter of Tenochtitlán, the quartile of the gods, where the imperial palace was found and the homes of the nobles
Teotihuacán	A large pre-Columbian Mesoamerican city dating back to 100 BC in the Valley of Mexico, about 30 miles from Mexico City
tequiua	A title bestowed to a warrior who had taken or killed four of the enemy; a tequiua was entitled to a share of the tribute
tlachtli	The I-shaped court in which the *pelota* game was played
Tlaloc	The Aztec god of rain
tlamacaztequiuaque	Warrior priest

tlapizque	An Aztec musician
Tlatelolco	The great market of Tenochtitlán
tlatoani	Supreme ruler
Tlaxochimaco	The ninth month on the Aztec calendar, the month of drum beat and dance
Tlazolteotl	Aztec god of carnal love and confession
tochti	Rabbit, also refers to the rabbit image seen in the moon
tzictli	Chewing gum from the Chicozapote tree
Uitzilopochtli	Aztec god of war, considered their most powerful deity
Xochipilli	Aztec god of music, pleasure, and games
xoloitzcuitli	A hairless breed of dog native to Mexico
Yacatecuhtli	Aztec god of merchants

Chapter One

RAIN PATTERED against the blue plastic tarp over Diego's worktable. Another gray day in Tenochtitlán. He pored over the maps again, having scanned them into his memory weeks before. He hadn't calculated so many rainy days into the grant projections, and he hoped the paltry funds would last for the time he and his team would need to complete the dig. Since his first childhood fieldtrip to the pyramids of Teotihuacán, he had been inspired to uncover the ruins of the Aztecs, a magnificent culture cut short by the pillaging of Hernán Cortés and the rest of the Spanish conquistadors. Buried beneath the dirt lay history and answers. Every mound or hill could be another lost temple. Every stone might have been carried by an ancestor. What would have become of the flourishing empire if it hadn't met with guns, metal armor, horses, and smallpox? He flipped the map over, accidentally tearing the damp, worn paper at its crease, and hoped that soon he and his team would be back in the soil at the dig, or the mud anyway.

"Professor. Come quick!" shouted an intern from below. Diego pushed his glasses up on his nose and sat up in his folding chair to see where she stood at the bottom of the stone stairs, waving her arms excitedly. "Come quick. You've got to see."

The huge smile on her face kept him from even donning his raincoat. It was his first field project in several years, and since they'd uncovered the small temple, they'd hardly found anything else. He had been afraid that he would be embarrassed in the archaeological community. *Patience.* He and all of his colleagues preached patience. But who didn't wish for the next big find? And his relatively young career being his primary focus in life—his *only* focus in life—such a flop would surely send him into a depression.

He rushed down the thirteen steep steps from his makeshift headquarters in the small dank room on top of the temple, the only stable structure around. One of thousands of ancient temples throughout Mexico, it unfortunately added little to the modern understanding of the Aztecs or any of the other pre-Hispanic civilizations. "Well, what is it?" he shouted, despite his otherwise dreary mood.

"Just come see...." She waited for him at the bottom and led him past a courtyard marked with stakes, yellow ribbon, and a complex of broken walls. He'd thought his team had gone off to town, but there they stood, eight of them in all, in a semicircle around a murky puddle that had formed in the dark, solidified clay.

"What is it?" he asked again, looking into the water like a witch into her brew.

The head assistant, Gerardo, stepped closer to it, grabbing the hands of the others for balance and watching the professor's expression. He dipped a booted foot into the brown water and swept it across the surface.

Diego saw nothing. Was it another prank? He could hardly blame them for trying to break the monotony once in a while, especially considering their low wages and stipends. They'd almost be better off in a factory or at a taco stand. But many shared his passion for the past and his curiosity for clues to all that was and all that might have been. "Ha-ha. Very funny. I don't see anything." He ran his fingers through his wavy black hair and began turning around to head back to his perch on the temple.

"No, really. Do it again, Gerardo," someone said.

Again Gerardo pushed the water from one side to the other with his boot, a boyish look of happy anticipation coming over the five o'clock shadow on his brown face. This time instead of brown sludge, Diego made out a round, white shape, and then another only a step away. Craniums. Telltale human eye sockets. At last.

He tried to get some words to come out of his mouth, but the adrenaline blocked any clear thoughts and dammed his speech. He put his hands up as if to settle the team and finally managed to say something. "Don't touch anything."

Now, if only the rain would stop.

Chapter Two

QUETZAZOZTLI FELT a dark premonition. The corn had tasted bitter, and a red ant had bitten her on the calf. She looked down at her stomach, swollen like a gourd. She had hoped the pulses would start before the end of the eighteenth month of the year so that her child would not be born during the five hollow days before the beginning of the new year. Or, gods willing, the child's birth might have waited until after the empty, cursed days. Yet just as her fellow citizens enclosed themselves behind their stone walls and wooden doors, the movements began and the babe descended.

The midwife lit the incense and began to quietly sing the prayer of childbirth.

> *We sing here*
> *Delight for the sun*
> *Above the highest mountain*

> *We sing here*
> *To the brave warrior-woman*
> *And the budding flower*

The old woman knew better than to sing loudly and pronounce to all that the new one was coming on this unfortunate morning. Yet the gods had decided. She clapped her hands softly as she circled the room and the mat where Quetzazoztli lay. Sweat was beginning to bead upon her brow. She clenched her teeth and restrained her moans behind pressed lips.

> *We sing here*
> *To a new heart and new blood*
> *A welcome song*

Quetzazoztli had taken great care not to look at red things while her belly grew. She had worn loose clothing and stayed indoors at night. She hadn't eaten beetles. She'd pierced her tongue thrice. Nevertheless, what the gods desired must come to pass. And at the end of a long morning, when even the birds remained silent, the baby was born in a puddle of blood, and he cried loudly—to the chagrin of his mother.

She heard her husband pacing outside the door. She saw him peer inside, as if he were wondering if she was still alive, or if she would join the fallen warriors who followed for eternity in the path of the sun. Quetza held the baby in a cloth and showed her husband its face. "A boy-child," she said. She expected to see him smile at what would be the last of many children, but they had been worried about this omen, and all he did was stand in the doorway and look at it from a distance, massaging his brow.

> *We sing here*
> *To welcome the sunrise*
> *And life like purest jade*
>
> *We sing here*
> *Where you are now among us*
> *Where your parents live in toil*
>
> *We sing here*
> *Not knowing your destiny*
> *Blind to your fate*
> *But we welcome you*

Quetza would wait till the new month, *Atlcaualo*, stopping of the water, before welcoming him to the social order or taking the unnamed boy to the priest. Children would be sacrificed to Tlaloc, the rain god, during these twenty days. Life required death. Not her baby, though. She kept him close to her and had the midwife surround him each day with fresh flowers from the rooftop garden. Let the captured children or the slave children, for whom tribute was paid—baskets of corn or fattened turkeys and dogs or an entire *quachtli*, twenty large pieces of cotton cloth—have their chests split on the temple stones and their blood spilt on the stairs of rock.

As the boy-child suckled with a vigor she had not seen in any of her other children, he gazed at her in wonder, and his tiny lips seemed to form a grateful smile. She skipped the traditional feast, knowing that relatives and friends would be hesitant to come during the hollow days, but she did prepare for the child—that he might be a great warrior—a miniature bow and tiny arrows to bury along with his birthing cord.

Despite her initial fear, a new premonition began to fill her bosom. This child was different. He would be a great merchant like his father, traveling far and scouting new lands. Or maybe a powerful warrior, even a jaguar-knight or an eagle-knight. And perhaps a father of many children. He would repay the gods for their benevolence.

She gathered payment for the priest—her best quachtli, the finest cotton cloth with the most exquisite embroidery and bright feathers woven into it—so he might sense in her child the same greatness she sensed. The old woman accompanied her to the priest's dwelling in their quarter of Tenochtitlán, toward the right-hand side of the world— Cuepopán, the place of the blossoming flowers. When they arrived at the abode, she agreed to wait for Quetza outside. As the first light of dawn appeared over the horizon, Quetza stepped inside, as she had done with each of her other children. But none of the others had been born in the hollow days.

The tall man came out from a hallway in his home, the grooves in his aging face much deeper than when he had named her first child. His cape was such a dark green that it appeared black in the shadow of the room. As he turned, Quetza noticed a white skull embroidered on it. He donned a red wooden mask that had been hanging on the wall, with brown feathers standing straight up on the top of it, and a long tongue jutting out from between pointed white teeth. He tapped two sticks together rhythmically and then held out his hands. She handed the baby to him.

He put a hand on its face as if to read the infant's soul. Then he pulled back the cloth to its groin. Next he inspected its belly where its cord had been severed. He groaned, peered at her through the eyeholes of the mask, and said in a gruff voice, "This is no newborn. His belly is nearly healed."

She did not quaver. Instead, she tilted her head to one side and took the pearl earring from first one ear and then the other. She stepped toward where she had set the quachtli and placed the magnificent, iridescent pearls on top of them. "No. But he is not of the ordinary world."

He looked at the pearls and back at the baby in his arms. He then laid it down on a mat on the floor in the middle of the room, disappeared into back room and returned with a clay pot. The lidless vessel held dried kernels of yellow and purple corn. These he flung around the baby on the mat. He knelt to interpret them as they had fallen. She whispered a prayer.

He took the red mask off, set it beside the mat, and rose.

"What?" she asked desperately. "What do you see?"

He put up his hand to silence her. "Nothing," he said. "Wait." He walked to the door and went out to the street. In a moment he returned.

"Your baby was not born under a favorable sign," he said with gravity. He looked down again at the pearls and cotton capes before lifting his head. "But there is another sign in this series, in the divinatory calendar. Seven *tochti* of the Four Hundred Rabbits, a decent date, and a definite sign of abundance. And look outside. Can you not see? Both the sun and the moon are watching. I was at first confused, but then I saw the rabbit's face in the moon, and I am certain. You are right. Not of the ordinary world, rather a boy-child of two worlds. And he shall be named Metzín, for the tender, respected moon that has come to welcome him."

When she took the child Metzín in her arms, the baby smiled again at her, his black eyes round like those of a rabbit. She returned home and ordered the servants to prepare a feast for her child of two worlds, her child of abundance. The all-knowing gods had destined him for humility and greatness.

Twenty Years Later

THEY HAD traveled for many passings of the sun, far from Tenochtitlán, to the far reaches of the left side of the world, where the reborn warriors would appear as hummingbirds to fill their sunlit hours with songs of war and flit from flower to flower. Here water flowed freely in streams and poured from the steep mountains of soft earth covered with tall palms and buzzing with shiny black insects. The growls and clicks of spirits and demons lurking beyond the yellow glow of the fire filled the black jungle sky at night. This was a savage place. And they were among savage people.

Metzín waited out of hearing distance from his father, whose soiled cloak and long hair must have made him appear as barbarous as this strange tribe they had encountered. Aside from their small temple, little more than a shrine, they had not a single stone building, but rather huts of leaves and sticks and fronds, and several of their men stood in a half circle around his father, talking to each other in what seemed like grunts and coughing noises. Metzín could barely distinguish the leader from the others, save for his loudness and white whiskers, for they all wore the same coarse skirt below bellies swollen like those of pregnant dogs. Even the women's bare breasts hung like the flat, flaccid tits of bitches.

The thick black hair of the savages was cut short and round, making them appear as if they wore charred coconut halves on their heads. Some wore necklaces of shells and bones, or triangular fish teeth, though they also had skill with gold whose flakes Metzín guessed they gathered in the nearby streams. A shorter man, who wore glimmering, golden shapes on his ears and whose chest sagged like the women's, kept glancing in all directions, as if he worried that an attack party would pounce at any moment. But Metzín knew his father came in peace, intending to negotiate fairly like the proper merchant he was.

The short man pulled on the shoulder of the old, loud one, coughing more words into his ear. Though Metzín could only imagine what he was saying, the sounds seemed less than friendly. He lifted his gaze to the immense wall of rock that surrounded them, a sheer cliff that could serve to both protect and blind this village. A group of warriors could gather on top and these wild people would never know, unless they had warriors posted in the woods. Judging by the simple appearance of these people, he doubted they were that sophisticated, and figured they spent most of their time foraging, hunting, and digging for food. Anyway, if Uitzilopochtli would require their blood, he would decide that in his time. If the great Aztec empire of Tenochtitlán were meant to extend its reaches this far to the left of the world, then no one—not Metzín's father, nor the emperor, nor these pitiful people— would stand a chance against that most powerful god.

Finally his father leaned in toward the old man and the two clutched forearms—the men had come to an agreement. *And in good time*, Metzín thought, his stomach growling. The somber faces of the elders brightened, and Metzín's father smiled at the men of the village before signaling for the porters to bring wares, and for him and his brothers and the other merchants to approach.

Metzín's father called for his books of agave paper and colored inks to begin the laborious process of recordkeeping. One by one, porters plopped sacks before the old man: sandals of fiber, seeds, herbs, obsidian tools and mirrors, coils of rope and twine, salt, colored powders for dyeing, bright feathers, and even jugs of *octli*. The drink's relaxing, dizzying effects would most certainly woo these people and leave them begging for more.

The newest servant-slave of Metzín's family brought the octli. The slender young man had been sold to them by his family, poor farmers from the Moyotlán quarter of Tenochtitlán, an area aptly named for the abundance of mosquitoes there. Metzín had yet to hear him speak more than a word or two at a time. The servant-slave kept his head bowed, always averting the direct gaze of others, as if one were about to send him to the sacrifice stone at any moment for the slightest wrongdoing. Though he had a lean physique, he had managed his given load without ever faltering or requiring extra rest. And though he usually kept up and followed directions, he seemed utterly lost inside, his eyes often glossy like those of a child left alone at market, which, in his case, wasn't far from the truth.

Metzín could empathize with the dull pain of being far from one's family. Well, at least far from his mother. As much as he loved taking adventurous treks with his father and brothers to distant lands, he longed for home and he wished to continue his lessons in the house of the young men, the *telpochcalli*, back home. The revered warriors spoke time and time again of his bright future, his dexterity and anticipation, and hence his destiny for greatness in battle, while his mother often mentioned the serenity his presence brought to her. But his father had insisted on him coming along again and leaving the tutelage of the warrior-teachers as well as his mother's bosom. Thus, despite their contradictory social statuses and even their physical differences—Metzín boasted a formidable, muscular physique—he felt an unusual kinship with the young servant-slave, who had also been torn from his mother's hearth like a plant ripped from the garden, roots and all. He watched the slim man secretly, for no merchant or noble would ever fix his eyes upon a servant-slave as he had, and he felt a strange impulse to protect him.

The village suddenly bustled, the people bringing armloads of firewood and broad bowls of fruit, berries, and dry insects. Small animals and birds skewered on sticks stripped of bark to be cooked over the fire. From the looks of the people, Metzín guessed they were bringing forward a sizeable portion of their stores. Before long, the merchants, Metzín, and his brothers all held food in cones of leaves, and after they began eating, the porters and the villagers were served. As he had witnessed before, the young servant-slave stood in the margin with his head hanging down and with no food or even a cup of water in his hands.

"You!" Metzín shouted more threateningly than he intended. "Come eat. You also must rest and nourish yourself."

The young man looked at Metzín timidly, like a frightened dog, and stepped toward the spread of food.

"Come here." Metzín said. The servant-slave instantly changed his course and stood in front of Metzín with his head still bowed. "Who are you? What is your name?"

The young man looked up, his dark eyes innocent and deep. He answered with an unexpectedly confident voice, "I am Tototli... he of the birds."

Chapter Three

THE TEAM quickly constructed a rock perimeter around the burial site and built a makeshift roof over it with another blue tarp. Diego brought his generator down from the temple and, from the nearest town, rented a low-powered pump to clear the site of water, a better alternative to the butchered plastic juice jugs they'd been trying to bail with that could potentially damage the fossils. Anabel, the designated photographer, snapped hundreds of shots from a tripod during every step of the excavation, the best motivators for continued funds from their less than patient sponsors. There were active digs all over Mexico; sponsors demanded results.

Thank you, Tlaloc, Diego mused, as the god of rain had now granted them two days of dryness.

The young team, balancing precaution with productivity, had managed to expose most of the two skeletons with no incidental damage. It was a rare find indeed—most deceased Aztecs had been cremated, leaving little to posterity. And the density of the clay in which they sat preserved them in what appeared to be their resting poses, unlike piles of bones found at most other digs.

From the nature of the burial, Diego had already ruled out Aztec nobility—the deceased hadn't been buried in a temple chamber, and the team hadn't found the lavish adornments of gems, jade, and gold usually associated with the ruling class. In fact, these two seemed to have been buried in the middle of nowhere. Even the temple and walls, simple structures of Toltec design, appeared to have been built during an earlier era. Drowning victims? The mystery was part of the allure, and he was certain that they'd find more clues regarding the pair as the dig proceeded. Already it was a triumph, and a big relief as well.

"Congratulations, Professor," Gerardo said, taking a place beside the leader at the gravesite. "I think it's time to celebrate."

"Sure." He nodded. "And take another look at the budget. Maybe we'll finally get a much-needed increase. The little temple is a minimal find, not much more than an obstruction to local building permits," he laughed. "But these… who knows? These skeletons could find their way into the Museum of Anthropology."

"So, it warrants a celebration, right? Let me get you a beer."

"No argument there."

AN HOUR later at a roadside restaurant in a small nearby town, the two sat at a plastic table with a faded beer logo in the middle of it. The rest of the team had stayed behind at the dig, so Diego and Gerardo had a generous plate of melted cheese and mushrooms all for themselves. Gerardo tore a bite-size piece of a fresh corn tortilla and pinched some mushrooms, pulling the stringy white cheese from the chipped terracotta plate. He followed it with a swig of cold beer. "I have to hand it to you," he said to the professor, "when I first saw you… how young you appeared… I had my doubts about how this project would go."

"The whole team is young. We're called cheap labor," Diego said. He pushed his glasses up on his nose and rubbed his palm on the breast of his plaid button-up shirt.

"Maybe. But you've turned it into a great success. Who'd have thought we'd turn up intact skeletons?"

"Hmm…. I didn't have much to do with it. I think it had more to do with a little luck and a lot of rain. You and I both know that we'd done little more than pull weeds from that site."

"Don't be so modest, Professor. You'd said from the start to be patient, to have faith, as if you knew something fabulous like this would turn up."

"Yeah, right. Most of the time I was trying to convince myself as much as any of you. It was my duty to keep you going, but I had no idea. The most I hoped for was some unbroken pots. Anyhow, we still have a lot of work to do. We know nothing about those bodies. For all we know, they're victims of the drug war from a decade ago."

Gerardo laughed out loud. "Don't be so reticent." He chugged his beer again and looked askance at the professor. "You know we've got something, don't you? A little rain and this is suddenly an important dig. I won't be surprised if we have half the curators in Mexico out here before the end of the month." Gerardo bit his thumb excitedly between his slightly crooked teeth.

"Well, maybe we've got something. Time will tell."

"All I can say is that your wife ought to feel pretty lucky to have someone as successful as you at your age... a good-looking professor at the university, a successful archaeologist—"

"Wife? Who told you I have a wife?"

"Oh." Gerardo tilted his head and raised his eyebrows. "Sorry. I just assumed...."

"No wife, no friends, hardly even any family. I'm pretty much married to my work."

"You never mentioned it. I mean, I've always known you work a lot, but I didn't realize...."

"No pity, please. I like my work. Goodness knows I don't make enough to support a partner, and—"

"You've got to come meet my family, then."

Diego shook his head and chuckled. "No. That's nonsense. I said no pity. I'm fine... I'm busy."

Gerardo clunked his beer down on the table. "I insist, Professor. You can't pass your time at work among the dead. And you may be from the big city, but out here in my part of the country, we still have old-fashioned ways, like getting together with family and friends. We get together every Sunday at my parents' place not far from here in Xonacahuacán. They've heard all about you and the excavation site. I'm sure they'd be thrilled to meet you." Gerardo lit up like a schoolboy with a brilliant idea.

Old-fashioned ways, Diego thought. His own family had lost its cohesiveness long ago. The busy lifestyle in Mexico City had made maintaining family relations nearly impossible. His father had died, his siblings had headed north, and his mother had followed them. Yet the family bond was central to Mexican mores and had been as long as history could tell. It seemed that his passion for archaeology and anthropology had taken the place of those bonds he had lost before he even entered higher education. Strangely, he didn't miss his family, though admittedly some part of him longed for a closer connection to live people and in a capacity beyond the roles of students and underlings.

"Fair enough," he answered. "I guess we've made sufficient progress to merit a little time away. I'm sure some distance from the project will do me good."

"This Sunday you're off the hook. My niece is getting baptized, and I'm guessing you don't have a suit out here. The following Sunday it is, then."

"Okay," Diego said with a smile that emphasized a shallow dimple in his left cheek, "but let's keep clear boundaries. Family is family, and work is work."

"Yes, boss," Gerardo responded with a military salute. "I didn't realize you were such a slave driver."

Chapter Four

AFTER MANY nights in the jungle amidst the wandering spirits and roaming creatures, and as many days of walking beneath the hot sun in humid air that made water drip down Metzín's back, the huge oval leaves on the trees gave way to smaller ones, the dark, moist soil turned to dry dirt, and the trails made by sporadic travelers became the roads meticulously tended by the men of the Aztec empire—men from Tenochtitlán, Coyoacán, and Xochimilco. The party had been hiking uphill toward the Lake of Texcoco, past many villages and a few small cities where temples rose to gods of which Metzín had not yet learned. The temples were nothing like the colossal temples in his quarter, where nobles met and leaders watched the citizenry and honored the gods. Still, it seemed his father knew cotton-wearing men in every place of significance, no matter how far from the great city.

In front of Metzín, Tototli marched in a line of many porters. His brown body was bare save his loincloth, and sweat dripped down the groove of his narrow back, making meandering traces between red mosquito bites. He alternated balancing a load of seashells that he carried in a basket on his head and hauling it in his arms, depending on the terrain. The big conches sounded like empty jugs when they hit each other while the smaller ones jingled at the bottom of the basket.

"Wait," Metzín said. The servant-slave did not alter his pace. "Stop." But the young man continued. "Tototli!"

Finally, he stopped moving and turned around to look at Metzín from beneath the basket, as if it were a large hat. "Forgive me. I was elsewhere."

"Use this," Metzín said, pulling from beneath his cloak a piece of spotted fur. "Put it on your head under the basket."

Tototli set the basket down and accepted the fur. "Thank you, beneficent master. I had thought to try a folded banana leaf, but I didn't want to lag behind."

"No, do not call me that. I am not more than a year or two your elder."

"My master's son is also my master."

"Call me Metzín."

"Yes, Master Metzín."

Metzín laughed, the tips of his long hair rubbing his shoulders. He brushed them off with his hand and looked forward to cutting them upon his safe return. "Let's get moving. Like you feared, we've fallen behind."

Tototli nodded and curled his lips in the slightest smile.

AFTER MORE grueling walking, as the sun neared the end of its journey, they finally reached a summit. From between the trees, Metzín beheld the black, glimmering surface of Lake Texcoco, which stretched as far as he could see. The smaller section, Lake Chalco, sparkled nearer to him, beside the colorful fields of flowers of Xochimilco and separated from the larger body of water by an enormous land arm. Smoke rose from temples and homes on the fist at Culhuacán. The three broad causeways that stretched in different directions from various spots on the lakeshore to the island of Tenochtitlán appeared to be little more than tan termite tunnels on a darker tree trunk, and the city of Tenochtitlán a massive white nest. They wouldn't make it to the city today. Metzín's father was surely considering a camp for the night, but Metzín longed to fly like a heron and land on the roof garden of his home, lie on his familiar mat, and gaze on the warm face of his mother.

IT WASN'T until almost twilight of the following day that Metzín, his father, and a few of the other merchants and porters walked the length of the closest causeway. The lake extended far on either side, and people in flat-bottomed boats paddled methodically along, carrying flowers, greens, or stalks of corn. Men trudged along the broad land bridge carrying loads of wood or brick on their backs, while others worked with tools on the upkeep of the public road. Women walked along with children at their sides or in their arms, likely headed home to prepare the evening meal.

The party reached the towering gate, open now during peacetime, where a small group of warriors stood guard, carefully observing all who entered. A jade pendant hung from one's neck and colorful feathers dangled at his side, all signs of accomplishments, rank, and wealth. Metzín's father led his party in nonchalantly, which didn't keep Metzín from noticing the disdainful glares of the guards. How the people despised the *pochteca*, envious of the liberties the merchants enjoyed, and the veiled luxuries. Metzín had been taught at an early age to never flaunt wealth, as the slightest offense could be sufficient pretext for an impromptu execution. Though they often wore cotton in public, they wouldn't dare parade around in ostentatious jewelry, overly adorned clothing, or expertly embroidered cloaks. Treasures from foreign lands were traded, warehoused, or appreciated within the privacy of their brick-walled homes. Also for that reason, they'd left the rest of the porters at a meeting place on the lakeshore to await boats for transport under the cover of darkness.

Metzín had requested permission to accompany the men into Tenochtitlán, and he had chosen Tototli to carry water jugs for the trip. Soon they would arrive home, and he'd be able to let out a sigh of relief for a safe return from a long journey, a favor granted by Yacatecuhtli, the god of merchants. They had thoroughly honored him, sang and danced his praises, lit the finest incense, and given of their blood to grace him.

As they approached the grand island of Tenochtitlán, human activity increased. Men waded out to their *chinampas*. Dredging mud from the lake bottom with hardened gourds and piling it onto their family plots, they virtually created land above the lake surface such that it looked as if they were floating agricultural parcels. Most of the chinampas were built along the shore of the lake, but as the empire grew, space had become more and more scarce, and chinampas now appeared along the causeways with only narrow canals between them. Women cooked fish and algae in pots over small fires near the water's edge, and naked children splashed around, having returned from their daily lessons in the local telpochcalli.

So many cycles of the sun had passed since his people, scorned and shunned, had founded Tenochtitlán on nothing more than chinampas. Thought of as little more than beggars, they had fulfilled the prophecy of the god Uitzilopochtli and had become the lords and kings he had promised they would become. They had toiled, creating their empire from nothing but soot and mud, like all of these poor farmers now along the causeway. Stone by stone, maize plant by maize plant, and childbirth by childbirth. His ancestors had been no strangers to hunger and hard work. *The gods are great, as is Tenochtitlán, the heart of the Aztec empire.*

He turned around to find that Tototli had fallen behind again. "Not much farther," Metzín said to him. "We will rest."

"It is not that I am weary, Master Metzín."

"Oh, then what?"

Because his hands were occupied with the jugs, he pointed at a chinampa with a nod of his head. "Those people… I used to know them."

And then an image came to Metzín of Tototli as a young child wading happy and naked with his siblings in the shallow water. He'd have imagined his future was to tend the chinampa, transport fresh water in, and honor Tlaloc so that he might bring rain. *One's destiny often seemed to be little more than a game of chance, our lives like pips on beans in a* patolli *game. The gods sitting around like gamblers, entertaining themselves, and betting away our very breath. We can little comprehend, and not at all control, the power of divinity.*

Metzín turned back to face the city and beheld the splendor before him, Tenochtitlán. The first buildings were humble rectangular homes with white walls and flat roofs. Even the smallest of them boasted a garden on its rooftop, vegetables and flowers in their seasons. The white buildings—homes, shops, public buildings, and warehouses— could be seen extending down the stretch of the straight road, and there in the distance, presided the palace and temple of Motecuhzoma, their wise leader and revered warrior. Smoke rose from the top of the temple where priests gathered in their constant duties to worship and appease the gods.

In the streets, hordes of people walked to and fro, many heading toward the market, and others returning from it. Between the buildings, Metzín caught glimpses of the many canoes floating along the system of canals that ran parallel to the earthen roads. His pace increased behind his father, who had to be as eager to complete the day's tasks and take a well-deserved rest at home.

Beside him, Metzín noticed a blue-handed man in a trancelike stride. The captive or slave headed toward the temples in the city center, having bid his captor or owner good-bye as tradition dictated. "You know the fortune for me today," he would have said, perfectly aware of his fate. "I am going and I shall wait for you beyond."

His owner would have opened the door for him, and the slave-captive would have stained the family's doorway with a blue handprint, grateful to have been treated as a god during those final days. Thus he would be prepared for his inevitable end. "I give my son to you," the owner would say to the god.

Then, to the temple, and up the steep stairs to the round stone, where his blood would be spilled and his heart wrenched away as an offering to the sun god. The man's blood would fuel Uitzilopochtli's fire, allowing him to once again travel across the sky. Every Aztec man understood the need to sacrifice thusly, so that the precarious world and all the insignificant people inhabiting it might continue to live for one more day. The songs would be sung, the tributes paid, and soon, the chest split open and the beating heart willingly given to the powerful being in the sky. Metzín, and all men, could only hope to die in such an honorable way, traversing the sky each day thereafter in Uitzilopochtli's wake.

The party stopped at a small dock near a junction in the road where a wide bridge and a stone aqueduct converged. Fresh water from the aqueduct was being poured into enormous pots on a water boat, which would glide through the city canals, to be used by the citizens. The lake water was too salty for drinking. Metzín's father yanked his son's shoulder, pulling his ear close to his mouth. "Tell your mother to prepare for our homecoming," he said in a muffled tone. "Get the warehouse and food ready. We've got to see the administrator before darkness falls. We will return tonight with the goods." The man signaled for a transport canoe, boarded it along with the other merchants, agave books in hand, and drifted away, leaving Metzín and Tototli alone in the road.

"Let's go, then," Metzín told Tototli, who was filling the jugs he carried in the aqueduct. The young man's shoulders sagged with the heavy containers. "Give me one of those."

"No, Master Metzín. I can carry them."

"Come now." Metzín held out a hand. "We'll arrive more swiftly."

Farther down the road, the houses became grander. The white two-story homes of dignitaries were a welcome sight for Metzín, their gardens like overflowing refreshing waterfalls. His weary feet felt rejuvenated as he walked more briskly, eager to finally arrive. The light from beyond the horizon faded as Uitzilopochtli prepared to return to the other side of the world and, hopefully, grace the empire on the morrow with his fire in the sky once more. They turned a familiar corner, crossed a small bridge of thick branches and beams, and entered through the front door of the family house that was nearly identical on the exterior to all the homes on the block. The interior, however, was like a precious flower to him, his mother the sweet nectar.

He entered quietly to find her sitting with two of his older sisters and their young daughters in a sleeping room on earthen platforms covered with mats, the bed-curtains tied back during daytime activities. Each of them held a spindle. His mother, Quetza, was instructing them in spinning thread from maguey and cotton. Beside them lay a cloth she had begun at the outset of their journey. At that time, she had little more than a few strands of cotton string attached to a dowel. Now the extravagant white cloak reached from one end of the mat to the other, adorned with careful designs of interlocking circles and embroidered images of flying birds. The young girls would learn their craft from one of the best.

After a moment she noticed Metzín in the doorway, and her serious instructor's face softened in the yellow light of a torch on the wall. All the girls looked over and instantly became an eruption of glee. They dropped their lessons and rushed to him. "You're back. You're back."

"Shhh," Quetza said. "Composure… composure." Yet she too seemed unable to contain her excitement. She clasped her hands together. "Thank the gods for your safe return."

The girls circled him and hugged him, bombarding him with questions. "Did ghosts haunt you? What did you bring back? Did you find jade? Was anyone captured? Tell us everything."

Quetza's voice silenced them all. "You look tired. You must rest. And girls, put your spindles away. We've got cooking and preparing to do. Your grandfather will be back tonight with his goods. You"—she pointed at Tototli—"get the fire for the *temazcalli* ready for a steam bath. Metzín needs to rest and clean and purify himself."

The young servant-slave nodded and disappeared to the back of the house and outside where the dome-shaped temazcalli was located, as the girls and young women left to bring fresh food to the hearth. Metzín stood alone before his mother. She approached him and placed the palm of her hand on his cheek.

"Back from some other world to this one. Brave son. Sit down so I can cut your hair."

He sat down and closed his eyes as she cut his hair, leaving it long over his right ear. "You lost your *piochtli* with your first captive," she said, tugging the lock of long hair on the right side of his head, "and soon you may cut it all short." The first bundle of his hair still hung on a wall in a sleeping room, commemorating the battle victory to which she alluded.

"My father expects me to trade with him. Perhaps I am not meant to return to battle," he said with disappointment.

"We will see. You are of two worlds. Not all of the codices apply to you. The warriors have taken you in training. They have made an exception already. Besides," she said with a deeper, more serious tone, "you will soon be a man, and we will find a wife for you." As she completed his haircut, she said, "We will speak of this later. Your foot will step on the path the gods have chosen for you. For now, go and relax. Let us prepare food for you, and let you enjoy those things you most love about home."

"The fire is ready, Master Metzín" came Tototli's timid voice.

Metzín walked outside, behind the house, to the opening of the brick structure. He felt the heat from the wood fire behind it and heard the crackling. He looked forward to some solitude inside, away from everyone except, of course, Tototli, who would attend to him.

In the dark night air, singing and drums could be heard in the distance—likely a ritual to a deity or entertainment in the *cuicacalco*, the house of singing and dancing, where the young men went after a day of instruction. Metzín would have to reacquaint himself with the current goings-on. He'd lost track of the calendar.

The sound of moving water could be heard from the canal behind the house. A pair of full-grown turkeys stepped out from between plants in the garden and faced off. Metzín sighed, relieved to be at home. He handed his cloak to Tototli, who stood near the narrow entrance of the temazcalli, and then got on his knees to crawl into the domed steam bath.

He crawled into complete darkness, went directly to the mat on the far side of the small space, and lay facedown. He could hear Tototli enter behind him and listened as the young man ladled water onto the hot wall. *Pffff.* The water instantly boiled, and the room filled with hot steam that burned his nose at first as he breathed in a chest full. As he got used to the heat, he began to relax, while images of his travels appeared in his head—the tireless walks, the newness of unknown places, the strangeness of foreign people, and the brown skin of Tototli, who sat within his reach.

He felt a hand on the small of his back and flinched even though he had anticipated the sensation. Tototli's skin felt soft with the delicateness of youth, despite the physical work he performed every day. "Ready for your massage?" the young man said.

Metzín breathed in deeply and exhaled, preparing to release his corporeal tension and purify his spirit. Now Tototli planted both hands on his back and began to move up and down, rubbing the muscles along his spine and ribs. He breathed in and out again. *Sacred Uitzilopochtli.* The hands reached his shoulders, working the tissue slowly, expertly. *Blessed Quetzalcoatl, smother me in flowers and tranquility.* Then they arrived at the nape of his neck, Tototli's fingers and thumbs making deep circles. Metzín now could do little more than focus on the sensations, trying to ignore the hardening of his member in the front of his loincloth.

Tototli granted him a respite as he went to throw more water on the wall. But the touch returned, as did the swelling. *Thank you lords of the night for darkness.* Metzín tried to recall the names of the nine deities, but he could not think as those hands made their way to his buttocks.

"Shall I remove your loincloth?" Tototli asked innocently.

"No," Metzín choked out. He cleared his throat. "No. I will leave it on."

He had no need to feel embarrassed with a slave, he reminded himself. Anyway, one had little control over his body, as in the morning when he would awaken as stiff as a dried fish. Naturally, he presumed, all of the other young men from the telpochcalli would have the same experience. And the slave could not see him here or feel the front of him, not in this position. Yet what a strange discomfort, one that he had hoped for in a way. He wanted to covet the young man, and be coveted. He wished to be touched. But what an unnatural thing to desire. And here, of all places, in the temazcalli, where he was supposed to cleanse himself inside and out. Though Tototli could not see him, he knew the gods could, especially Tlazolteotl, the goddess of carnal love. Metzín knew he could be stricken with a death spell for thinking unclean thoughts of another man. So was this young man a snake shrouded like a butterfly? Was he an enticing demon, a test of discipline?

The balls of Tototli's hands pressed down on the mass of Metzín's buttocks, which made him inhale deeply through clenched teeth. He had been harboring a weariness there of which he had not been aware. Tototli seemed to know. He seemed to read Metzín's body as a scholar reads glyphs. He of the birds, beautiful in his own way, like the most colorful of guacamayas, his fingers soft as feathers, and his voice a chirping song. How could he be anything but good?

When Tototli finished with Metzín's legs and feet, he said, "Would you like to turn over now?"

Metzín was fearful to reveal that part of his body that was still betraying him, yet he did not have the courage to say no either. So he lay there, as if asleep, trying internally to make those immoral impulses wash away like dead leaves in the swift current of a river and wondering for a moment if Tototli had suffered the same unnatural condition. *Tlazolteotl, goddess of confession, cleanse me, and draw away temptation from my loin.*

"Brother, the canoes have arrived," said a sister from the entrance of the temazcalli.

Metzín hurried out, but not before his swelling had subsided. The night of unloading, storing, and organizing the goods for market became a reprieve, and he felt normal again in the company of his brothers and father, outside in the cool night air and away from the steaming heat within the dome of bricks.

Chapter Five

A LONGER bout of dry weather allowed a small brigade with miniature shovels, picks, and brushes to clear the dense dirt from the fossils and the immediate vicinity. Diego had expected to find a number of artifacts beside the bodies—jewelry, writings, weapons, or incense—typical items buried with the Aztecs. Almost none of those things had turned up except for a single, simple jade pendant around the neck of one of the skeletons, and Diego wondered if grave robbers hadn't beaten them to the find some time in the last four or five centuries.

If they had, why would they have left the pendant, a piece that was, based on the style and craftsmanship, undoubtedly from the Aztec period? Could it be superstition? Doubtful.

Also strange was the clothing on the pair—one had remnants of a cotton cloak indicative of a higher class, while the other wore the tatters of a loincloth of cactus fiber of a commoner or slave. Yet the individual in the fiber loincloth bore the pendant. It was not uncommon for slaves to choose to die with their masters. Yet the two, apparently males according to their bone structures, appeared quite close in age. Were they brothers? But why then the difference in class of clothing?

And what caused them to die so young? They didn't appear to have been sacrificed, because none of their limbs were detached, nor were their chest cavities hacked open. The one in the cactus fiber did appear to have a serious wound in his skull. Every piece of evidence appeared atypical, creating more questions than answers, and only further forensics would solve the riddle.

The rainy days of late summer would soon become the drier, albeit cooler, climate of fall. Diego had chosen to keep the news under wraps until they had a few more clues. The grant would run out soon, since this was on such a small site, one with few prospects of getting on the tourist circuit. Besides, Diego would likely be expected back after the New Year to give a full semester of classes. Through his years of training, he had learned to be patient with the process of excavations, yet the dwindling numbers in the project account continued to pressure him. *Patience. Patience.*

Diego had felt tempted to cancel the visit to Gerardo's family in Xonacahuacán due to the unexpected pressure from work. However, a deal was a deal, and Diego wasn't one to renege. Early Sunday morning, after reading through his copious notes and questions once again—ever the workaholic—he found his cleanest jeans and newest plaid shirt, and revved up his ailing Subaru.

"We'll make good time in your car," Gerardo said as he closed the passenger door. "Usually, if I can't convince one of my brothers to come get me, I have to walk out to the highway and wait half an hour for a *combi* to pass, or a passenger bus headed out to Teotihuacán. Sure, they're greater targets for the bandits, but the cushy seats make up for it," he laughed. "Besides, I don't have anything they would want."

Half an hour later, after traveling straight, single-lane highways in the heart of Aztec territory, they stopped in a dirt parking lot across the street from an old church. They were somewhere in the middle of the bed of the great Texcoco Lake that had dried out or been drained over the centuries. Most of the cars in the parking lot were also from long ago—worn out pickup trucks and junkers with cracked windshields, rusty doors, and dings. Judging by the architecture of the church, its brickwork, steeple design, and the sagging of the doorframe, Diego placed it around the middle of the seventeenth century. He hated the habit at times, always thinking with his archaeologist's hat on. "I thought we were going to a house?"

"Well, we got here so quickly that we're just in time for mass. Anyhow, if we head over to the house now, no one will be there." Gerardo checked the time on his cellular phone and pointed at the church. "I'm sure they're here. You don't mind, do you?"

"No, I guess not."

"It'll do you good. You probably haven't been to mass in—"

"Years," Diego completed his sentence.

"And confession?"

"Let's not even go there."

An arrangement of blue and peach-colored plastic flowers sat near the door beside the receptacle of holy water where Gerardo and Diego dipped their fingers and crossed themselves as they quietly entered. Inside, thirty or forty churchgoers knelt at tiny pews, the mass having already commenced. On cue, they all said, "Amen," crossed themselves, and sat up in the creaky benches to listen to the sermon of the bespectacled father. Typical gaudy adornments between small buttresses on the walls depicted the stories and suffering of Jesus and the disciples.

The father began his sermon as Gerardo led Diego toward the front, where he directed Diego into a pew. Gerardo responded to a slew of handshakes and whispered greetings from a dozen people or more in their immediate radius, and he awkwardly introduced the professor to people who compensated for their hushed voices with exaggerated expressions of delight. The father paused and gave them a firm "Ah-hum," and they all faced forward again in respectful silence.

Even a small church, a humble offshoot nevertheless built in proportion to the titanic cathedrals of Europe and downtown Mexico City, transported Diego to a childhood of ingrained obedience and respect. One barely listened to the sermon, only filtering the words for cues to sit or kneel or stand or chant, "Praise to the Lord, blessed be his name," and then shake hands with one fellow churchgoer in each of the cardinal directions. It made Diego feel like dropping the role of professor and adopting an air of familiarity with Gerardo's friends and relatives.

After the final prayer, hushed vocal tones became normal again, and the introductions were repeated as Gerardo presented face and name, face and name, face and name, followed by a cordial, "Nice to meet you," over and over again, from brothers, sisters, uncles, and aunts. The scientific, professional side of him preferred the stoicism of the dead, but he did appreciate the obviously warm welcome from the living.

"I'll never remember all of their names," Diego whispered to Gerardo.

"Don't worry, they'll only talk bad about you behind your back."

"Oh, here are my parents." Gerardo greeted a woman dressed more formally than the rest. A silver rosary hung around her neck. A thin man with salt and pepper hair stood close beside her, but did not seem to notice them. "Mother, this is Professor Diego, my boss. I mentioned him to you. Professor, my mother, Eunice."

"Señora, delighted to meet you," Diego said.

"How do you do?" she responded with a confident voice, raising her lips in a tight smile. "This is my husband, Vicente." She indicated the man whose arm she clutched, squeezing him as if to regain his attention.

"Oh," he said with a carefree tone, "I must have been thinking about the soccer game... must be in the second half by now." He chuckled, shaking hands sociably. "Welcome to Xonacahuacán, Professor."

As Diego and Gerardo followed them out of the church, Diego leaned over and said softly, "Their names I won't forget."

"You'd better not."

After a few minutes driving behind several cars down a dusty road, they followed Gerardo's family through a gate in the middle of a long stone wall, behind which stood a plain white house. A lengthy rectangular vegetable garden sat to one side, a patch of green in an otherwise drab dirt lot, though a few citrus trees grew near the far end of the property. As they walked toward the house, Diego watched a hen and her chicks peck around near the wall. He couldn't help but notice the geometrical shapes in the brick—patterns of small diagonal rhombi—reminiscent of a building style of peoples in the more western state of Oaxaca. A few remaining patches of red fresco completed the wall. It had likely been built around the same time as the little church— by indigenous hands under the whip of a Spanish invader seeking to mark and protect his new property. If so, the wall would have survived countless storms, floods and droughts, earthquakes, and hundreds of years of weathering, and now served only to keep out the noise of passing cars. Contrary to the common European and Western opinion that the Aztecs were a disorganized and primitive people, the natives knew how to build edifices comparable, or even superior, to the Roman structures of their time.

"Beh-eh-eh-eh-eh," a sheep cried from where it was tethered near a water trough not far from the front door.

"Good morning, Barbie," Gerardo answered.

"Barbie? She's hardly blond and beautiful."

"No," Gerardo said, turning the knob on the front door. "Barbacoa." He took his hand off the doorknob and stopped, apparently in thought. "That's it. You're going to have to come for the Christmas feast."

"What are you talking about?"

"Well, you said you have no family around here. And I've got plenty to spare. See? We do a big barbacoa every year on Christmas... the whole family gets together and we slaughter a sheep to make my mother's specialty. We'll be quite insulted if you don't come."

"Let's see how today goes before I make any promises."

"Of course, Professor. The scientific method... trial and error."

"I think it's called 'one step at a time.'"

"Sure." Gerardo put a hand on Diego's shoulder and squeezed. "However you like." He dropped his hand and walked inside.

Chapter Six

B-ROOOM. THE sound of conches rang out from the temple tops, first from a distance, then coming closer and closer from the various temples in the many sectors of Tenochtitlán, and more still from the far side, a passing wave of monotones. *BONG... BONG... bong... bong.* Gongs reverberated in dual tones, blending with the continuing sound of conches. Light of dawn broke. Uitzilopochtli was bringing daylight again, thanks to those who had sacrificed their precious life water, quenching the perpetual thirst of the gods.

Metzín rose from his mat. He now felt the accumulated soreness of the trip of many months. No matter, instruction would begin as early as the birds began to fly. He stepped out to the back patio, where yellow and pink flowers hung down on vines from the rooftop. A pair of hairless xoloitzcuitli lifted their lazy heads without moving from where they lay in the dirt or even so much as wagging their tails.

He knelt down beside the canal, scooped water in his hand, washed his face, and rinsed his mouth. He sprung awake with a cool splash of water. His grumbling stomach reminded him of the many dishes his mother had prepared the night before. There was nothing like the familiar, succulent dishes his mother had made for as long as he could remember. He'd wait till the second sounding of the conches to break his fast with the rest of the students.

He walked into the main room, where he saw his mother coming in from the hallway, gripping a broom of dried reeds forcefully in her hands. Her brow was furrowed, her stride swift.

"What is it, Mother?"

"Nothing." She began to sweep the main room with fury, starting in the center near the hearth. "Out... out," she said under her breath.

"You're not cleansing for nothing. I know your face."

She stopped to adjust the bracelet of brown stones on her wrist. "Your father may be leaving again... back to where he just came from. He awaits word."

"Oh." He hadn't expected another trading expedition until at least after the next merchant festival.

She waved her hand at him, and continued her brusque sweeping, looking down at the floor. "You mustn't concern yourself. You go to the telpochcalli. You don't want them to make you breathe the fumes of the hot chile fire."

"I'm not a child anymore."

"No, but they will expect you before the sun becomes yellow. Go on now."

He shuffled down the street, attempting not to attract the attention of the citizens beginning their daily tasks around the city. He arrived at the telpochcalli as the other young men were seating themselves in a semicircle. They sat in a covered patio in the interior of the house of the young men. He sat near the rear, crossing his legs in front of him. They waited quietly; the daily oratories would soon begin.

"Metzín," said the master warrior who sat in front of the group. "Yours is a welcome presence." He smiled gently, the scar on his lower lip separating it into two distinct, purple bulges against his dark Aztec complexion, a disconcerting flaw at first, yet now a scarcely noticed feature on the friendly face of a tranquil teacher.

Near him, Peohuatac blocked the view of smaller students with his massive back and enormous head. He turned to regard Metzín with a silent sneer, which reminded Metzín of one of the few things he found distasteful at the telpochcalli. He regarded the hairy spot that grew on Peo's cheek like a bitter black slug. Peo had been a rock beneath his sleeping mat since they had entered instruction together as young boys. Even back then the oaf used his large physique to establish his superiority over others. Metzín returned his gaze to the learned countenance of the instructor who, with the slightest hand signal, commenced a chorus among the young men:

> *I am the warrior Uitzilopochtli*
> *No one is like me*
> *In my cloak of parrot feathers*
> *In my fiery blaze*
>
> *I am the warrior Uitzilopochtli*

No one is like me
Hungry for the eagle's cactus fruit
And thirsty for precious water

I am the warrior Uitzilopochtli
No one is like me
Come Tlaxochimaco—month of drum beat and dance
At my highest, hottest place
There is none like me

After chanting choruses and hearing lectures on the duties of men and warriors, they ate their maize cakes and broth and began the duties of sweeping the communal house. A younger group left to cut wood, while Metzín, with a group of older students, carried digging tools and brushes outside to the closest causeway. Peo assumed a supervisory role, ordering some to dredge a canal and the others to scrub the dry side of the aqueduct as he took shade at the side of a nearby building. "Look at these long-haired farmers," he teased the other students, "who will never make jaguar-knight. Send them back to the chinampas from where they came."

"Peohuatac," said the master warrior, appearing from behind the corner of the building where Peo was leaning, "your mouth is the beak of a toucan and your body that of a vulture. But you have neither stealth nor grace. How do you expect to return from the south a hummingbird and fly with the god of the sun?"

"Master warrior, surely these children who pretend to be brave will need a strong leader to follow."

"Yes, they will. But you carry just a pair of minor battles and a single captive. Your hair is not yet cut short either. So be a leader now and take a brush to the thickest grime there." He pointed to a slimy section of the aqueduct, to the silent delight of the students, including Metzín, who knew of Peo's lowly past, the one he tried so desperately to hide. He'd grown up on the humble, makeshift plots like many of the others. Often plants could barely grow in the salty, dry mud. If he hadn't tried to hide it, if he had preserved a bit of humility, he might not be so loathed. It must have been due to some pity of the gods that

Peo had grown to be such a beast. Yet none of them dared to look Peo in the eyes or let their smiles of vindication show, for later in the afternoon, they would be drilled in combat tactics, and he would surely let loose his wrath.

Metzín recalled the first confrontation he'd had with Peo not many years before. They wielded *macquauitl*, and practiced fighting techniques with the wooden swords with sharp obsidian edges fixed along their lengths. The objective, as always, was to capture the enemy alive. Stop had been called. Metzín lowered his weapon, opening himself to Peo's stiff elbow, which knocked him down. With a deadly rage in his eyes, the brute raised his macquauitl over Metzín, who lay defenseless on the ground. If it hadn't been for the master warrior stepping in to restrain Peo, Metzín could only imagine what might have happened. "Fortunate woman," Peo had blared at him as he turned away under the master's orders. Metzín had never forgotten, and always wondered at Peo's animosity. Had he been envious because of the masters' praises of Metzín? Had he been bitter at the gods and seen Metzín as an easy target? Or was he nothing but a mean brute to all he encountered?

Now Metzín did his best to stay out of Peo's way. Later in the evening, as the young men sang in the cuicacalco, some embracing one another as they danced to the music of drums and flutes, Peo seemed to flaunt the *auianime* who clung to his arm. Despite her face carefully colored in a soft yellow hue and her teeth painstakingly dyed red with cochineal, her shape resembled that of a papaya and her breath, notwithstanding the *tzictli* she constantly chewed and clacked, was notoriously foul. The misery and defeat he wished on all seemed to seep malodorously through his skin, most noticeably from the pits of his arms.

As difficult as it was to ignore Peo's menacing presence and his desperation for power, Metzín joined in with the gleeful jumping and dancing of the others. Elders watched them, as if enjoying their bygone days through the young men, and Metzín grabbed the shoulders of one and another, some slightly older and others younger, until the fire finally burned down. *Let Peo go off and sleep with his auianime.* He left the group behind, unable to clear his mind of the leaner, more enticing physique of Tototli.

Chapter Seven

"THE DNA evidence is back," the professor explained to his assistant. "Not only do the results confirm what we already suspected—that both bodies were males—but they also prove, to a 99.998 percent certainty, that the two were not siblings. In fact it is almost certain that they had no relatives in common for at least six generations."

"So this is not a family burial?" Gerardo confirmed.

"Not from the looks of it. Moreover the initial bone scan shows their approximate ages—both were in their late teens or early twenties."

"Killed in battle? A warrior and his slave?"

"No—they'd have been cremated. And since when would a twenty-year-old have a slave the same age as he?"

"So, does this mean you have a hypothesis?"

The professor paused like a politician during a tough interview. "Nothing I'm willing to bet on yet. I hope whatever we can gather from the autopsy… about the cause of death… and any other artifacts from the gravesite will fill in some of the missing pieces."

"Whatever we've got, it seems like an unusual find."

The professor nodded pensively. "That goes without saying. Let's keep moving on the dig… careful as ever."

"Of course."

"And let me know as soon as you find anything new."

"Right…. And you?"

"Me? I'm working on the write-up. Got to keep the money coming in."

"We're counting on you for that," Gerardo said, dismissing himself from the temple top office. He popped his head back in. "One more thing…."

"Yes?"

"My family said they really enjoyed your company. 'Professional and intelligent,' they called you, 'an impressive yet humble man for a light-skinned *mestizo.*'"

"Thank you. I had a nice time too. It was good to get away for a little while."

"You understand that this means they're expecting you this coming Sunday too, right?"

"What's that?"

"Oh, yeah. My mother, of all people, insisted you return. She said you barely touched the food. How were you ever to judge her cooking?"

"Are you kidding? I left as stuffed as those *chiles rellenos*."

"Mother's orders. You can't let down the family now. Study the dead, enjoy the living, right?"

"Alright. But maybe we could skip mass this time?"

"A heathen mestizo at that."

"PROFESSOR. WHAT a surprise," Eunice said as she greeted him with her customary air-kiss on the right cheek.

"Surprise? I was told you were expecting me… adamantly so, in fact."

"Umm…." She looked quizzically at her son.

"Well, no," Gerardo said. "What I meant is that you're always welcome."

"Ah, I see," Diego said with uncertainty.

"Of course," she said, "you never need an invitation. Mi casa, su casa."

"I appreciate you having me again."

"And," added Gerardo, "I mentioned the annual barbacoa to him, so you won't think I'm inviting anyone without your consent."

"Like I said," she confirmed to the professor. "Mi casa, su casa. We would be happy to have you for our Christmas feast. What's one more added to the horde I have to feed? That's if you don't have any prior commitments."

"Actually, I—"

"He doesn't. His family lives far, far from here."

"Well, then I suppose it's settled," she said. "And I think we can see where the adamancy was coming from."

"Great." Gerardo said, ignoring her jibe. "And to celebrate, I brought some tequila." He pulled a double-sized bottle of aged liquor from a paper bag he'd brought in.

"Wow… your father is going to love that. Why don't you go outside and pick some fresh green lemons?"

"Sure. Let me go get some scissors."

"In the kitchen—"

"I know," Gerardo said, leaving Diego in the front room with his mother.

"He seems to have a fond… a lot of respect for you," she said with an indistinct expression.

"He's been a great assistant."

She smiled politely. "Didn't see you two at mass this morning?"

"Speaking for myself, I wanted the extra time to sleep in this morning."

"Yes. I understand you've been busy on an… *intriguing* project."

"Definitely."

"And Gerardo? He slept in as well this morning?"

"I… I assume so. To be honest with you, I'm rather far removed from his sleeping area."

She smiled more sincerely. "Well, that's good to know."

Gerardo returned with some scissors and pushed the professor out the door through which they had entered.

Diego followed Gerardo toward the citrus trees and asked, "Am I mistaken or did I sense a little animosity from your mother?"

Gerardo spoke without looking back. "I know I'm a grown man and all, but she can be a bit protective of her family… especially after what happened with my sister…." His voice seemed to drop off on the last words.

"Oh? Is there something I should know?"

"Watch out." He veered quickly to one side of the path, stopping in place. He pointed down at the ground and lifted a tarp camouflaged with sand to reveal a rectangular hole. "Damn sand-covered pit. It looks like some kind of wartime trap."

The professor knelt to look inside. "What is it, some kind of well?"

"No." Gerardo pulled the tarp back further so they could get a better view. The hole extended about a meter into the ground, the walls lined with red brick and mortar. "It's the barbacoa pit."

"Ah… I've never been to a real barbacoa. I've only had barbacoa tacos on the city corner."

"Then you're in for a treat. There is nothing like fresh barbacoa cooked in its fiery pit," Gerardo said. "Though I do know one individual who would prefer we didn't do it."

"Is your mother really that worked up?"

"Don't worry about my mother right now." Gerardo shook his head strongly, pointing at the sheep across the yard. "I'm talking about Barbie."

AS THE afternoon became early evening, any sense of animosity had subsided, perhaps related to the way the entire family sat around the huge dining-room table, sipping the last of a few bottles of tequila. Diego hadn't drunk more than a glass or two of wine for months, or maybe a couple of beers. Now, each time he looked down, his shot glass was refilled.

"We'd better be getting back to the site pretty soon," he slurred.

"I don't think you're up to driving," one of Gerardo's sisters said.

"No, no… I've got to get back tonight. We start first thing in the morning."

"You're welcome to stay here, Professor," said an older brother, whose name Diego could not recall. "Gerardo's got his bed and we've got a spare."

Diego waved his hand at them, politely declining. "Thank you, but no." He stood up, swaying in place, and pulling the keys from his pocket.

"I'll take those," Gerardo said, grabbing the keys from Diego. "I'll drive us back. Don't you all worry." Though he'd had his share of tequila, he appeared more composed, and his family voiced no qualms about the prospect of his driving the professor back to the dig.

Diego woke some time later in the passenger seat of his car, the night sky pitch black. He heard the sound of curtains closing. He sat up, dizzy and confused. "Where the hell are we?"

"Come on. Get out," Gerardo said as he opened the door. "Time to go to bed."

Diego put his feet down on a concrete floor. "This isn't the site."

"No, the site is too far, the night too dark. I thought I could drive alright, but I decided it was better to pull over."

"Where are we?"

"Just a little motel."

"With a curtain in the carport? What kind of sordid place is this?"

"A cheap place… with a bed." He pulled Diego up to his feet from the passenger seat. "Come on. We can leave first thing in the morning."

Diego, staggering a bit, grabbed Gerardo's arm like a prom date and followed him up the stairs in the carport to the bedroom. His eyes immediately fixed on the single, queen-size bed, with an ashtray on either nightstand. He approached the bed and noticed that each ashtray held not a pack of matches, but a small packet of personal lubricant and a foil-wrapped condom. "Is this what I think it is?"

"Don't think of it like that, boss. It's just a place to sleep." He started to unbutton his shirt. "Do you want me to help you get undressed?"

"No, I'm fine." Diego lay down on the far side of the bed without taking off his clothes. "What would the team think of this… or your mother?"

"They won't care about what they don't know about."

Diego turned off the small night-light, leaned back, and closed his eyes. "Okay. Whatever."

"Anyway, we're just going to sleep, right?"

Diego barely heard him as he drifted off.

SOMETIME LATER a hand on his chest woke him. The alcohol had worn off a bit, but the strange environment of utter darkness, an unfamiliar bed, questionable odors, and the touch of his assistant's hand were bewildering. No way had he ever slept with a coworker. In fact, he hadn't slept with anyone at all since before he'd entered the university. Yet he didn't immediately push Gerardo's hand away. In truth, though he hadn't at first felt an attraction to his assistant, he now realized he didn't have the aversion he might have expected either. On the contrary, he felt a certain curiosity about which direction that hand might go. Perhaps Gerardo was only asleep, unaware of his movements.

Gerardo shifted his weight closer, as if reacting to the fact that his hand hadn't been rejected. He began to rub up and down Diego's chest. Diego turned his face toward Gerardo's, and caught a whiff of tequila. It reminded him of Gerardo's house. And Eunice.

Bad idea. Before he could act, Gerardo slipped his hand inside Diego's shirt and moved his mouth closer. Diego did not withdraw, and when their lips met, he pushed his mouth harder against Gerardo's. Their tongues intertwined and their hands began to caress and explore.

Eventually, they shed the rest of their clothes and made heat in the darkness.

Chapter Eight

SHHHH... SHHHH... shhh.

Metzín awoke on his mat to the telltale sound of his mother sweeping. She paused, had some stern words with his father, and furiously began to sweep again.

He hated when the two were so far apart, like the sun and the moon at opposite horizons. And even when they were together, one often tried to eclipse the other. Naturally, his father had the final word, or at least his mother would figure out a way to let him believe so. Metzín had hoped to enjoy a free day with them both; they were so seldom together. If his father wasn't on a trading expedition, then civic duties and other business always seemed to separate them.

Metzín stood and approached the door, wondering if he could wash his face and leave for the market unnoticed.

"I'm telling you he is to be a merchant like me. He knows the business. He reads the signs." His father's emphatic voice carried down the hall.

"You've got plenty of sons to accompany you." Metzín could hear the frustration in her voice, as well as her attempts at reason and composure. People thought poorly of yelling matches.

"Such are the dictates of the codices," Metzín's father said.

"Yes, but you know he is no normal boy."

"'Of two worlds.' You will never let me forget. Two worlds—yours and mine. But in my world, a merchant's son becomes like his father."

"And if I were to lose you all to a foul mood of Yacatecuhtli?"

"Then so be it. The god of merchants decides, not you or I."

"And he may be married soon. How would he raise children?"

"I have."

"Axa." Her voice became more tender as she pronounced his name. "The master warrior has already taken him in the telpochcalli.

He attests to Metzín's potential. Axa, have a warrior son. Let him stay this time."

"Very well. He stays. This time." Metzín's father let out a long sigh. "But now I go. Like the gods, the nobles never sleep, or the merchants."

"Will you be leaving again?"

"That is what I hope to find out."

Shhh… shhh. The broom strokes slowed, fading to the farther regions of the house and then the patio.

Metzín tied his cloak, grabbed a small pouch of cacao beans from his wicker chest, and went quickly to the cooking area to splash water on his face. He found Tototli there scraping the fine thorns off the oval leaves of nopal cacti.

"Come with me to the market," Metzín told him.

"And the cacti?" Tototli asked with hopeful, raised eyebrows. "I am not finished yet."

"The nopales will wait." And he tugged the servant-slave out the front door.

THE GREAT market, Tlatelolco. They walked toward the far-right side of the city, moving along with countless canoes and droves of people transporting goods: earthenware, bags of jewelry, lengths of cloth, fruit and vegetables, turkeys cuffed at the ankles, cut flowers, and any other tradable item one could imagine. They walked in line with the citizens in the usual orderly and subdued fashion, but Metzín carried a secret jubilance inside, along with the slightest pang of guilt. He ought to have told his mother where he was heading. More importantly, he ought not feel so content for having Tototli at his side. But a trip to the market, especially the grand market every fifth day, which always brought him a sense of liberty, was sufficient to explain his happiness. And he had just returned from the trading trip and a couple of long days in the telpochcalli.

As they neared the entrance, the masses of merchants and buyers slowed. A crowd of people waited to be admitted by the impassive guards. They checked for suspicious goods, fake cacao beans, and unacceptable weaponry and were ready to haul any scammers or accused criminals to the market court, where judges waited. Once inside, the multitudes dispersed to their destinations—livestock in one direction, clothing in another, cooking wares and jewelry in yet others.

Metzín paused to find that distractible Tototli had fallen behind, his mouth agape and his eyes wide. "What happened? Haven't you ever been here before?"

"Only as a small child. And then again when…."

"When what?"

"When you bought me."

"As the gods desire," Metzín said, pulling on his arm. "Now come along. You will someday be a free man again."

Tototli followed as directed. "Yes," he said. "I hope someday so."

"And if you were? What would you do then? Go back to the chinampas and pray to Tlaloc for rain?"

"No," he answered determinedly. "I believe my destiny is to be a musician."

"A musician?"

"Yes," he said with a surprising, dreamy smile. "I was meant to study in the *mecatlan*. I would play the flute or shake rattles before the emperor and dance the ceremonial dances along with all the tlapizque for the nobles. We would play through the night till the hint of dawn, offering rhythmic beauty as tribute to the gods."

"And you would be a great musician, I am sure."

"I know it. I am of the birds. It is my nature."

"There may still be time."

"Let Xochipilli decide. The god of music and games surely has his chosen ones."

"That is most certain."

As he neared his destination, Metzín focused on the many goods laid out on cloths and displayed in large baskets. He could smell incense burning, so he knew they were in the section where spiritual items were sold. He stopped before the merchandise of a familiar old woman. Her wrinkles were the hieroglyphics of her history.

"Greetings, wise mother," he said to her, looking over an assortment of pointed, carved stones, shiny chips of obsidian, triangular shark teeth, fish spines, and thick cactus thorns nearly as long as his thumbs.

"What will you take, my son?"

"These," he said, picking up a handful of the cactus thorns. He tested the point of one with the tip of his finger.

"Sharp and durable," she said.

"You always have exactly what I'm looking for." He handed her the thorns, which she placed in a small envelope of thick paper. Then he gave her as many cacao beans from his pouch.

"And so we are both blessed."

Metzín turned to hand Tototli the envelope, but the servant-slave had wandered a few stalls down. He strolled over to see what his companion was looking at. Enthralled, Tototli had the expression of a child at the sweet berry and nut stand. Metzín followed his gaze to the ground where the vendor, an older man with white hair, had flutes of all sorts for sale in wood, bamboo, and clay.

The vendor looked at him, certainly noticing his humble clothing, bare skin, and worn sandals. "Futt." The man shooed him away.

"Which do you like?" Metzín asked, pulling him back by the elbow and squinting indignantly at the elder.

"Well, all of them."

Metzín picked up a small clay flute in the shape of a bird. The black instrument had four finger holes on the top, and its tail doubled as a mouthpiece so that the sound would come out of its beak. Its tiny spread wings served as handles and the entire figure was adorned with painted designs of white. Metzín put the device to his lips and blew. A deafening shrill ensued.

Tototli held out his hand deferentially. Metzín gave him the flute. He raised it to his mouth and proceeded to play a simple tune, which elicited a delighted smile from both Metzín and the surprised vendor.

"How much?" Metzín asked.

The man showed his ten fingers. Metzín returned with eight. The man nodded and Metzín paid him the beans.

A few steps down the aisle, Metzín presented Tototli with the flute. "A gift for a magical musician."

Tototli accepted it modestly. He played a few more notes before tucking it safely into his loincloth.

They spent the rest of the afternoon browsing around the market and had a small lunch of maize cakes and grilled frogs. When the conches sounded, the vendors began to pack up, and the many buyers headed toward the exit. Metzín and Tototli followed the flow back toward Metzín's home, but when they reached the aqueduct, Metzín turned onto the causeway that led outside the city.

"Your house is back this way, is it not?" Tototli asked.

"Just follow."

After another long walk, the two were on the shore of the lake, near the lower-class suburbs of the fishermen and farmers.

"This is Chapultepec, the city of grasshoppers."

"Do you need to buy something here?"

"No. But I want to show you something."

Inland from the shore, past smoky fires from the one-room huts, Metzín led Tototli off the walking trail. "Hurry," he said nervously, noting Tototli's tired appearance. "We don't want anyone to see." And they disappeared into the trees and canyons of the foothills.

"Where are we going?"

"Quiet," Metzín whispered. "It's a private place I found during the battle exercises. You are not to tell."

"Yes, Master Metzín."

Soon, they were out of sight of the entire city.

Metzín found the tree he'd been looking for. It stood upon a slope and bent out strangely. "Over here," he said. He knelt on the ground, dug his hands into the dirt, and pulled away a dry branch that he had placed there some time before. Leaves fell away from the fan of tiny branches and twigs. He set it to one side, revealing an opening in the earth about as wide as his hips.

"I hide in here at times to evade my opponents," he explained to Tototli. "Follow me… and make sure no one sees you."

Metzín lowered himself in and guided the thin legs of Tototli in until they hit bottom.

"What is this?" Tototli asked.

"Just a hollow made by a fallen tree, I guess."

"How far back does it go?"

"I'm not sure. I've only gone as far as the light would allow," Metzín said.

"Do you pray here?"

"Sometimes. Or think."

"Okay. So have we come to pray and think?" Tototli asked.

Metzín could barely make out the form of Tototli's body in the scant light. He had been thinking very punishable thoughts—and he was losing control over some of them. A glint of light shone in Tototli's black eyes. The temptation was overcoming Metzín. Finally.

"Come closer," Metzín said softly.

"Why?"

He touched the young man in the darkness, afraid he'd soon suffer overwhelming regret. Yet he had to know. He had to taste it. And perhaps then the desire to devour the young man would dissipate.

"Turn around."

"Alright."

"You'll never say anything."

"No."

"And take off your loincloth."

"If that is what you wish," Tototli whispered.

"Do you not also wish for it?"

"In truth, I do."

Chapter Nine

IN THE morning the rain returned. Diego's head throbbed. It was all he could do to get his assistant dressed and to the car. He decided to return to the driver's seat after listening so long to Gerardo's raspy snores, which, along with his thoughts, had kept him awake. In a way he had hoped that something might happen between them, and he'd followed Gerardo's moves while feigning sleep. Most of his associates at the university regarded Diego as nothing but a dedicated professional, a fanatic of archaeology. And he was those things. But he felt lonely at times.

That didn't excuse the imprudent events of the prior evening, his logical side argued. Loneliness was an inadequate reason to threaten the cohesion of the team and therefore the entire project. Romance was the root of many evils, especially romance among coworkers. He began to feel remorse.

He pulled over at a roadside restaurant for coffee and the waitress pointed him to the north. But they had come from the north, so he realized that in order to arrive at that particular motel, they had passed the excavation site where they could have slept. No wonder he hadn't recognized it.

He looked at Gerardo, passed out in what appeared to be a very uncomfortable position. His beard showed a few days of growth, and his mouth threatened to drip saliva any moment. Diego had found him to be an attractive man—an easy smile, the classic curved nose and dark complexion of the Aztecs, a witty sense of humor, and a reassuring enthusiasm for work. Yet this instant he found solace in the fact that Gerardo was asleep, unattractive even; it made it that much easier to avoid the awkwardness of the morning after.

He realized now what Gerardo's mother might be afraid of. After all, it is said that mothers always know. They had all seemed to love him, but there had been the strange mixed messages from Eunice—the initial hesitancy before the welcome, the uncertainty in her voice as she had acknowledged Gerardo's regard for him. The protectiveness was there. But why, unless she sensed a vulnerability and, in Diego a—

what? Corruptor? Abuser of authority? And what would she think of him now? What would they *all* think of him if they knew?

He thought for an instant of Gerardo's estranged sister. What had happened to her? Would Gerardo and she share the same fate? Was that what frightened him into such secrecy and evident shame? He wondered what other pieces of the story were missing.

The rain began to pour down hard, slamming on the windshield. The wipers exerted themselves uselessly, and the windows filled with fog. He maximized the defroster to little avail and considered waking Gerardo to ask him to wipe the humidity away. *No, better he remain asleep for now.*

In the silence Gerardo's unconsciousness allowed, Diego's thoughts drifted to the past. By the last year of his preparatory school, he still hadn't had a serious romance of any sort.

As his schoolmates had lost themselves with their girlfriends or boyfriends, he had plunged himself more deeply into the books. It had paid off—he always scored close to the top on exams and report cards. He had entered easily into the university and earned a full scholarship along the way, having convinced himself that those adolescent relationships were meaningless distractions from life's more important goals.

Even back then he had considered the idea that he was homosexual. Or asexual. It was as though his body had not experienced the spurt of hormones that teenagers were known for. Gay or straight, he'd found sexuality of little import. And he'd had the sense that, had he spoken to his mother and siblings about it, they would have reacted with the same indifference they had to most of his aspirations. Since he didn't turn to drugs or crime or drop out of school, they had pretty much left him alone. In the end he realized they left him more alone than he'd ever imagined. Yes, his past had made him a professor—quite the expert on many things a studious and responsible nature can lead one to master—yet quite the novice of human relationships.

A few more minutes down the road, he pulled off at the familiar site of the project, hoping to God that he wouldn't continue to regret… anything.

He tapped Gerardo's shoulder. No response. He checked the seat behind him for an umbrella. Nothing. The rain had let up a little, but he'd have to make a dash.

"Gerardo, we're here."

"Mm-hm." Gerardo stirred in the seat but did not sit up.

Diego looked outside and saw nothing but rain, mud, and his blue tarp on top of the temple flapping in the breeze. More importantly, he saw no one. He hurried out of the car and ran up the steps to his headquarters, as if fleeing the scene of a crime.

On top of the temple, he adjusted the tarp that had been brought down by the weight of the water. It extended from the entrance of a small room on top of the pyramid where he stored his personal items and had set up a cot. He pulled his nearly obsolete laptop from a case in the back and dragged the card table into the little room where he and his computer would be safer from the rain, albeit in almost total darkness, except for what light the doorway allowed in. When his eyes adjusted, he could make out a few bats that hung noiselessly on the ceiling—he wouldn't bother them if they didn't bother him. The dank little room smelled of moisture and fungus, but that fit perfectly with his role, following in the footsteps of his counterparts who had carried out their studies decades earlier, commandeering as studios the ceremonial rooms restricted in their time to the Mayan priests of the famous site at Palenque.

Its history notwithstanding, the dark little room provided a place for him to steal away from the rain, from the people, and from Gerardo. He hadn't completely discounted the chance of romance, yet the possibility of some terrible consequence—scandal in the workplace, drama with Gerardo's family, or a plain old broken heart—weighed far more heavily on him. He'd hidden away, safe from intimacy, for so long in his life that one more day wouldn't hurt.

The showers continued throughout the day. The only faces he saw were the groggy little mugs of the bats. He trusted his team would find a way to advance the project despite the trying weather. By nightfall he'd barely completed two pages of his report, further proof of the deleterious effects of his undisciplined actions.

He hadn't stopped thinking of Gerardo. He remembered the day he had stepped into his office, visibly excited and nervous about the interview. Diego had liked him from the start, sensing he'd contribute zeal and important skills to the project. In these few months, they'd come to know each other and work together well, as one hand coordinates with the other—and somewhere inside he had wondered where and how deep the relationship might go. When he allowed himself to admit it, a small part of him had wished, or merely daydreamed, about seeing Gerardo's lighthearted face happy and blindly smitten. So he felt quietly disappointed by the inevitable letdown after a night in a sordid motel. Yet an even bigger part of him felt more disappointed because, somehow, someway, so many people out there still fell in love.

"WE'RE HAVING a hard time keeping the water out. I'm afraid we're going to lose what's left of the fiber cloth," Gerardo reported first thing the following morning. "Once it dries, it may disintegrate."

"What have you done to protect it?" the professor asked.

"We spent all day yesterday building a dam around Jade and Handy, but we're working against gravity and erosion. The topsoil is fine, so it washes away."

"Jade and Handy?"

"Oh, sorry. We named them yesterday. You know, the one with the jade and the other... well, it looks like his hand was placed on top of the other's. Could have happened afterwards, of course; some shifting could have occurred. Anyway, a stream of water broke through the wall."

"I'm counting on you to fix it. You've got to protect them." Diego surprised himself with the severity in his voice.

"I know. I'm on it. We'll have to get better materials brought in. We're trying to work wonders with a single pump that has half the capacity it ought to have."

"More materials aren't in the budget."

"Is money all you're worried about?" Gerardo turned around and quickly descended the stairs. Diego watched him as he made the walk all the way down. He crossed the clearing and disappeared into some trees without once looking back.

Diego stayed in the shelter of the temple, his laptop and the bats his sole companions. By early afternoon he felt more like an accountant than an architect. His tables and worksheets displayed costs and balances, special attention paid to those incidental items not projected in the grant. Even with his reading glasses on, the boxes blurred, and the numbers became a sort of alphabet soup. As much as he tried, he could no longer concentrate on his reports. He had to go face his true preoccupation, especially since that particular preoccupation hadn't come to face him.

When he arrived at the burial site, he found Jade and Handy almost completely exposed, lying together as if on a bed of dry earth. The crew had managed to pump out all the water, dig a sort of moat that channeled the water away, fortify the tarp, and construct a wall about knee high to protect the archaeological treasures.

"Now *that* looks fit for *National Geographic*," he said cheerfully, imagining that they might not look at him the same for having lost his professionalism and shown bias for a team member.

The crew stood up from their respective tasks, satisfied expressions on their faces.

"Ready for the next downpour," one of them stated with a genuine smile.

"Nothing should happen now, unless we get a hurricane," another said.

"Do not incite the gods," said a third, Hugo.

"This is a top-notch job," Diego praised, relieved by their tones and their focus on the work. They appeared oblivious to his internal turmoil.

"The design was Gerardo's," someone added.

"Yeah," confirmed an intern who was putting finishing touches on the wall. "We've got to give credit where credit is due."

Gerardo stood on the opposite side of the burial from Diego, who had yet to look him in the face. And when he did, Diego's gaze was met by a timid but penetrating stare. Diego grinned at him in acknowledgement. "It is fabulous. I couldn't have done it better myself."

"Thanks," Gerardo said quietly.

Diego stepped over to get a closer look at Jade and Handy, his professional focus rejuvenated. "Alright, let's continue the photos and brush away the dirt. There have got to be more artifacts. They left them, now we find them... but carefully, patiently, methodically."

One of the interns looked at him, wiping her forehead with the back of her hand and leaving a big smear of mud on her face.

Diego reconsidered. "Well, enough for today. You all look pretty tired from a hard day's work. Double-check the stakes on the tarp, and let's call it a day. We can get a fresh start on it tomorrow."

They all let out a relieved sigh at once. They checked the stakes, stacked the tools, and headed off to get cleaned up and rested. Except for his assistant, who stepped closer to Diego.

"Crushed?" Gerardo said.

The professor, who had kneeled down to examine Jade's cranium, turned to look at Gerardo. "Excuse me?"

"Crushed? I said. Do you think his skull had been crushed somehow?"

"Oh, yeah. Sure looks like he may have suffered a fatal blow to the head." He stood up in front of Gerardo and risked a couple pats on Gerardo's shoulder. They both jumped a bit at the physical connection. "Uh… you did a great job here. I'm… uh… I'm sorry if I wasn't too cool the last time."

"No. You were right. I should have taken the proper precautions."

"Well, you've certainly made up for it and then some. Let any of our sponsors come out for an audit now. They'll double the grant when they see this dig. It's amazing work."

"I learned from the best."

"Well, uh, it's getting kind of late," Diego said. "I guess I should go and finish what I was working on." He turned to walk back to the temple.

"Professor?"

"Yeah?"

"Count on you for Sunday again? My family's getting used to seeing you."

"Sure, right. You know… about that…. I think it's best if we keep it on a professional level, you know?"

Gerardo smiled awkwardly. "Yes. I guess we let the tequila get the best of us." He paused a second. "So, strictly professional? But professionals have to eat too."

"True."

"Sunday it is, then?"

"Yes. Sunday it is."

Chapter Ten

THE CONCHES and gongs of dawn. Metzín hurried off his mat for the start of *Etzalqualiztli*, the month of maize and beans. He'd have to be down at the lake with the rest of the telpochcalli for cleansing. *B-ROOOM, BONG, bong.* As he scurried around his room in preparation, the house filled with a pleasing melody, as if a bird had taken the home for a nest.

Shhh….shhh. His mother had woken early too and started her cleansing. "Where did you get that, boy?"

Metzín went into the kitchen to answer her. "I gave it to him. Can you not hear his talent? He was meant to be a musician."

"This is no time for it," she scolded Tototli. "Put that whistle away before I crush it beneath my foot. This is a month of penance. Go outside and bring me back a turkey to slaughter for the feast."

Tototli tucked his flute away and went to the back patio as instructed.

"And you, my youngest child, what has made you buy presents for a servant-slave? What were you thinking?"

"Did you not hear? He has taught himself to play."

"This is no time for play," she said sternly as she swept. "You will soon be a man and you will take on a man's responsibilities." She stopped moving her broom and looked at him tenderly. "My dear son of two worlds. You are so often in some other than this one. This is One Etzalqualiztli. Your father is leaving today, and he is letting you stay. But there could soon be war. And for now, you must get down to the lake lest you be punished. In the time of penance, infractions are not taken lightly. My dear, what will you do when you have a wife and children to worry about? Now, walk quickly. The conches are sounding again."

"Yes, Mother."

He looked at the shrine his mother had made in the front room, beside the hearth. It was made in a nook in the wall that had been designed for praising the gods. The shrine centered around a large ceramic vessel that bore on one side a mask of two faces—the one of life enveloped by the one of death. Life came from death. The vessel sat upon three legs. When he was younger, she had often shown him those three legs. "It stands on three legs," she would say, "like people, who cannot always stand on just their own two." She maintained the shrine appropriate for the given month, and found ways to make it beautiful, as she loved things of beauty. This time, she had adorned it with dry corn and beans, long cornhusks, and bean sprouts arranged with her usual flair.

Metzín splashed water on his face and left. He walked as briskly as he could toward the lakeshore, running not being permitted in public. In the bathing area, some of the students were wading in the water already, and the master warrior was pacing on a wooden catwalk above. He had begun the chants. The master warrior lifted his eyes when Metzín arrived. With a slight movement of his head, he directed him into the water. Metzín stripped off his cloak and loincloth and entered the cool water with careful steps, trying not to splash.

The students were spaced a few steps apart. Metzín waded to the closest end where Peo stood, his arms following the movements on the master warrior. He took up the end of the line beside Peo. When the instructor chanted praises to Tlaloc, they repeated.

"Late as usual," Peo said under his breath. "Your mother didn't shake you awake?"

Metzín ignored his comments.

"And always the exception, cared for like a delicate sack of eggs."

Metzín closed his eyes, trying to concentrate on the chant and the cleansing.

"Or a wounded snail. Is that what you are?"

But Metzín continued to focus, knowing the importance of purification, and that ignoring Peo was the only way to handle the heckling of the big boar. More importantly, if they would soon be off to war, he'd need the blessing of the gods.

He returned home as the sun began to descend, hungry after the fast he'd endured throughout the day. The feast would not begin until well after darkness had set in. When he stepped into the house, he encountered a bloody scene. Precious water had been spilt all around the house. Confused, his heart began to pump faster. He searched the house for Tototli, wondering if he'd ever hear the sweet melody of the young man's flute again. Had he been offered to Tlaloc?

He looked back at the frame of the door, scanning it for a blue handprint. There was none.

When he turned back, his mother walked out from the kitchen, precious crimson water splattered on her face and streaking down her bosom and skirt. Even her feet were stained red.

"Mother, is everything as it should be?" he asked, restraining his initial panic.

"Yes, son."

"And Tototli? Is he here?"

"No. He has gone," she answered stoically.

He maintained his upright posture, though inside his heart sank.

"You mustn't worry," she said.

No, Metzín knew that he would meet him again in the path of the sun.

"He has gone for firewood."

"Firewood?" he asked, this time suppressing his hopefulness.

"Yes, I imagined you'd need a steam bath after a day in the lake."

"Ah. Yes. And the precious water? What happened? Did you offer your own to Tlaloc?"

She laughed. "No, son. I did not. And neither did the turkey agree to offer his own to us. Even without a head, he managed to find his way around the whole house."

His tension subsided instantly. "Let me help you clean it."

"You rest. I will have the boy call you when the temazcalli is ready. We have a long night ahead of us."

"Okay."

Within minutes he lay sleeping on his mat, and a disturbing visitor came to his dreams. A black bird with foul, fiery breath and a beak of obsidian. It squawked at him unintelligibly, its gaze piercing the skin on his chest like so many cactus thorns. It was angry. He asked what it wanted, but it did not answer, and he tried to run away, but he could not. Then he woke up to a gentle voice, "Master Metzín, the temazcalli is ready." Still aggravated by the visitor in his dream, Metzín felt a discomfort in his chest. He rose to check his mat and found little mounds where he had been lying. He lifted the mat to discover a pair of small rocks where his chest had been. Had the gods put them there? Were they like the black bird? Were they an omen?

"Master Metzín, your steam bath is ready."

"I heard you," he snapped, glaring at Tototli with eyes as sharp as javelins. "I will be right there."

The young man quickly sucked in a breath and looked away, bowing his head in acquiescence before retreating and leaving Metzín with the bitter echo of his own voice. Metzín recalled too, the words of his mother about the impending war and the prospect of him starting a family. What if she knew about the sickness that had come upon him? What if anyone found out? He trembled at the thought of an execution, where his insides would be spilled like the turkey's. And the disgrace his family would suffer, especially now in the month of Etzalqualiztli, when one ought to be most penitent. He would have to find a way to ward off this powerful, evil malady.

"Metzín," his mother called from the main room of the house. "The fire is waiting. We mustn't waste."

So he got to his knees outside the temazcalli, where he had shed his cloak in the waning daylight and where, it seemed, all his good and healthy intentions had also remained. As he crawled into the darkness, toward the hot and steamy interior and toward Tototli, who awaited him, that crude, carnal stiffness seized his groin again. He found the waiting mat and lay upon it face up. Tototli's hands soon rested upon his chest. And Metzín could not control the urge to pull the young man toward him, scour his body with his hands in a mutual massage, taste the flesh, smell the hair, and brush the lips and eyes with his mouth. A demon, sweet and spicy, possessed and tempted him within the confines of those bricks. And he could not stop as Tototli's slender body matched his gyrations until that demon had been satisfied, leaving him upon the mat, satiated and expended.

BELOW THE temple of Tlaloc, people gathered. Torches on top of the pyramid, one of the largest in all of Tenochtitlán, lit the faces of the many priests who danced the sacred dances of the Rain God. The people watched in awe as the ritual to one of the most revered gods unfolded.

Drummers lined the stairs, beating in perfect unison. A high priest dressed in a dark, feathered cape—the plumed serpent—rose above the others as if in flight. He raised his arms to the sky, praising Tlaloc, and then he lowered them, waving his arms at the people below, bestowing upon them the messages of the god. "Purity of life. Knowledge of doctrine. Severity and scrupulousness in morals!" Another came forth in the same plumed form, his arms stained the same blue as the feathered cape. The high priest continued, "Humility. Compassion. Earnestness. Morality!"

The other priests brought the blue-armed serpent closer. The drums beat deeper, louder, and faster. They raised the blue arms of the serpent, turning him around, as the high priest, with awe in his eyes, greeted the god before him. He continued to bellow the virtues of Tlaloc, but as Metzín gazed upon the scene high above him, all he heard was "Morality. Morality. Morality!"

Finally, the serpent-god was laid upon the stone, his arms held by a pair of priests, his legs by others. The high priest praised him for his precious water, that he might bring the life-giving rains, the bounty, to the people. "Water and rain. Maize and beans. We honor your sacrifice, your great gifts!"

He raised an obsidian knife above him. It flashed with fire. And the knife came down into the serpent-god, and precious red water surged out in two high waves, drenching the high priest as Tlaloc might drench every field and chinampa. The drumming continued as the priest twisted the knife in the writhing body until he cut loose the eagle's sacred cactus-fruit and held the dripping organ above his head to the cheers of the people.

Another priest approached the sacrificial stone, clutching a broad wooden sword edged with obsidian. The blue arms were stretched out and the sword struck down on the shoulder once, and again, until the arm detached from the body. It was swung in circles over the heads of the priests and launched upon the stairs, where it fell and rested lifelessly. The crowd continued to cheer over the sound of the drums as the other arm, legs, head, and torso followed down the stairs, meager gifts to a powerful, benevolent deity from a humble people.

Then they returned to their homes to feast and honor the god with their own small sacrifices, hoping to be so moral that they were worthy of his generosity.

And in the patio behind their house, Metzín and his mother gave of themselves tributes to Tlaloc. Metzín pulled sharp spikes from the envelope of thick cactus thorns. He closed his eyes and prayed inside for morality as he cut into the skin of his legs and arms until blood dripped down his calves and forearms. Then he pierced his earlobes, tolerating the pain in a silent, personal plea for health, normality, and morality.

Let me be no longer afflicted with this ailment. Let me be rid of unnatural temptation.

Chapter Eleven

"WHAT ABOUT your family?" Diego asked Gerardo as they drove down the highway to Xonacahuacán.

"Oh, they'll be there. Like every Sunday."

"All of them?"

"Yeah, my mother and father, Uncle Layo, my cousins Chapín, Joaquín, and Alejandrina, my brothers—"

"And your sister?"

"Of course, they should be there too."

"All of them?"

"Everyone usually goes if they can make it."

"Are you putting me on?" Diego said, starting to get frustrated.

"Why? Not everyone can make it all the time. They have in-laws."

"Okay, so I guess your family got over the problem with your sister?"

"Ah… you're talking about Ruth."

"I don't know. You never told me her name."

Gerardo paused. "Let's say Ruth was the black sheep of the family."

"*Was*? You speak of her in past tense?"

"It's just that I haven't seen her for a while now."

"I see. Black sheep. What was she, some sort of devil worshipper or druggie or something?"

"Well…." Another pause. "She veered from my parents'—or *our* beliefs."

Diego took a long turn on the curving highway, waiting for Gerardo to continue. He finally looked over. "Am I prying? Is it something you just don't want to talk about?"

"She is bisexual," Gerardo finally spit out. "She let herself be influenced by this short-haired marimacha in high school. Then she got a tattoo and wore black all the time, definitely not the norm in these rural parts. She brought the girl over to the house. That didn't go over well. She argued for days with my parents about how her girlfriend ought to be accepted just like any of our boyfriends or girlfriends."

"And?"

"My parents wouldn't consider it. They offered therapy and prayer and said no, the girl could not visit. When Ruth turned eighteen, she left for Mexico City with the girl."

"And they're still together?"

"No. She's actually married to a man now, living down in Xochimilco. We found out she just had a second child this year."

"And she hasn't come back?"

"No. We haven't seen her since she left."

"But you seem to know a lot about her."

"She's close with my sister Ofelia. They write e-mails. In fact, my mother told Ofelia to invite Ruth back after she got married. Ruth's response, in short, was hell no."

"Pretty tough. Your family seems so cohesive."

"Good, old-fashioned family values."

"And," Diego asked, "is that what you're worried about?"

"What?"

"That you could get disowned?"

"Disowned, for what?"

"Because you're gay."

"Gay? I can't be gay, I'm Catholic."

Diego looked at him askance. "You're kidding, right?"

"Well. I don't know," he answered, nervously searching for words. "I mean, I just, uh…."

"Confirmed. You're afraid you'd be rejected," Diego said decidedly.

"Okay, okay." Gerardo held up his hands protectively. "I guess I'm gay," he explained. "But I'm not a *gay* gay, you know? I'm from a small town. People notice. They talk."

"They judge."

"Exactly," Gerardo said, finally letting his hands down.

"So, you're in the closet?"

"I'm private." They drove in silence for a long kilometer. "Well," Gerardo said, breaking the awkwardness. "You're private too."

"I'm professional."

"Fecal matter still smells like shit to me."

"You know how it is. People in the professional world can be… irrational."

"As families can be."

"And here we are, two grown men, limited by fear instilled in us by those around us." He shook his head at the sad truth.

"Basically, Professor." Gerardo pointed to the left. "Here's the turn. Let's not miss it."

As the afternoon unfolded, Gerardo's family seemed to be seeing Diego in a new light. The many family members had warmed up to the professor, losing some of the initial formality with him. They still called him "Professor," and most continued to use "usted," the formal "you" pronoun, but their topics of conversation had begun to change as they got to know him.

Diego couldn't help but appreciate the quaint closeness of the traditional family. They seemed so genuine and trusting, enjoying one another's company over food and drinks. Much of that family-centered feeling had been lost in Mexico City, where Diego had grown up, and where so many families struggled to make ends meet in a metropolis of twenty million or more. People were little more than anonymous ants in an enormous anthill, with few opportunities for family get-togethers. Crime was a factor too. It meant that neighbors developed an unfortunate, impenetrable distrust for one another. Gone were the days of open festivities in city neighborhoods. However, in Xonacahuacán, those endearing traditions endured. As he sat among Gerardo's family, he felt as if he'd stepped back through the pages of time.

He could hardly imagine such a harsh rejection of their kin from such a warm family. But he was well aware of the cultural effects of strict adherence to religion—both its benefits for the preservation of a society and its detriments to its evolution. Woe to the black sheep.

More than ever Diego now noticed Gerardo's relaxing charm. An easygoing character, he had a delightful sense of humor, which made talking with him an effortless task, provided the topic was not a sensitive one. He was modest, even self-deprecating at times. He was thoughtful and dutiful, quick to assist his mother with the kitchen and cleaning chores. Diego certainly had seen all of those characteristics in his job performance, and now he understood where those habits had formed. He wondered too, if Gerardo's family suspected anything, or if they watched him watching Gerardo. But no, they appeared carefree and even jubilant, doting on the professor in any way they could. "Have another drink, Professor," and, "Don't hide your appetite."

"So, Professor, tell me more about the project you're working on." Gerardo's mother, Eunice, finally had the chance to sit down and be sociable. "I trust my son is performing his duties well."

"Oh, yes, I know the boys are in good hands."

"The boys?" she asked.

"That's what the team has taken to calling them—Jade and Handy, actually."

"Ah, well, I assume there was nothing out of the ordinary. I mean there are Aztec graves all over the place, right?"

He felt as if her gaze were starting to penetrate him, as though she were an archaeologist on her own dig. "In truth, we believe we may have come across an unusual circumstance," he said, choosing his words carefully and wondering why he should. He was only sharing the facts about a gravesite, after all. Yet he feared that she had suspicions about her son and him that mirrored his suspicions about Jade and Handy. "What I mean is that most Aztec bodies were cremated, but these were buried. And, uh, there are some contradictions... mysteries, if you will, regarding such things as their clothing and juxtaposition."

"I see. Juxtaposition? Interesting."

"As with so many details regarding history, we may never be able to put all the pieces together."

"What is it that you're thinking?"

"Señora, it's just hard to speculate."

She perked her head up alertly as a couple of her grandchildren headed into the kitchen behind them, and she put on a polite smile. "I'm looking forward to hearing more about it. I think."

"I'll be glad to tell you as much or as little as you want to know." He let out a nervous laugh as she excused herself to investigate some racket the children were making.

"I APPRECIATE the weekly getaway," Diego said, feeling a bit tipsy as he zoomed down the highway. "Thanks for the invitation."

"You're becoming a permanent feature at the table," Gerardo answered.

"I have to say, I'm not sure how much your mother likes me."

"It's not whether she likes you. She may be afraid that another of her flock will get away."

"Might that happen?" Diego asked.

"What do you mean, Professor?" he asked with feigned ignorance.

Diego's hand lay on the knob of the stick shift. Gerardo's knee was temptingly close. He glanced over at Gerardo's leg, trying also to keep his eyes on the road. "I'm not sure where this is going, but—"

"*This?*"

"Us. I'm not sure where this thing between us is going, but I am certainly feeling closer to you."

"I know," Gerardo said, shifting his glance nervously from Diego to the night sky.

"Yet somehow, despite my better judgment, it still doesn't feel close enough."

"What do you propose, Professor?"

Diego grew frustrated by Gerardo's vague expression, something between flirtatiousness and fear. He found it hard to believe that a grown man could behave so blindly, and force him, a relationship novice, to make all the moves. "I don't know," he finally answered. "I'm just worried about you and your mother. Seemed like last time, you took a giant step away from me and back toward her."

"And you in your shelter in your temple of bricks."

"Maybe." A silent pause ensued. "I know I get worried about things at work. I just can't risk any problems."

"So, what do you propose?"

Diego shot a glance at his leg again, wanting to grab it though his fingers clung desperately to the gear shifter. He took a deep breath, set his eyes on the road, and forced his hand to make the seemingly distant, frightening leap to Gerardo's knee. He grabbed Gerardo's leg more forcefully than he'd intended, wordlessly awaiting some response, some rejection. *It's not a good idea*, he imagined, and *I can't let my family down.* Instead, Gerardo's hand gently covered Diego's, then flipped it over. Gerardo's darker fingers contrasted with Diego's lighter ones as they slid together. Diego breathed a sigh of relief at the soothing feel of Gerardo's gentle hand.

"We can be private," Diego finally answered.

"And professional," Gerardo added.

An impressive multitude of stars shone in the unusually clear night sky—a brilliant streak of the Milky Way and a sliver of the moon that seemed to wink upon them as it hovered high above. Before walking to his tent on the far side of the courtyard, Gerardo accompanied Diego to the temple, as if seeing him to his doorstep, like a boyfriend keeping at a safe, appropriate distance after a first date. They stopped when they reached the base of the stairs.

"Thanks again, Professor," Gerardo said, his voice an official bass tone. No one besides Diego was around to hear them. "The discussion was particularly enthralling."

"Don't be sarcastic," Diego said, reaching out to shake hands.

Gerardo smiled. "Good night, then."

"Good night to you." Diego started up the steep stairs. In the moonlight he noticed that his blue tarp had collapsed outside the temple. He stopped midflight and turned around. "Say, Gerardo."

"Yes, Professor?" Gerardo responded, having walked only a few paces.

"Would you mind assisting me with the tarp? It appears that the wind has toppled it."

"I'd be most delighted. I am your assistant, after all."

Diego waited as Gerardo caught up to him and they climbed the staircase together. At the top they surveyed the fallen sheet. Yet Diego couldn't help but start to survey Gerardo instead, considering a change in the immediate itinerary. He looked down past the courtyard and knew they were alone. Standing at that height renewed his slight wooziness from the liquor and bolstered his confidence. He wrapped his arms around Gerardo and pushed him toward the dark room covered by the tarp. They turned around and brushed their lips together in the darkness. They explored with their hands as though they had just been released from shackles. They unbuttoned their shirts and undid their belts.

"I'm not sure alcohol is a good thing for us," Gerardo said, catching his breath.

But Diego continued his pursuit. "Or perhaps it's precisely what we need."

Chapter Twelve

IN TWO months' time, forty days, Metzín's father would return with word. As decreed, the elders of that primitive tribe to the far left of the world would be allowed one month to respond. Would they peaceably become part of the Aztec empire? If they agreed, their required tribute would be minimal. Though Metzín doubted their wisdom, he knew that most tribes did not readily agree to their destiny. Did the rat turn over its life to the snake without a fight, even when the struggle was futile?

Should the tribe refuse, they'd be given another month after renewed discussions. Would they then see their inevitable future and the uselessness of resistance? The price of the tribute would increase and more resources demanded of them each year—cloth, furs, victuals, gold, or gems. Should the poor souls continue to refuse, the precious water of their leader would be demanded, their temple toppled, and their warriors slain or captured. Only Uitzilopochtli, great warrior and god of all war, knew what the choice would be.

Meanwhile, in the telpochcalli, the young warriors prepared, hoping for a chance at advancement. All prayed for a capture to honor the god. They prayed to become jaguar-knights or eagle-knights. Or, should honor in life not be the will of the gods, to spill their own precious water in battle and travel each day across the sky, and bid farewell to constant peril and to mortality.

Bolster the stores of the tlacochcalli. Fill the racks and storerooms. Fix obsidian blades upon the swords. Sharpen arrowheads and javelins. Carve bows and launchers. Build shields and armor. Prepare the rope for binding the captives and offer to him, Uitzilopochtli, their precious red water and their beating eagle cacti-fruit. Great Aztec, may the empire flourish!

METZÍN DUCKED his head as he crawled ahead of his cohort. They'd come to an uninhabited space in the canyons to practice, and Metzín knew the area well. He had practiced there before, and hunted rabbits, chasing and trapping them in the ravines. Soon, warriors would be the objective, and nothing honored Uitzilopochtli more than a live capture.

He had killed a man before. Excited and frightened, he'd dodged a blow and swung his heavy sword. The man's leg had snapped and was held together only by skin. He'd opened his mouth widely as he cried in agony. Then another blow to the open mouth and his head nearly came off above the jaw. It was a great day when the master warrior ordered Metzín's hair cut in recognition of his achievement. Yet it had only inspired him to further conquest, and soon he would have his chance. What he wouldn't give to one day don the jaguar suit and roar like a mighty beast at Uitzilopochtli's next sacrifices. And what honor to his mother to have given birth to a jaguar-knight.

Below, coming up the canyon, Peo led a rival group of six. This drier landscape did not offer the thick camouflage of the jungle, although the big boar could hardly hide anyway, much less hope to surprise. Instead, Peo would rely on his tusks and his power. Indeed, they didn't attempt to sneak. They appeared to walk casually, as if headed to the market at Tlatelolco. But even a boar had its weaknesses, and Metzín remembered the teachings of the master warrior—patience, stealth, and intelligence—and the old saying, *the hare could vanquish the python.*

Metzín crawled backward toward his group and indicated instructions to them with hand signals, as they had practiced. They doubled around toward the higher part of the canyon where the trail from below met the rim. He gave his team a few moments before he appeared at the ledge with a conch. He sucked in a deep breath and blew hard. *B-ROOM.* It rang throughout the canyon, begetting a flurry of screeches and hollers from Peo's team below. "Attack!" Peo yelled. "No mercy!" And his entire squad lifted their shields and began a sprint directly toward him. Metzín stood valiantly to show them his fearlessness and to anger them. But before they reached the top, he disappeared behind a tree in a small grove.

When he heard them top the ridge, he reappeared with the conch. *B-ROOM.*

"Behind the trees. Prepare your bows," Peo directed. And his team nocked leather-tipped, pitch-stained arrows and moved in without hesitation. "Watch your flanks!"

Dropping his conch to where it dangled at his waist, Metzín lifted his wooden sword and pointed it directly at Peo's face.

"Attack!" Peo repeated, and Peo's squad ran toward the grove and fanned out behind the trees. They must have expected to find Metzín's entire squad hidden behind the trunks, but there was no one. They looked up, likely expecting attackers to pounce down upon them. Still no one. So they began to rush in toward Metzín, encircling him. They closed in.

Ffft. An arrow whizzed toward him. It broke against the trunk of the tree, leaving a black stain where it had hit. *Ffft.* Another ricocheted against the shield on Metzín's forearm. He'd avoided the stain of defeat on his armor. But he wouldn't be able to hold them all off alone.

"Now!" he shouted.

Suddenly, the earth rose up around them, as if leaves and dirt rained upward, a dry fury of Tlaloc the rain god.

One of the rival team cried out, then another and another. They were pinned on the ground, legs and arms wrapped behind them like the four legs of captured deer. The snares had worked, and the young men had pounced upon them so quickly that they'd had no chance.

Ffft, ffft. More arrows whisked through the air. One hit dead center in the back of the opposing bowman. He fell to the ground defeated.

Metzín's team, having vanquished their first victims, circled the last of Peo's team. He had drawn his sword and swung it in all directions, as if trying to fight off a swarm of bees. But they were many against one, and he must succumb to the multitude.

Peo, closest to Metzín, who still stood near the tree from behind which he had appeared, dropped his bow and shield. He drew his sword and brandished it with both hands, rage flaring in his eyes. He gnashed his teeth as if baring his tusks and then screamed out like a desperate beast. He rushed toward Metzín, who raised his shield to withstand a blow.

Crash. A heavy swing nearly disjointed his arm at the elbow. *Bang.* Another swing from the opposite side as Peo swung without restraint. Each hit threw Metzín to one side, then the other. Between each swing, Metzín saw the big, exposed body of Peo. He wanted to draw his sword, but his rival was too fast. He could do little more than protect himself.

Finally, Peo raised his sword high with both arms, leaving his entire body vulnerable. But Metzín could only match his move by raising the shield above his head. Though these were only games, an unblocked blow from this boar would send him to Uitzilopochtli before his destined time. He closed his eyes, bracing his shield above him with two arms. *Thud.*

He heard the crash of a blow but felt nothing. Instead, Peo was on the ground before him. Metzín's final team member, the smallest and youngest one, had climbed the tree beside them during the melee, and stood over Peo, triumphantly flaunting the eagle feather he had pulled from Peo's hair. Metzín gathered his group, and they chanted together and danced. Victory!

As Metzín's team helped to pull the rivals up from where they had fallen and began to loosen the fiber ropes, Peo stood up. The little warrior gave Metzín the long feather, which he stuck into his hair. Then, Metzín extended his arm to Peo, whose arm rose to meet his. But the open hand became a closed fist and the big arm moved fast, a solid blow to Metzín's face. He fell heavily to the ground.

WHEN HE awoke, his head throbbed. He opened his eyes for an instant but closed them again when the light stabbed his brain. He raised his hand to his forehead, recalling the time many years ago that his grandfather had passed out and left a gourd of octli on the table and the headache it had caused him. For good reason, only the elderly were permitted to drink the otherwise forbidden liquid, well known to cause cursing, riotousness, rape, and crime in all its forms. Also for good reason, its use was severely punished. Metzín could hardly imagine who would ever want to imbibe—like particular, despicable members of Peo's family were known to do at regular intervals. That loathsome family was often seen at games of gambling too, a certain explanation for their well-known predicament of poverty. If Peo thought he'd gain respect through the telpochcalli, he ought first to adopt a sense of honor.

"It's only a welt, Master Metzín."

The gentle voice was an elixir. He heard the swish of water and felt a cool cloth against his face. He dared to open his eyes again, hoping to see—yes, the face of Tototli. He could not keep from smiling. But then he wondered where he lay. His eyes jumped around to see the faces of his team. He remembered now that Tototli had accompanied him to the game fields, not far from their little cave. He had needed Tototli, he'd told his mother, to carry his weapons. As he'd never been a team leader before, his mother had given Tototli permission to go with him. His team sat around him, watching and listening to the voice of the master warrior.

"The losers," he was saying to all the vanquished groups, "will be washing and sweeping." A moan came from half the crowd.

"It is everyone's duty to clean the telpochcalli!" complained Peo, who stood up in defiance. "Even the tricksters'."

"So you will not be cleaning, Peohuatac," clarified the master warrior. Peo sat down smugly. "Instead, your team will row the excrement canoe to the manure field and prepare the night soil."

"But master—" Peo protested.

"And I am sure your family in the chinampas will appreciate it!" the master warrior said with a rare tone of impatient authority.

"The winners"—his voice became celebratory—"will be in the house of singing and dancing."

Cheers and howls of the winners erupted, splitting Metzín's head in two. Though he was happy for his win, the pounding again overcame him. He pulled Tototli's ear to his mouth. "No singing and dancing for me. Just get me home."

Chapter Thirteen

"FLESH—SKIN, organs, and muscle tissue—when preserved, is extremely telling," the professor explained to his young team as they sat outside in a circle for their daily review. "It can offer answers to questions about nutrition, flesh wounds, body adornments—"

"Which can, in turn, indicate social status and religious beliefs, right?" an intern asked.

"Absolutely, because tattoos, piercings, pigmentation, and even scarring, all often provide clues about such things as family or social roles. Farmers tend to have thickened skin in their feet and hands, and even darker complexion on the shoulders and back, whereas a warrior might have battle wounds, and priests, self-inflicted sacrificial cuts."

A couple of the students scratched notes.

"In cases of mummification or freezing, forensic archaeologists have uncovered tremendous information, particularly with today's technology. Unfortunately in the case of our dig, no traces of flesh have been found, which means many of those details that flesh might have revealed are next to impossible to determine.

"Thanks to our expert forensic photographer—" Diego pointed at Anabel "—who has been painstakingly chronicling the entire project, we know the exact positioning of the bodies and will be able to place them as they were in the case of any accidental or purposeful movement." The team gave her a small round of applause, in response to which she raised her digital camera and snapped a picture of the professor and the team. "It seems we've become so accustomed to her constant clicking, we hardly notice her anymore—a mini reality show—but her work will help us on several fronts. We prevent lost information due to mistakes, we share information with other experts around the world, and we procure funding. I'll worry about the funding. You continue your great work on the dig."

Another intern raised his hand.

"Yes, Guillermo."

"Do we have a cause of death yet?"

"Thank you. I was getting to that." The professor pulled up a document on his laptop and scrolled through several written pages, until he reached the close-up photos of Jade's cranium. The team waited as he read through the accompanying paragraphs, pointing to the screen with his finger. "Okay. Here's what I'm talking about—the need to bring in other experts. Basically, our colleagues have hypothesized that the young man, whom we've named Jade, was killed by a trauma to the head."

"Does that mean he was killed, or might it have been an accident?"

"Well, it's sometimes hard to tell. However, it appears that the force of the blow was severe." He blew up the picture on the screen, focusing on the bone fracture. "We have sometimes seen this sort of breaking in falls. But where could there have been such falls in Tenochtitlán? It was mostly flat ground and two-story buildings. There were temples, of course, but a person in a fiber loincloth wouldn't likely have been in a temple, unless he was sacrificed, in which case the wounds would be entirely different. Even then, if he had fallen from a perilous height, we would generally find multiple broken bones. You don't just fall on your head. You fall on your side or faceup or facedown. Even if you fall on your head, you break your neck too."

"There was damage to other bones, though, right?"

"Yes, but let's take a closer look at the skull first." He zoomed in further, revealing a jagged line across the fragmentation. "We've had some wearing here, but the line measures about six point four centimeters."

"A weapon," answered Guillermo, his eyes wide with wonder.

"Yes. And despite the wear, we were able to salvage some chemical samples, which we sent to the lab. They came back as?" He waited for anyone's guess.

"Ferrous oxide." Vilma, a shy, bespectacled student conjectured.

"Actually, ferric oxide, in traces," the professor corrected. "And silicon oxide."

She snapped her fingers. "Obsidian."

"Exactly. That's what we expected, and that's what the lab confirmed."

"So, he got smacked upside the head with a chunk of sharpened obsidian," Guillermo concluded.

"That's what it looks like. And by someone pretty strong. Of course, warriors practiced and drilled. They knew what they were doing. They could deliver serious blows. Plus, judging by the angle, the blow came from above his head, which could indicate that either the guy was tall—"

"Or the victim was kneeling," Vilma said. "Might he have been sacrificed?"

"Well," said Diego, "you bring up a good point. Sacrifice victims generally had their chests ripped open and their hearts dug out, not necessarily their heads bashed in. But they did vary the style of sacrifices, depending on the month and god being made an offer to. Sometimes women had their heads lopped off in the middle of a dance to the goddess of the earth. They danced away, feigning unawareness, and... chop."

"*Off with her head*!" someone quoted.

"What do you mean, then? We've ruled out an accidental falling. So was he sacrificed or killed in battle?" Anabel asked.

The professor shook his head. "Are those the only choices? Will we ever be 100 percent sure? The more evidence we gather, the more we can argue for a theory. Killed in battle? It's a weak argument now, based on his clothing. He wasn't dressed for battle."

"Is he wearing what he died in?"

"Good question. Then again, given his wounds, it supports a fight."

"*Wounds*? I thought you said there was just one."

"Ah, we didn't get to the other yet. And this both assists and confounds us." He scrolled down another couple of pages on the computer. "There was another wound on his tibia, a seemingly smaller wound. There were also some traces here of silicon oxide, though the smaller, triangular-shaped wound suggests the tip of an arrow."

"If only we could find the arrow."

The professor nodded. "It appears to have been removed. Indeed, I'm a little surprised we haven't found more artifacts."

"But the other wound means—" Guillermo started.

"That he was in some sort of battle," Vilma finished.

"And what about the other body?" another student asked. "What did we find there?"

"Handy." The professor sighed. "This only goes to show what an unusual find we have here."

"Any evidence as to cause of death?" Guillermo asked, looking up from his notes.

"Nothing yet. A single injury to a carpal on the left hand—"

"The free hand?" Vilma clarified.

"Correct. Seems to have been healed. The bone tissue had been well bonded. It had mended before he died. That was likely some sort of accident in his youth."

"And the cloak?"

"You mean what was left of it? Definitely cotton, abounding with skilled embroidery. Someone cared when they made that cloak. It follows, then, that someone cared for him. Definitely upper class. Still, cause of death is unknown on this one."

"Blood stains!" The entire group turned to Gerardo, who walked excitedly into the group meeting, pulling a written report from a manila courier envelope.

"You were right, Vilma!" he said. "We had argued over the staining on the cloak. It was quite disintegrated and soiled. But look." He held up the papers. "The darkened splotches were definitely blood. And, based on the DNA evidence, it was his blood. This guy may have died in a violent, or at least bloody, way."

The professor reached out his hand, eager for the report and gave it a cursory read as they all sat watching him.

"I doubted her," Gerardo said. "I was sure it was plain old dirt. But she detected it."

"And this is just one more piece of this puzzle," the professor said gleefully. He held out his arms to receive Vilma and Gerardo, one wrapped in each arm. He planted a big kiss on Vilma's proud face and a kiss on Gerardo's cheek. *CLICK*. Anabel snapped a picture.

Chapter Fourteen

A RING of shadow around his eye did not keep Metzín from participating in the battle practice, nor did a cheap, embarrassing wound inflicted by Peo. As the sun rose each day and the gongs sounded, the warriors gathered at the lake for early morning purification and chanted invocations to Uitzilopochtli. After a ration of maize cakes, they crossed the causeway parallel to the great aqueduct, returning to the canyons for drills and training. Evening time was spent in the house of singing and dancing, except for every fifth night, because they were granted these days for duties at home.

The house seemed particularly empty. Though most of his brothers had been paired with wives and lived in their own homes, and his sisters had also been matched and had left home, they often came by to spend time with family and to allow the grandchildren time to learn their duties from their grandmother. With the men away on the negotiation mission, the women tended to their homes and also spent time with the families of their spouses.

Each day since his father had left, his mother's sweeping of the packed earth floor became more desperate and frequent. And when, one morning in the middle of the month, a number of shiny flying insects the size of the black eyeballs of deer entered the house, she had become convinced that a bad omen was upon them. Spirits were watching, she had said. The success of the mission was in peril. Or someone would not return.

"Will you go to the market today?" she asked Metzín with a stoic, subdued tone and an atypical lisp.

Metzín noticed a cactus thorn in her tongue, reddened saliva filling her mouth. Her forearms bore fresh cuts and traces of blood that had meandered down to her wrists and up to her elbows.

"Yes, Mother, as you wish. What shall I bring back?"

"A pair of large turkeys."

"Are there none left in the patio?"

"They are dead."

"Will you sacrifice another?"

"No, my son. I have made ample offerings to the gods." She looked up to the ceiling. "May they hear me. May they bestow upon us again their benevolence."

"Recall, then, there is no need to cook for many."

"But there is. I will be meeting with the *cihuatlanque* today to negotiate for your bride. The old woman will then visit the administrator and his wife. Will they not be swayed by my turkey and chile porridge?"

"Without a doubt," he answered with a polite smile. "All wish to know your secrets."

"A woman reveals her secrets at careful intervals."

"So, you will say no more about *which* administrator the cihuatlanque will visit?"

"No, son. First we will allow for the gods to do their part. Then she will see the signs that show you are a good match for their daughter. And the turkey porridge will guarantee the arrangement."

"Then I will bring the turkeys as you wish." She handed him a small bag of cacao beans. "And I will bring Tototli with me," he added.

"I believe you can handle the turkeys by yourself," she said.

"Of course I could," he said, glancing at the wall behind her. "But I would like to show him how to purchase the turkeys so that he might run the errand alone."

She smirked. "You have had him accompany you daily to the canyons."

"I have been entrusted with a warrior group. I must focus on my prayers and purification, and not concern myself with hauling weapons and bearing weight."

She shook her head. "Young son, soon you will leave such carefree and childish thoughts behind. How else will you provide for an administrator's daughter? And without a slave of your own."

He put his hands together in front of him, feeling as if she could see right into him, and he looked down to the floor timidly, ashamed. He swallowed hard, but his throat felt as if it were dammed up.

She stepped close to him, raised her reddened arms, and placed her palms on his chest. "The last of my children," she said with a tender smile. "Relish the final days of your childhood. I have done my best to protect you for all of your days, but one day I will no longer be here."

He returned her smile. "I will go now, before the biggest turkeys are claimed."

"HURRY UP." Metzín pulled Tototli along, walking as rapidly as possible without causing suspicion.

Tototli fell a half step behind. "Are we not going to the market at Tlatelolco?" he asked when they turned the corner onto the causeway.

"Quiet."

"But your mother sent us for turkeys."

"Yes, but we are going to the canyons first."

"But there are no lessons there today, Master Metzín."

"I know. I said to remain quiet." But when he looked at Tototli's disconcerted face, he could not resist offering an explanation. "We will first be rabbit hunting." In truth in the previous few days, he had been finding it harder and harder to resist his impulses concerning Tototli. Though the gods had granted him fortune with his training group, they had also instilled in him a temptation that he could no longer bear.

"We did not bring javelins or your bow and arrows."

Metzín signaled a canoe passing along the causeway. It pulled to one side to allow them to board, and they sat on the floor of the small boat near the front. A cargo of calabashes separated them from the standing pilot. "We will snare the rabbits in the cave."

Tototli turned his face away from Metzín, toward the female side of the world, where Uitzilopochtli would set the sun. Metzín tapped his elbow, and Tototli turned his face back toward him, his gaze now on the floor of the canoe. "You do not mind, do you?" Metzín asked him.

"I do as I am told, Master Metzín."

Metzín shook his head, squeezing his elbow. "Then I am telling you to answer me. You do not mind, do you?"

Tototli looked up bashfully. "I like snaring rabbits as much as I enjoy playing the flute."

An uncontrollable smile came to Metzín's face, forcing him to turn away. A canoe with a small group of whispering women passed them as they drifted in the direction of Tenochtitlán. Could they see the crimson in his face and sense his secrets? Were they talking about him?

Should a master be talking to his slave that way? He killed his smile. Inside, however, his heart thumped excitedly, eager for the darkness and an opportunity, against his moral thoughts, to release the blaze inside him that burned quietly and hotly like a fire with no flames, only red coals left in the pit late into the night with no one watching.

Once on the shore of the lake, they hurried to the canyons and to the cave. Inside, Metzín let his desire loose. He had begged the gods to liberate him from those urges. He had spilled his blood in payment, anticipating the granting of his request. But the gods did not rid him of the impulses. Instead, they had sent Tototli to him in his dreams and daytime imagination. So, then, the gods continued the mystery. It must serve some purpose, he knew, though whether the purpose was a test of self-discipline or a revelation that could only be discovered through indulgence, he could not yet know. Now, in the darkness, the cave was a void where no eyes could see, and perhaps even the gods themselves did not enter.

He pushed Tototli farther into the black space than he had ever been. He could not see to what depth it extended, but perceived, from the absence of echo and the stuffiness, that the space was quite limited. Within only a few steps, he felt Tototli hit against a wall. He took his hands off Tototli's chest for a moment to feel the rock wall—an enormous, curved boulder. Reaching out to the side, he felt another rock wall close to his shoulder, and he realized how the placement of the boulders so close together had allowed for the creation of this private corridor. His focus, however, was not cold rock, but warm flesh.

As he slid Tototli's loincloth down his waist and legs, he felt his companion's hands untying the knot of his cloak. The two were naked. At first ravaging and frantic, they slowed their hands. They found places on one another's backs and buttocks, and they intertwined their tongues like a pair of slithering serpents. Slower yet, Metzín relaxed, and the hardened member between his legs throbbed in contrast to the soft solace he found in the arms of the man in front of him.

His mind flashed for a moment on the turkeys, the task requested of him by his mother, and the turkey and chile porridge, the administrator, and his daughter. Yes, he knew that soon he would become a man, and that sooner he might be sent off to battle, or even to the wake of Uitzilopochtli's path in the sky. But Tototli's wet mouth brought him back to the present, to the void, where they concocted a spicy stew of their own.

Afterward, Metzín retied his cloak and peered out of the small, brush-covered entrance. As if Uitzilopochtli had quickened his pace, the sun seemed to have sped across the sky. They'd have to hurry so as not to arouse suspicion or anger his mother. He held Tototli's hand for a final touch and began to remove the cover of branches. His eyes became wide and his ears alert. He'd heard movement outside. He hunkered back in the darkness, listening. No noise followed. Had a rock rolled their way or an animal passed by? Nothing.

He waited another moment before removing the branch. "Help me out," he said to Tototli, who pushed up on his backside. Still alert, he saw nothing, so he put his hands on the ledge of the exit and pushed himself up. With his torso outside the cave, he turned to one side and saw a pair of feet. Startled, he twisted, falling sideways outside the cave and onto his back. He looked up and the lowering sun blinded his view of all except for the outline of a head, raised arms, and the threatening profile of a thick sword. The person's head moved and, he read, like an unforgettable glyph, the incensed face of Peo. He looked up again at the sword and imagined it smashing down, breaking his head in two like a coconut.

"Grrr!" Peo grunted in angry frustration. But the sword did not come down on Metzín. "Stupid dog! I could have killed you. I thought you were a rabbit coming out of its hole. You almost became the stuffing of tamales."

"What are you doing out here?" Metzín said in the absence of another ready response.

"Hunting. What do you think? I should be asking *you* what you're doing, you useless clod, besides looking for a quick end to your misery." He pulled Metzín away from the cave entrance and peered inside. "Is this where your family has moved to? Your father finally punished for his cheating and arrogance?"

Peo crouched to take a closer look. "Well, then? Who else is in there? A demon whore? I knew I heard some slapping noises going on in there. Show yourself."

The face of Tototli came into the light. Obedient boy! He should have hidden. Then Peo stepped back and became silent. It seemed as though his sluggish brain was suspended in thought, as if finally comprehending the use of a stirring paddle in a pot. And when his face lit up, Metzín had never missed his sword like he did in that moment.

"I see what I have found," Peo finally composed.

And before Metzín could respond, the big boar skittered down the canyon, as if this time *he* had captured *Metzín's* feather.

ON THE return trip to Tenochtitlán, Metzín practically jogged to the market, leaving Tototli far behind.

Repugnant boar. He was likely in the canyons hunting rabbits because his family has squandered away the little wealth they had been endowed on gambling and octli. Undeniably Peo, who was once an irritating brute, was now a terrible threat. If confronted, Metzín could attempt to lie, but truthfulness was a virtue deeply instilled in him. Yet the punishments for men caught in unnatural acts with others were hideous and unthinkable. The entrails of one citizen had been yanked out of his rear for the mere accusation of activities with his son. Worse, the denigration and humiliation his family would suffer were more than Metzín could bear. His father could lose his place as a merchant. The entire family could be displaced to the chinampas. No, this he could not allow.

"Master Metzín. Wait. Please."

In that moment, Metzín abhorred Tototli's whiny voice. He knew then that the feelings he'd had for the servant-slave were like the evil, irresistible influences of octli. And he realized that the gods had not filled him with such desires for any purpose of enlightenment. Rather, they had been testing his resolve and his willpower. He had failed. Why hadn't he understood before what was so obvious to him now?

Upon his arrival at home, he could lift his sharpened sword and smite the wicked temptation as simply as smashing a gourd of octli. No more would this snake disguised like a fluttering bird impede his true destiny. His mother had sensed an evil, unbalancing force. As always, she had been right. And she had sacrificed her blood to ward off the malevolent omen. Now, it was up to him to extinguish the burning heat like an unwanted fire.

Chapter Fifteen

"SNAIL SHELLS. All I keep getting are snail shells." Hugo scratched his growing bald spot, which was too big for his young age, as was his waistline. Despite his frequent whining, the accuracy and detail of his data records were flawless. He also added character to the team. He was quick to turn up the volume on the speakers of a run-down stereo and start a dance in the dark of the night, brightening the long, weary faces. But he had shown outright disappointment when he had been assigned to the perimeter of the skeletons. Diego understood his discontent. The actual skeletons would be considered by most as the center of attention and, like dinosaur diggers, they all wanted to discover the next big beast, the revolutionary find, or the missing link. Yet often the artifacts farther removed from the focal point shed the most light on history and culture.

"How many?" Diego asked.

"Hundreds."

Diego nodded pensively.

"Hundreds upon fucking hundreds." Hugo clenched his teeth together. "Oh, excuse the language, Professor. It's just that I'm so tired of crumbly gastropod fossils."

"I understand, Hugo. Have patience. You've got to realize that every detail is an important piece of the puzzle."

"Mollusks." Hugo curled his lip. "It was a lake. Of course there were mollusks. What's that got to do with forensics and battle wounds? Where is the history in that?"

"Hugo," Diego said, patting the big guy's shoulder. "You've got to ask yourself what those mollusks tell us."

"I don't know. Someone was ready for some escargot, I guess."

Diego laughed. "Actually, it might mean quite the opposite. In fact, you may have discovered more than you realize."

"How do you figure? I was hoping to find a murder weapon or a dead baby or something."

"First of all, ask yourself this. Where must they have been buried?"

"Well, by the lake. The whole damn place was a lake."

"Not exactly true, right? Parts of the area were lakebed or lakeshore, while others were dry land, and others were a sort of ancient landfill."

"Okay."

"And that there were so many snails in the immediate area perhaps shows us that the snails were there."

"Pretty obvious, Professor. You're just trying to make me feel better."

"No. If you think about it, if the area had been more populated, as was the area where bodies not cremated might have been buried, then the snails would have been gathered and eaten. So, we might suppose that despite the relative closeness of the even more ancient temple, the area may not have been inhabited. Why?"

"Maybe they died there."

"Perhaps. But, by the style of burial, we know that somebody cared. Somebody buried them deliberately. We saw an arrow wound but we found no arrow. It had been removed. The two were buried lying on their backs, not necessarily in death poses. They were placed there."

"Okay. So a volcano didn't bury them."

"More importantly, they were buried with a certain amount of attention, yet in a sparsely inhabited section, not in Tenochtitlán. Given their clothing we can assume that at least one was of nobility or a higher class, maybe a merchant or some sort of leader—not everyone could wear cotton—so his burial, already unusual because they were normally cremated, would have been more formal. The snails give us important information—for some reason they were taken away to a place far removed from society, where even the snails weren't gathered for sustenance. They also help us date the find."

"Professor! We've got visitors." The volume of Gerardo's voice increased as he trotted toward the site. "Were you expecting someone?"

"Who is it?" Diego asked.

"I'm not sure, but they look, uh… academic."

Diego spotted a group of four people walking across the courtyard, toward the temple. He immediately recognized the stout figure of Dr. Pedraja, the chairman of the archaeology department at the National Autonomous University of Mexico, under whom he worked. Diego had always appreciated his casual style of leadership as a direct supervisor. He knew that the man's heart was more often in the digs the chairman had directly overseen for the first three decades of his career. He found budgets and publications far less interesting, though they occupied the majority of his time lately in his cramped office in the archaeology department on campus. That same office was filled with pictures and artifacts from a time, not that long ago, when the excavation of the ancient Mexican civilization had become a popular movement. The frenzy to find world-renowned tourist attractions had spawned generous funding of sites all over the vast territory. Times had changed. The country now had too many sites, thousands of them, to deal with. Even with fairly generous endowments and international support, all of the sites could not possibly be funded. But every archaeologist in Mexico knew they had only scratched the surface. A wealth of information far greater than what had been uncovered still lay buried and hidden beneath the earth.

Dr. Pedraja wore the only tweed sport coat that Diego had ever seen on him. The little man had always been afflicted with excessive perspiration. He'd be in agony now. Beside him were three people, none of whom Diego recognized—two men, one in a sport coat and the other in a black shirt, and a woman in a smart, blue pant suit. Two of them carried legal pads and another toted a briefcase. They appeared to look back and forth from the temple to the trees—trained observers on an official audit.

Diego straightened his shirt and quickened his pace to catch up with them. "Dr. Pedraja."

At once they stopped and turned around to greet him.

"Ah, Professor Alvarado," the stout man said, offering his hand for a firm shake. Diego could tell this was an important visit. "This is Dr. Estudillo from the Museum of Anthropology, Dr. Ramirez-Johnson from the history department at the University of Veracruz." They shook cordially. "And this is Brother Esteban Shoemacher, a biblical archaeologist from the Archdiocese of Mexico."

"Pleased to meet you," Diego said, making note of the clergyman's neatly trimmed gray hair, tweezed eyebrows, and limp handshake. He also noticed his blue eyes and fair skin before fixing on the large silver cross suspended from his neck by a chain. Above the cross, a white clerical collar stood out on his black shirt. "I didn't realize you'd be visiting."

"Standard protocol, Professor Alvarado," Dr. Pedraja explained. "Your request for additional funding requires an on-site visit. These are members of the oversight committee. We've reviewed your report but have come to see it firsthand."

"Well," Diego said modestly, "I didn't expect you all to travel so far for our little project."

"As you know, we're all accountable to ensure that every precious peso is spent for maximum historical value. There are many sites competing simultaneously."

"We're not asking for much, just enough to finish what we started. We believe we've stumbled across an unusual case. Let me show you around, and then we can go on up to my office and I can answer any questions you might have."

As they headed toward the main attraction, Diego walked beside Brother Shoemacher. "I didn't realize the Archdiocese had a member on the oversight committee," he said to him.

"The church contributes a lot of money to projects that offer insight and hard evidence in regard to the history of the church. Needless to say, sixteenth century Mexico is of great importance."

"Yes. Well, we think we're looking at late fifteenth century here."

"I am aware of that."

By the time they made it to the skeletons, Gerardo had assembled the entire team and had them pick up some scattered tools, tighten the tarp, and put the finishing touches on a small piece of the wall that had collapsed.

Diego began to explain the various findings of the dig, watching their eyes more than anything else. Each of them walked around Jade and Handy, jotting down some notes, while Brother Shoemacher pulled a camera from his briefcase. He raised it to his eye, first standing farther back, and then focusing in on the hands of the skeletons. "Handy and Jade. Curious choice of names," he commented with an interrogative look. "I don't suppose you've named him Handy for his agility with a toolbox?"

"Not exactly, Brother. Um… as you can see, we've removed the jade pendant from the other for security and study. It's a simple piece, relatively small."

"I recall. I've seen the photos from the project updates you've sent."

After a few more minutes viewing the skeletons, they headed back to the temple. "What have you got on the pyramid? Not period, is it?" Dr. Estudillo asked.

"Based on the clothing, and the quality of the jade design, we estimate the construction of the temple at several hundred years *prior* to the burial. In fact, the grant was originally written for a class project on temples, not skeletons. The pyramid turned out to be pretty deteriorated. Finding the skeletons was a total surprise."

"It's so often the case."

Dr. Pedraja began to huff halfway up the stairs. "Not like the old days," he said, patting his round stomach. "Too much bookwork and not enough legwork."

The group laughed. Upstairs in his makeshift office, Diego pulled a couple of folding chairs around his plastic table. "Sorry, I don't have enough for everyone."

"It's alright," Brother Shoemacher said. "I'll stand." He pulled a binder from his briefcase, and set it on the table. He opened it so that everyone could see it, flipped a few pages, and stopped on a spreadsheet of digits. "Professor Alvarado, I must tell you that we're concerned about the number of personnel you have on such a small site. You said yourself that the temple is in shambles, and the fact that you've uncovered two isolated skeletons does not convince us that the ultimate contribution will be significant."

"Brother, the majority of the staff are students receiving nominal stipends. They do need to eat. And two of them left part-time positions to participate in the excavation."

"But how do you explain the equipment expenditures?" He turned the page in the binder and began flipping it to various pages of photos of the project.

"Equipment expenditures? The generator was the most costly item, purchased for the entire archaeology department. The last one, which was about fifteen years old, broke down on us. We spent some money renting the water pump, and we bought some outdoor lights, building supplies, and cookware. The tents are all but useless, yet we're making do."

"So, what can we hope to achieve here?"

"It's hard to tell, Brother, until we've completed the project."

"You know," he nodded at each of them. "And I think I can speak for everyone at the table. We are dedicated to preserving and excavating as many sites throughout Mexico as we can. The ancients left an amazing story, and they still have more to tell. Every time we deny a project, defund one, or have to shut one down—" He put his hand on his heart beside the crucifix. "—it hurts in here. But we do have to make decisions."

"I understand. I'm sorry the projections were inaccurate. I had no idea we'd stumble on this."

He flipped another page to display several pictures of the pair of skeletons. "Yes, one can never tell."

The party waited through an awkward moment of silence.

"So," he continued. "In what ways could you reduce expenses? Perhaps on personnel?"

"The equipment we need is already purchased. Office supplies and stipends are definite necessities. Besides my own salary, my assistant is the only full-time staff member, and his pay is a fraction of that of a project director."

He flipped to the last page in the binder, a blown-up photo of the professor and Gerardo, the former's lips firmly planted on the cheek of the latter. Diego was stunned by the image, and his voice got caught somewhere in his throat. He tried to place the picture, fogged by this unexpected shock, this incrimination. The blood, the excitement about the blood, he recalled, and he began to piece together an explanation.

"This man?" Brother Shoemacher said, crouching to read the label beneath the picture. "Gerardo?"

Diego cleared his throat, wishing he could also clear his head of all the blood that seemed to have rushed into it. He wished the clergyman would flip the page again, but he left it in all its splendor on the table. Embarrassed, Diego smiled, "Um, yes. It's… it's not what it looks like."

Brother Shoemacher smirked. "I'm sure." He finally closed the book. "Gentlemen, Dr. Ramirez-Johnson," he said, looking at the other visitors but not at Diego. "I think I've seen enough."

"You know, the professor has quite a positive reputation," Dr. Pedraja chimed.

"Yes," said Dr. Ramirez-Johnson. "I've read a number of his papers. Extremely thorough."

"I think there may be a storm coming on," Brother Shoemacher said, looking up at the sky. "I'd really prefer to return to the city before we get caught in a deluge."

Chapter Sixteen

As METZÍN entered the telpochcalli, he almost expected a storm of guards who would haul him before a panel of judges for sentencing. His peers would stab him with their penetrating gazes, and they would taunt him with hisses and jeers for his weakness and immorality. The master warrior would not be able to bear the disappointment. And his mother, father and family, victims of his imprudence and impurity, would send him to a horrible fate before accepting their own punishment. All would be lost.

But that was not the case. All appeared normal in the early morning. A few groups of students prepared javelins and arrows, while others practiced drills with their shields and wooden training swords. Peo's group and Metzín's group chatted with each other in a small circle, waiting for the master warrior to begin a lesson. Metzín sat with them, looking intermittently at Peo's face for any sign, but the big man showed none. On the contrary, he seemed to meet Metzín's gaze more infrequently than ever, and his typical scowl had disappeared. In a way Metzín felt relieved, as if he had dreamt the episode or even the animosity between them. Something inside warned him, however, that a downpour could fall when least expected.

When he arrived home, his mother appeared to be in a pleasant mood. She sat at her loom, patiently adding lines of thread to a new cloth and humming.

"Mother, have you seen better signs?" he asked.

"No," she said. "But there has been an absence of bad ones."

"And how was your meeting with the cihuatlanque? Did she find favor in your choice?"

"Are you anxious about it?"

He paused before he answered. "Yes."

"You must be hungry."

"Yes."

"Then we will talk over our food."

He waited where she had been sitting as she went to the kitchen to bring a prepared dish of axolotls in a sauce of red and yellow peppers. With one hand, they each tore tortillas and dipped them into the pot to scoop out the delectable newts.

"One of my favorites. Is this a special occasion, the two of us at home alone?"

"You will become a man soon. Can a mother not squeeze juice from the fruit while it is still ripe and within her grasp?"

"And so, your meeting with the old woman went well? Did she return with an answer?"

"Of course she did. The administrator insisted his daughter was too young and as stupid as a bonefish. He said we had made a mistake, that the girl was not worthy of a fine boy like you."

Metzín dipped a tortilla casually in the pot for another newt and peppers. "And when will the cihuatlanque revisit?"

"In a few days' time."

"And they will again refuse?"

"Naturally. My parents, for civility, said I was as ugly as a stink beetle and as simple as a fly. They refused for two months!"

Metzín let out a loud laugh. "How polite they were."

"Very polite indeed."

"But then they agreed?"

"Yes, in the end they agreed, seeing, they said, that your father's parents had set so much store by it. They consulted with my aunts and uncles before they made the promise, as will the administrator and his wife."

"Will it be soon?"

"I cannot say. They may wait until your father comes back, or even stall for your return from battle. They are as smart as they say she is stupid, and they will not wish for her to be widowed so soon."

"Let's hope my father does not become frustrated and angry." Metzín began to massage his hand where the finger had healed crookedly. He'd never forget the punishing blow his father had inflicted on him as a young child, when he destroyed the best flowers in the garden with a toy sword. "We wouldn't want him to lose his temper."

"No, he has become a more peaceful man since his younger days, and more so now that he deals directly with many administrators. He always considers his honor first."

"I hope also to bring you honor."

"And I hope to bring you happiness and purposefulness. Soon you will see your bride as your father saw me—dressed in all colors of embroidery and adorned with feathers like a bird, and the brightest flowers."

He looked away from her at the mention of a bird. "As you wish, Mother."

"Not as *I* wish, son. It is as the gods have decided."

He nodded.

"Finish your food. I will tell the servant-slave to prepare the temazcalli."

"No, I do not want that."

"Are you not in need of a steam bath?"

"Yes. Only I do not wish for Tototli to prepare it. Have him trade tasks with the neighbor's girl-servant so that she might make the preparations."

"Oh? Has he displeased you? Should he be punished?"

"No." Metzín shook his head. "He has not adequately honed his skills for massage."

She nodded knowingly. "Very well, then. I will have it done."

When the fire was ready, he crawled inside the temazcalli. He was nervous, but also relieved to have the object of temptation removed from his proximity in the heat and darkness. Surely the natural desire for women that had eluded him in the presence of Tototli would now find him. He heard her come in behind him, and he lay facedown and naked on the mat, waiting. But the fire was not hot enough, and when she threw the water upon the wall, it fizzled briefly and died, barely warming the room.

"Shall I add wood to the fire?"

"No," he answered. "Just rub me."

She approached him, straddled his back, and pressed her hands against his shoulders. He rested his head on the mat and closed his eyes, hoping. She began to work his muscles awkwardly, like a girl child wielding a mano and metate for the first time. She would struggle to grind the corn, making instead a masa of maize full of corn chunks. She continued to struggle, pressing down painfully on the depressions in his spine. When she reached his buttocks and legs, he wished to send her away. For this girl only his shoulders had hardened. Instead he wondered where Tototli was and what he might be doing. Could he be tending the neighbors' temazcalli? The thought made him furious. Against everything he believed, he could not help but long for the young man's touch.

"Would you like to turn over now?" she asked.

But he did not answer, feigning sleep. And he lamented his cursed body and his continuing, corrupt fantasies. He did not have the integrity of a warrior. He did not deserve the jaguar suit. He did not deserve a beautiful bride. How could he criticize Peo for his lack of integrity, when he carried something far worse hidden inside? Might he be sent to war and be struck down or captured because of it? However, he did have perseverance and the determination to destroy that immoral scorpion that lurked inside him. He no longer saw another choice.

Chapter Seventeen

INCREDIBLE, DIEGO thought as he sat alone at his table, feeling as if he had lingered in a courtroom after he'd been severely misjudged. He fiddled with a pen, tapped the plastic table, sighed hopelessly, then sighed again. He had half a mind to track down Brother Shoemacher and hang him by that damn crucifix, or call Dr. Pedraja to lobby for his assistance. He knew that acting irrationally or defensively could make him appear more guilty than he already felt. Another long sigh. How had he let it get this far, and all over an innocent, albeit incriminating, kiss?

Ironically, the situation was exactly what he had feared—that a relationship with Gerardo could jeopardize not only the project but his entire reputation. His laptop buzzed and powered down after having timed out. His November project report was due. He had to get to it. He kept tapping his pen, unable to conjure the energy or the motivation to work. It all seemed like a lost cause. *And over a fucking picture. A kiss on the cheek. And two skeletons holding hands.* Everyone at the table had to know that the gesture revealed nothing more than camaraderie and excitement. *That prick.*

Still, wasn't he entitled to a personal life? He'd dedicated so much time to the university and never pursued a personal, *private* relationship. And most of that time he had worked with colleagues who were married and had families—he had even taken them to events and out to sites. How about an audit on *their* expenses? No, the bigoted eye was focused on that which it most feared.

What could he do now? What *should* he do now? His modus operandi when distressed was to crawl into the dark room of the temple behind him, wallow in loneliness, and hope the powers that be would feel for his wretched plight.

He sat back in his chair, listening to the birds and the wind around him. Suddenly he felt a noose around his neck. Literally. Or a snake. Instinctively his hands grabbed at a sensation on his throat. His fingers hooked a thin cord. His panic had him up in the chair in an instant.

"Ha, ha, ha! Got you!"

Diego turned around to see Gerardo, who must have sneaked up the stairs behind him. "Very funny," he said reproachfully.

"What's the matter? Did we get defunded?"

"An asshole, that's what." Diego surprised himself with such vulgarity. It felt good to let it out, and to have someone with whom to express himself.

"Oh, you mean that closet case."

Diego laughed, his only consolation in such defeat.

"Come on," Gerardo said. "Do you really think he's a threat?"

Diego looked up at him with a snarl. "Yeah, if he controls the purse strings. I mean, did you see that picture?"

"I saw how freaked out you were over it. I'm trying to forget about it and wait for that clergyman to take a bus back to wherever he came from," Gerardo answered.

"Imagine what they could do with that picture in the archaeological community." Diego shook his head and slammed his fist on the wobbly table. "Or in *your* community, for that matter. Imagine if your family saw that."

"Come on," Gerardo responded. "That picture's not going anywhere that any layperson is going to see, much less my family. Relax."

"Still, can't you see what he must have been thinking about this whole project? He snapped close-ups of their overlapping hands for God's sake!"

"Well, maybe it's what we've all been thinking, Professor, but haven't had the guts to declare."

"Right. And now with that photo, we've got the gay professor and his lover making claims to Aztec homosexuality. Great. I've been playing the devil's advocate all along, just to make sure I wasn't projecting my own fantasy on them. But the possibility is getting harder to deny. Maybe that's what Brother Shoemacher's freaking out about."

"*Lover*? That's the first time you ever called me that."

"Well, I'm just saying it from that bastard's point of view."

"Oh." Gerardo bit his lip lightly, as if trying to hide his hurt feelings.

Diego reached for his hand and replaced it on his shoulder near where Gerardo had nearly strangled him a few minutes before. "That's not what I—hey, what is this anyway?" He peered down and pulled up the cord with his free hand.

"It's the pendant. We got it back."

"Gerardo, you know this isn't protocol for the artifacts."

"Gee, Professor, is that what you're terribly concerned about now, when your entire project could be reburied?"

"No. It's not."

"I just wanted to tell you what they came up with."

Diego took it off his neck, set it in front of him, and looked closely at the silver pendant and the striation of the rich green jade inside it. "Okay. Let's hear it."

"Mostly things we'd said before. It's a small piece for a noble, relatively simple. However, the grade of the jade precisely matches that of the Motagua River in Guatemala."

"Right. This would definitely not have come from any place around here, or even from the south in Chiapas."

"Confirmed. And the purity of the silver—you can see a trace of the luster—had to be from Otumba, where the craftsmen centered, north of here. This was brought in by a pochteca. So unless this was traded for locally, we're looking at a merchant, not a nobleman."

"We suspected that for the lack of artifacts."

"Yes. Nobody liked the pochteca to flaunt their wealth back then, so they mostly kept it quiet. Of course, the cotton cloak would have never been part of the lower-classman's wardrobe. Some fine embroidery. I guess it was used for ceremonial purposes."

"Or a burial."

"That's right."

"And the rope it was hanging on?"

"Almost totally disintegrated. It's been vacuum-sealed in plastic for now. If any of this ever gets to a museum, we'll replace it as it was."

"Big 'if' at this point."

"Let it go, Professor. Let's just do the best we can and trust in God for the rest."

"God? Seems like God has become our biggest opponent as of late."

"Nah, even I would tell you that God and his followers are oftentimes at opposite ends of the ring."

"Let's not even bring up the whole religious debate. I don't feel like talking sociology or theology right at this moment."

"Alright. We'll give it a rest. So, you feel like going out to Xonacahuacán tomorrow instead?"

Diego shook his head. "You know, it's nothing against your family. I'm not feeling all that social right now."

Gerardo massaged Diego's shoulder. "Let's skip it, then."

"No, you go ahead. They'll miss you if you don't."

"I don't have to go *every* Sunday. We can go someplace else."

"What do you have in mind?"

LATE THE next morning, after about an hour's drive, they pulled up to the town center in Querétaro, the heart of the ancient Otomíland. Diego had taken several groups of students to the area for field studies and was quite familiar with the local history. Here, in 1810, María Ortiz de Dominguez, the imprisoned wife of the governor, had warned her revolutionary comrades about the discovery of their movement, setting off an early start to the struggle for independence. Later that century, Emperor Maximiliano, who was backed by Napoleon, was famously executed by a firing squad on the Hill of the Bells. And also in Querétaro, the Treaty of Guadalupe Hidalgo was signed, handing over to the United States a great portion of Mexico, including Texas and California—while the Americans insisted that the Mexicans were the invaders. Details, details. Diego could hardly keep the events of history from running through his head.

From almost any vantage point in the city, the historical dominance of the Spaniards stood out. Soaring cathedrals, palaces, monasteries, and museums were all reminders of a people who had stumbled upon and obliterated a culture—greedy imperialists in the guise of missionaries and civilizers. One look at the Convento de la Santa Cruz was enough to remind Diego of Brother Shoemacher, making him feel queasy. "Did you suggest Querétaro to cheer me up?"

"Uh, yeah. A change of pace, no?"

Diego winced as they got out of the car. "Okay, where to, then?"

"I don't know. Do you want to check out the cathedral?"

"Seriously? I think I'd rather avoid anything Catholic right now."

"Okay. Are you hungry?" Gerardo asked.

"Yeah." As they walked through the fresh-cut grass and then around the rose bushes of the town square, they passed a small group of Otomís in traditional white garb embroidered with flowers in bright red, green, and yellow. Diego recognized their language, something between old-time Otomí and Nahuatl. These were the people who had always interested him the most—the indigenous people who had inhabited the land before the collapse of their civilization and the Spanish invasion. In fairness, he thought, the ancient tribes were constantly warring and attempting to dominate one another. But ultimately they always refrained from annihilating each other, unlike the Europeans. Instead, they found ways of accepting one another, folding new gods into old religions, and respecting the ways of others, human sacrifices notwithstanding.

Diego watched as the group of indigenous walked by and was perked up a bit by their sombreros and floral bags. "Alright," he said, nodding at the tribal folks. "Let's try some of their spiced turkey soup. I haven't had the Otomí version of *pozole* in the longest time."

On the far side of the town center, just opposite the cathedral, Diego and Gerardo found a vendor beneath a little tent supported by PVC pipes. They sat in plastic chairs at a plastic table, and a petite indigenous girl who couldn't have been more than twelve brought Styrofoam bowls of steaming soup served from a huge stainless-steel pot. As condiments for the concoction of turkey and hominy, the girl set down plates of sliced radishes, chopped cabbage, lemon wedges, and dry chile powder. The two promptly dumped the entire contents of the plates into their bowls and began to stuff themselves with the tasty delicacy.

Diego listened in as the girl spoke with an older lady behind the pot. From their conversation, he figured the older woman was instructing the younger one on the intricacies of the dish.

"What do you think would have happened," Gerardo pondered out loud, "if the Otomí had never seen the apparition of St. James or the dazzling cross in the sky during the battle with the Spaniards? What would have become of them?"

"I don't know. History is replete with stories of the strong taking over the weak. Don't you think their fall, their *conversion*, was inevitable?"

"Of course. I know it. I just wonder sometimes, what would have happened had Motecuhzoma put a swift end to Hernán Cortés, as some of his advisors had urged. The Spaniards were hopelessly outnumbered. If it hadn't been for their earthshaking cannon, shiny helmets, their horses, and their smallpox, history would have been entirely different. We would be digging up small arms between great pyramids, piecing together details of the brief visit of forgotten explorers."

"But then *we* wouldn't be here, would we?"

"Well, it's only conjecture. I just wonder sometimes." Gerardo put his spoon down and signaled for the young waitress to come to the table.

"And that's why we stick to the facts of it all, right? The science," Diego said.

"Yes, that's why," Gerardo responded to Diego before turning his attention to the black-haired girl. "More salsa please." He made a spooning motion with his hand. She nodded and walked away. "And I guess the strong will always bully the weak," he continued, "Regardless of constitutions, democracies, and courtrooms."

"There's the way it is and the way it ought to be. Look at the United States, South America, and Africa. History is full of conquistadores all over the globe. The more 'advanced' conquer. In the end we're nothing more than a huge pack of wolves. The strong prevail."

"True. And these days, money is the biggest weapon of them all."

"Without a doubt," Diego said.

"So, Professor, what are your plans, then? Back to the university?" He held up his hand, the back of it facing the girl in a gesture of gratitude as she placed a small bowl of hot chile sauce on the table.

"Well, it's not over till it's over. I intend to get out of my little slump and figure out a way to finish this project. But eventually, yes, back to the university. I've got courses to teach." He took another spoonful of pozole. "And you?"

Gerardo dumped a full spoon of salsa in his soup. "I'm going to finish up my degree, I guess. I never should have left it. It was harder for me to adapt to the life in the city than I expected. I missed my family."

"It's a big change," Diego said. He cleared his throat and pointed at the hot sauce. "That stuff will kill you."

"It adds flavor." Gerardo smirked. "Anyway, you think of archaeology as being out in the field all the time. I always loved to explore all the sites around my home. I never realized how easy it would be to feel lost in the metro, the infinite streets, the concrete jungle. I can only imagine how an Aztec felt out here, one tiny ant among nearly a million souls in Tenochtitlán. Can you even imagine it? An Aztec Rome!"

"It must have been an awesome sight to see. Anyway, so you're thinking of finishing up? I recall from your resume that you had only a year or so to go."

"I know. It was stupid to leave it. I guess I couldn't really see a future in it. But this experience has definitely motivated me to get back to it. I may as well finish what I started."

"May as well." Diego sat back and patted his full stomach.

"So," Gerardo asked. "Why'd you pick me, anyway?"

"Huh. Qualified applicants weren't exactly beating down the door, not for these wages. And besides, you lived so close to the site. I knew that would be an advantage. I needed someone who could help to get the resources we would need right away, maybe using some local connections."

"Strictly business, aren't you?"

"Strictly archaeology." They stared at each other for a moment. "Maybe not totally now," Diego conceded. "It started that way, but things have taken unexpected turns."

"I hope not regrettable ones."

Diego nodded. "I hope that too." He started to feel tense now that the conversation had changed direction.

"What do you hope for exactly?" Gerardo asked.

"I just hope to get through this for now."

"I mean, between us?"

"Well," Diego sniffed. "I don't know. I'm not really, uh, I'm not that good at all this. And there's your family. I know you're close to them."

"That doesn't mean anything, does it?"

"You're not about to tell them, are you?"

"No." He pushed around a turkey bone in the nearly empty bowl and lowered his voice. "No. I can't exactly say with certainty, I guess. It seems like maybe there is something here I'm not ready to let go of. You know, the closeness I've always had with my family? But it's kind of like what you said about the Otomí. If I don't come out, I'd always wonder what would have happened."

"And you said that their end was inevitable," Diego pointed out.

"I know. But history has its anomalies too."

"You never know. Maybe someday someone will be digging us up where we were buried together."

Gerardo smiled bashfully and let out a short laugh. "Yeah. Maybe."

They paid the bill and spent the rest of the day wandering through the quiet streets of Querétaro. They stopped for an ice cream and a coffee and then stumbled across an alley of Otomí art vendors. First they walked down a long row of colorfully woven clothes and tablecloths, and then they perused a few tables of jewelry displaying all sorts of rings and necklaces in shiny silver, gems of all colors, obsidian, and other stones.

Diego picked up a few pieces and inspected their craftsmanship. Here, as everywhere, attention to detail had diminished with the industrial revolution. Nevertheless, the Otomí largely maintained many of the styles he was familiar with from digs all over the state. Even the symbols hadn't changed all that much, as the indigenous clung to what remained of their religion. One piece caught his attention. He brought it close to his face and nudged Gerardo to take a look at the simple, round piece. Inside a circle of silver, an image had been carved from forest green jade. It was a jaguar knight from the waist up, his ferocious face peering through the open mouth of the jaguar head. The carving had been situated so that the dark veins in the jade appeared as stripes in the jaguar suit. He wielded a sword with an uplifted arm, its obsidian edges mere specks carved into the stone. Opposite the sword, above the knight's head, a hummingbird flew, representing the ultimate dream of an Aztec warrior.

Behind the jewelry stand, Diego heard the faint sound of trickling water coming through an open, antiquated wooden doorway. Above the door a hanging sign read "Pensión." He studied the building and recognized the Spanish-style construction—the plain wall, the rectangular shape, especially high ceilings and doors, and a large courtyard in the interior with arches around the perimeter.

"Would you care for another overnight stay?" Diego asked.

"Professor," Gerardo responded bashfully. "I believe we're due back at the site in the morning."

"To be honest with you, Faithful Assistant, I'm not entirely concerned about it. Anyway, we can get up early enough, have a breakfast of street tacos, and get to the site before anyone notices."

"You're really pushing that professionalism."

"Or maybe the *professionals* are pushing me. You suggested coming out here, and I think we've made the best of it. Now, let's cap it off. I don't think I can bear being back on the site so soon after such an enjoyable day."

"And it's not the alcohol this time?"

"No alcohol. Clear thinking."

"Well, we skipped out on my family. We may as well skip out on work too."

Diego led the way inside the pensión, past flaking paint and termite-eaten window frames. Flowers abounded in the courtyard, and an old well converted into a fountain accounted for the noise that had attracted him. Around the courtyard were a dozen or so doors with painted numbers on them. An old man attended to the enormous, rusted lock on one of them.

"Do you have any rooms for two, Señor?"

"Of course we do," he answered. "But they've only got one bed."

Diego looked at Gerardo and they both shrugged. "Alright. We only need one bed."

The old man shrugged as well. "Suit yourself." He pointed to several of the doors. "Take number four, seven, eight, or eleven. They're all open."

"Do we need a key?"

"Damn things haven't worked for a decade. Don't worry. Nothing gets stolen around here."

They chose a room away from the street and the reception area. Diego opened the door for Gerardo and followed him in. The room and its solid wood furniture reminded him of times long ago. And as he stepped inside, he couldn't help but notice the feeling of quaint romance, and felt a kind of companionable delight.

Chapter Eighteen

THE DEPRAVED impulses had taken hold of Metzín again, pulsing through his body in unstoppable waves. Tototli, Tototli. Despite all of Metzín's beseeching of the gods, the young man's face appeared to him in the night, as did his craving for the sweetest nectar, the most delicate flower. He entered the darkness of the temazcalli and found his fervent mate. Metzín stroked his slender back, clutched his gyrating hips, matching them with his own sliding javelin. Tototli. The young man clenched his teeth in pleasurable pain, bringing his lips up to Metzín's mouth, until their tongues slithered together, deeper and deeper, with unstoppable moans. Tototli. They became as one, the beak of the hummingbird deep inside the flower. Salty broth became sweetest broth as Metzín traversed the smooth brown neck and shoulders and back in front of him with his tongue, lapping up the sweat and drinking him to the sound of rapid whimpers. Tototli. Faster and faster. The heat inside grew. It was the hottest day, with the sun on high, but the two of them in the darkness. Tototli. Their twin movements became like those of wrestlers, yet their struggle was not against one another. Tototli. Faster and faster they made a sprint together, their bodies colliding and writhing, until they exploded in gushes of white.

And he awoke upon the mat, covered in sweat and sticky goo. He looked around him in the dim moonlight, afraid someone might have seen into him or learned his secret. He recalled the dream, the delicious dream, and remembered the sounds of the moans and whimpers. Tototli was not there in the room with him. He realized then that the sounds had been his own. He wished to purify himself and cleanse himself of this madness, almost as much as he wished to seek Tototli in the night, wake him on his mat, and bring him to himself, hold him in his arms, and tell him—

No. No. No.

Had he not made enough holy sacrifices? Had he not given all that he could give? Why had the gods ignored his pleas? He crawled to his wicker chest and pulled a knife from it. He would give them the precious water they needed, if only they would have pity on him.

He stood, wiped himself with his cloak, and walked down the hall. As he passed the sleeping quarters of the servant-slave, he regarded the door with contempt. Inside slept the object of his desire, the weakness inside him.

The moon shone on the patio. It was as if he saw himself in a white mirror, the great rabbit's face looking down upon him. Its look was still, stern, and penetrating. He looked away and took a seat on the edge of the canal, where the gaze of the moon was in the water—still upon him as it wavered in the current.

He pulled up his cloak and set the point of the knife on his thigh. Tototli. No. He dug the knife in and withstood the pain, emitting only a brief grunt as the warm, red blood began to stream out over his knee and onto the earth. He bowed his head and watched some of it make a small puddle beneath him. And he felt the rest trickle down his leg to his feet, where it began to drip into the water for the wavering moon.

Tototli. *Won't you leave me and drift away like those drops?* Tears came to his eyes—tears of sadness and quiet, tormenting rage. They gathered on the tip of his nose. He raised his hand to wipe them. There was only one more thing to do. He stabbed down powerfully into the other thigh and bore the shooting pain when the knife's tip hit solid bone.

"HAVE YOU begged the gods for guidance?"

Metzín awoke to the voice of his mother. She knelt beside him, laid a hand on his chest, and looked at his legs. He sat up, feeling unrested, recalling the plea he had made in the night for this torment to abandon him. He had waited and waited for a sign, but had seen none. It was as if his cries had dropped into the water like a rock, sank to the bottom, and disappeared.

"Yes," he finally answered. "I have asked them to make me a great man, a brave warrior."

"You are a great man," she said. "Yet you seem to be troubled as of late."

"I... I...." He had neither the words to express his fears nor the courage to confess his affliction.

"Are you afraid?"

"Only of disappointing you or dishonoring you."

She smiled tenderly. "You could not do such a thing. Who knows you better than I?"

"Mother, there are things a man carries that a woman does not understand."

"I sense your worries. You have been far from home, but you cannot be far from me. All men, all people, cannot help but feel frightened as they step up to the precipice. The gods will show you the way. We can see the present, but only they know what is to come for each of us."

"Do you think their plan will favor me?"

"I know the gods will. And you will need their favor. We have received word that your father will return within days."

Metzín sucked in a deep breath in anticipation. He could be leaving soon, going away from this house, away from Tototli, away from temptation, and into the wild. It would be a chance for redemption, ascension—and an end to torment.

"Will I go to battle then?"

"I cannot know. But I can hope for it."

"Then let us hope."

"And let us hope for your return, and that the gods have not yet decided to take you away from here forever. You have an important part to play yet. Be pure and brave."

He moved his leg and pain darted through his body again, a cruel reminder of the difference between the true, hard world, and that of fantasy.

MORNING BATHS in the lake, drills at the telpochcalli, and battle exercises in the canyon had become serious affairs. Word had spread that the negotiation party would be returning, so every warrior sought greater skills from the master warrior and grace from the gods. The expansion of Tenochtitlán and the greatness of the Aztec empire necessitated the annexation of land and resources. The lesser peoples who could not see their destiny as part of that of Tenochtitlán, or understand the futility of resistance, brought war upon themselves. Yet such was the will of the gods, and the *tlatoani*, the supreme ruler, who was charged with leading the people and appeasing the gods' thirst for precious water, must obey.

"Where is your breastless mistress?" Peo asked Metzín under his breath as they walked out on the causeway toward the canyon.

In his mind, Metzín drew his sword and struck first the knee of the beast to bring him down to the dirt. He then parted his face like a papaya, whose seeds spilled onto the earth. But he knew better than to cause any disturbance there on the causeway, especially given what Peo had witnessed. So he turned away, as if entrancing himself in concentration and prayers, leaving the hatred to rumble inside.

The following evening as the company of warriors sang solemn war chants in the house of singing and dancing, and oscillated between the excitement of glory and quiet, internal anxiety at an unknown fate, they were joined by a fire priest whom Metzín had never seen before. Deep vertical grooves lined the man's face like grim scars of time between his eyes and on either side of his mouth. His lips and gums were so dark that they appeared to have been colored. He wore a carved bone horizontally in his nose, and his ears hung down, stretched halfway down his neck by small skulls inserted in the lobes. The skulls at first appeared to Metzín to be those of unborn children, but the pointed teeth in them revealed them as the heads of little monkeys. The priest's dark cape was laced with black feathers that made the cape seem edged with crow's wings. In the middle of the back, more feathers made concentric circles, in the center of which glared the open-beaked head of an eagle.

The master warrior raised his hands to silence his pupils. "We welcome, Ixtomoc, the *tlamacaztequiuaque*."

Metzín sat in reverent silence, for he had never seen a priest-warrior in the house of singing and dancing, or even in the telpochcalli. He had only seen them prophesying from the heights of temples or assisting with the sacrifices of battle captives. The entire room instantly became hushed.

"After trials and travails, the party has returned from the left side of the world where Uitzilopochtli has yet to blaze." The tlamacaztequiuaque elongated each word as he spoke. He paused often and emitted a sort of hum between phrases. From beneath his cloak, he produced a book of bark pages—the codices. "The poor savages have not yet come to realize their destiny as children of Tenochtitlán."

The students continued to listen with anxious patience as the man inhaled slowly through clenched teeth and exhaled with a hiss. Metzín sucked in his breath in excitement, thinking of his father's return and his own approaching destiny. Metzín felt relief that he would no longer be concerned with childish worries or boyhood confusions. Yes. Over the precipice.

"The distant lands contain blessings, but there is an obstacle, an uncivilized folk of rugged ways." He opened the codex to a marked page. "And so we wait to see the path." Should the savage leader open his fountain of precious water? Should he offer his own fruit? Or should he, like the young maize seedling, be left idle, that he might one day share his fruit? He raised the book in one hand and placed a finger on a glyph. "It is decreed, but only the gods know. Only the gods can tell. Let them reveal to us, to Motecuhzoma, as with a hand of patolli beans.

"You, children of the sun, rest and pray, drill and strengthen, for your day will come to give or be given, to eat or be eaten, to smite or be smitten." He set the codices down, drew up his cloak like the wings of an eagle, and began to dance in slow steps around the room. He shrieked and squawked, fire in his eyes.

"Children of the sun, you have not seen what I know. You have not tasted the prickly pear, the cactus juice. You, miniscule seed, call on Telpochtli who protects the young warrior. You, tiny bird, fly with me to another world. Glory to Uitzilopochtli. Glory to Motecuhzoma. Take up your shield and sword and bow. Become a jaguar, become an eagle, become the sun!"

He waved his eagle wings and spun. Upon the floor, Metzín did not see from where, a scattering of white seeds flew out in all directions.

"Prepare. The battle awaits on the *pelota* field!"

He picked up the codex and flew out the door through which he had entered.

"So," the master warrior stated. "It will be decided through the games."

Metzín listened and wondered, imagining the pelota game and the hordes of people watching the players. Would the battle commence?

Somewhere unseen, Xochipilli, god of pleasure and games, would govern the tournament and the fate of many. Metzín leaned over to pick up a seed for good luck. He thought of Tototli again, and was angry that the slave possessed him. And yet he could think of little more than bringing the seed to the servant-slave. He wanted to both ravish and vanquish him. How could such a sweet flower be like an enemy in his own home? And yet if an enemy, how had Tototli's actions truly done him harm?

Xochipilli, is this a game to you as well? Am I nothing more than a toy with which you play? The temptations with which you torment me, are they challenges? Am I to pass a test? Or am I to taste the honey before me? Like the priest-warrior, the men of dual roles, am I meant to see the gifts brought by those of two cloaks? I beg you! Reveal to me, then, in this game, if I should recognize a serpent before me or a flower. Kill or covet? I must know.

He looked at the seed. It was about the size of a grain of corn, though he did not immediately recognize its strange pair of pointed spines. He held it between his fingers. It was as hard as a pebble. Then he set it in his palm and saw that it was no seed, but a tooth, a clean, white, human tooth.

Chapter Nineteen

DESPITE A late night, Diego and Gerardo woke up before the morning's first light. They dressed and straightened the room a bit before leaving. Near the reception desk, a gray-haired woman in a checkered apron swept the hallway vigorously for such an early hour.

"Señora," Diego said. "We'll be checking out now."

"Good morning," she said matter-of-factly. She straightened up, still holding the broom in one hand.

"My apologies, Señora. I meant to say good morning," Diego corrected. "We will be checking out now." He noticed a small gold crucifix on a chain around her neck. *What is with women lately? They seem to have it out for me.*

"Alright. Did you double-check the room for your belongings?"

"Yes."

"Well enough. I know your bill is paid."

They started to make their way down the hallway toward the street.

"Young men," she said.

They both stopped and turned around. "Yes?" Diego recalled a gay friend of his from the city who had told him of blatant homophobia out in the province. He'd been denied rooms in several little pensiónes a few years back. Diego half expected her to tell them never to come back.

"Won't you come to the dining room and have a cup of coffee?" Her face brightened.

"Thank you very much," he choked, pleasantly surprised by her offer. "We're in a bit of a hurry."

"Then we hope you'll at least come back soon."

He nodded politely, touched by her kindness. "We'll make a point of it."

"And tell your friends that they are welcome here too."

"Okay. We will do that." He walked out with a grin on his face, wondering why all the other women he'd dealt with in recent days couldn't be as agreeable as this one.

"SO, WHAT do you really think?" Gerardo asked in the car.

"The mattress wasn't as comfortable as it might have been, but I would definitely go back," Diego said.

"I'm not talking about the pensión, Professor. I'm talking about the dig."

"I think the facts are pretty well stipulated in my report. Don't you? Anyway, you know the details as well as I do," he said, stopping for pedestrians at the street corner.

"I am not talking about facts or details. I'm talking about what you think. I mean, you said something about making claims to Aztec homosexuality. So, what do you think?"

"I was rather riled up when I said that."

"I know that. But what do you think?" Gerardo said. He tapped the side window with his knuckles.

"I think the evidence is inconclusive in that regard." The car lurched as Diego throttled it.

"They were holding hands, for God's sake."

"One's hand was on top of the other's, as far as we can tell. Thank goodness for the clay, which seems to have frozen them in place. Still, 'holding' is an assumption. We cannot witness musculature of one hand physically grasping the other," Diego said.

"Well, no."

"So perhaps it is more what you *want* to see in it."

"There are just so many aspects here that are unusual. I mean, it looks and quacks like a duck, doesn't it?"

"And what if it is? What if it is a duck? A big *pink* duck? So what?" Diego let out a frustrated sigh. "The reality is that those particular details may be more detrimental to our project than anything."

"It's important." His tapping turned into a louder knocking.

"Why? Because it helps us show that there were gay Aztecs? We know that already. Everyone *knows* that already. It's not as if homosexuality sprang up in the twentieth century. And as far as I recall from a very limited number of studies on the topic, they weren't treated any better than we are today."

"I beg to differ. Holding hands or not is a moot argument. They were dead, after all, when they were buried. Someone obviously cared about them enough to bury them in the first place and, unless my vision is failing me, saw to it that their hands were put together. These men weren't brothers. They weren't cousins. And I doubt they were merely owner and slave. Since when did a slave get buried with jade around his neck?"

Diego started to laugh quietly in astonishment.

"What?" Gerardo asked.

"You're so worked up about it. Argumentative. I'm a bit surprised, that's all. And quit knocking on the window."

"Maybe it's time to just say it as it is, or at least throw out the possibility."

"If only…," Diego said.

"If only what?"

"If only you'd be so open when it comes to your own situation, your family."

"Let's leave them out of this."

"Well, don't you think it's a bit hypocritical to fight so hard for the rights to the identity of these guys, who may or may not have been anything *special* to each other, when they died hundreds of years ago, yet you won't stand up for your own identity?"

"Come on. You're changing the subject."

"No, I think you're bringing it up," Diego said, glancing in the rearview mirror but not at Gerardo.

Gerardo shook his head. "You know my mother. You heard about my sister."

"Hey. Handy and Jade had mothers too."

"If only they could be like the lady back at the pensión."

"If only we could know. There are enough mysteries about those two. Let's not even start to wonder about their mothers."

"What is it with mothers anyway?" Gerardo asked, his voice changing from one of debate to one of open discussion. "I mean, maybe it's an obvious point, but they are just such powerful people in our lives."

"Speak for yourself." Diego's contact with his mother had been reduced to courtesy calls on birthdays and Christmas.

"She must have been important to you at some point."

"I didn't say she wasn't important. I don't know. Sometimes it's as if *I* wasn't."

"I don't believe that."

"Or maybe I was just too easy. Didn't need that much mothering." Diego chuckled lightly.

"Maybe that's why you're standoffish."

"Who invited who to stay in the pensión last night?"

"I'm only saying that maybe you're a bit of a hermit crab. Correct me if I'm wrong, but you sneak away into your shell at any sign of a threat. Not exactly a social creature. Maybe you got that way because of your mom."

"Maybe. She did have her hands full with the rest of my family. But you know it's kind of funny, sometimes I catch myself doing things exactly like her, or saying things I hadn't heard for years and years until they come out of my mouth, and I do realize that, as distant as she might be, she's still inside me somehow. Even the hermit crab idea. None of us were brought up to deal with things head-on. After my dad died, she'd never let on to missing him, but she'd lock herself up in her room for days at a time and leave us to make fried-egg tostadas or noodles in a cup!"

"That's nothing like my mother. She's a bit more…direct."

"So, how do you deal with it? I mean, your father's pretty laid-back."

"Right. He just lets her have her way," Gerardo replied. He started to tap the window again.

"Even with your sister, Ruth?" Diego asked.

"Yup."

"So what do you propose, to live a secret life all the time?"

Gerardo paused in thought. "I'm not sure. I mean, my mother is so protective of her family, and that's the way it ought to be. But it's like she's terrified of change or loss. Yet what she did with my sister created the loss she was most afraid of. So, it's like you have to figure out a way of taking the threat away, of showing her there's nothing to be afraid of."

"Me?"

"No. Not *you* specifically. I mean anyone. Me, I guess."

"Oh. That doesn't sound so hard."

"Well, it's not exactly easy either."

"Makes me wonder which one's better—distant and seemingly uncaring, or close and overly protective."

Gerardo sighed. "Be nice to find a happy medium." He put his tapping hand in his lap as they cleared the traffic of the town and began to drive through uninhabited countryside.

THE TEAM spent the week at the dig preparing the skeletons for removal from the site. They had thoroughly excavated the entire area surrounding the bodies, but the painstaking work yielded surprisingly little, which lent ever more credence to the idea that this burial was particularly unusual.

The tops of the skeletons themselves had been almost entirely exposed—the compact soil came off in relatively solid clumps, allowing for its removal without jeopardizing the fossils. Of the limited clothing the two had been buried in, the cotton cloak on Handy had endured the worst. Though the team estimated 90 percent deterioration, the 10 percent that had survived was still a significant amount due to its considerable original size. It was of the quality of cotton known to be reserved for the upper class, and had rich embroidery and attention to detail that would have required many days, if not weeks, of work. Diego guessed it also required a fair share of old-fashioned tender love and care.

Diego had now been at the site for several months. He'd become accustomed to the dark, starry nights, the camp stoves and propane lamps, the youthful enthusiasm of his team, and the constant feeling of dampness in his clothes. He could hardly imagine returning to the city, the busy life amid smog and concrete, or the enclosed sense of the classroom. He did appreciate a few of life's modern luxuries, like a warm shower and a grocery store on the corner, but the thought of leaving certainly filled him with melancholy.

He could hardly imagine the removal of Handy and Jade either. The two had almost become a living part of the team. They had spent many hours—not unlike the weaver of the cloak—carefully and tediously discovering their secrets, discussing at length every precious detail, and hypothesizing about the lives and deaths of the two. Therein lay the artistic side of archaeology, in the wondering, fantasizing, and creating stories of lives around limited, weathered, eroded, and otherwise damaged evidence.

With or without an extension of the grant, these two would never be forgotten. But their final resting place might be a storage box in the national archives or just the backroom of some local museum. With a little luck, he'd at least get the bodies sent to the Autonomous University for classroom use in his department. He knew their entire story might never be known, and either way the project would eventually be over. But Diego would see to it that a full report and the entire range of hypotheses made it into the *Journal of Archaeology* in case someone, sometime, were to find corroborating evidence elsewhere and carry the torch for the gay hypothesis.

He had grown attached. He didn't want to see the bodies go. But still, as a scientist, he knew that their removal could reveal more pieces of the puzzle. Not only would there be the possibility of full-on X-rays and MRIs—the team wouldn't risk removing the clay from the inside of the skeletons, only high tech tools could do that virtually—but they'd finally have the chance to see if any artifacts existed beneath the bodies. The weather was growing colder. Time was ticking away. They'd have to work fast in order to find out.

BARBIE HAD fattened up, and her dark face protruding from her generous coat of white wool made her look like a gigantic cotton ball with a black fly stuck in it. "Baa-aa-aa." She fought against the tether that kept her from a few more blades of grass almost within her reach. Gerardo went to loosen it.

"Go ahead, little girl, you'll need it."

"Will she be clipped before her slau… um, beforehand?" Diego asked.

"Yeah. My parents will probably sell the wool to the local Otomí."

"Wool? They hardly had wool before the conquest."

"It's called adaptation, my friend."

When they went inside the house, Diego immediately heard from the living room the usual Sunday banter, laughter, music in the background, opening of beer cans, and clinking of glasses. As soon as they walked in, the many family members offered hugs—the macho, one-armed hugs and backslaps of the men, and the cheek kisses and more intimate embraces of the women.

"How about a beer, guys?" one of Gerardo's brothers offered.

"Where have you guys been?" someone else asked.

"Where's my mom?" Gerardo asked.

"The kitchen, I guess."

Gerardo nudged Diego. "Come on. Let's say hi to my mother."

In the kitchen, his mother stirred an enormous pot of boiling broth on the stove. Gerardo's sister, Ofelia, sat at the counter, cranking out tortillas from an iron tortilla press.

"Hey, Mamá," Gerardo said, walking to her for a kiss.

She smiled tersely. "Oh, you made it." As she reached her face up for the cheek kiss, she regarded Diego and nearly rolled her eyes, but then closed them. "You might have called."

"Sorry, I meant to," he answered.

"You didn't call?" Diego asked, approaching Gerardo's mother for his greeting. She gave him a tepid air-kiss and a barely passable brush of her cheek on his.

"No. No call. I was worried about you," she said, looking at Gerardo. "I guess I'm lower on the list."

"Oh, Mother. We were busy at the dig. We had some work to catch up on."

"I'm sure."

"Professor, I hope you like ribs. My mother's ribs are delectable," Ofelia said perkily.

Diego smiled. "I do, thank you. Everything your mother makes is delectable."

"And wait till you try the barbacoa," Ofelia said.

Diego turned to Gerardo's mother. "Truly, Señora, I thought he had let you know we wouldn't make it last week. Bad form. Anyone ought to feel lucky to have a family as close as yours."

"Well," she said, appearing slightly appeased. "At least you're here today." She shook her finger at her son. "Go get yourselves some beers. The food will be ready shortly."

"THE RIBS were delicious," Diego said to Eunice as he brought in dirty dishes from the living room.

"I'm glad you liked them," she answered.

Standing beside her he lowered his voice. "I hope you don't mind me coming here."

"Not at all. I just hadn't realized I'd be competing with you for my son."

"*Competing*? I hardly think we're competing," Diego said.

"If it takes him bringing along his boss from work to get him here, I suppose that's okay."

"No, Señora, I think he's quite determined to maintain the strength of his family ties. I sometimes feel like a zero on the left of the decimal, myself."

"Huh. I've never seen him so excited about a job," Eunice said.

"And I have rarely seen such family cohesion, especially in the city."

"My mother instilled it in me, I guess, and so I like to keep my family close."

Diego thought of Gerardo's sister Ruth, and bit his tongue to keep his foot far from his mouth. "It shows. If only all of Mexico would retain your family values."

"Come now," she said, "would you mind helping me serve the flan?" She passed him a stack of paper plates and a handful of plastic spoons, and he followed her into the living room. The men stood around watching the end of a football game on the TV while the women gabbed on the sofa. From a large round tray of flan, they served dessert until everyone had some. "Here you are," Eunice said, handing Diego the biggest piece.

Chapter Twenty

"WOULD YOU like for me to tend your wounds?" Tototli asked as he set down a calabash of water beside Metzín.

The cuts on Metzín's thighs were raw, his legs exposed, as he lay on his mat. He'd been limping for the past few days.

"No," Metzín answered tersely, imagining the young man's slender fingers and soft hands on his legs. "I can tend to myself."

"As you wish." Tototli said softly, his eyes teary like those of a rejected child. He began to leave.

"I do need a clean cloak, however."

"Yes, Master Metzín." The servant-slave raised one side of his mouth in a barely discernible smile and bowed his head. He left and returned with a folded white cloth, which he set beside Metzín. "The games are today?"

Metzín began to untie his bloodied garment. Unable to keep his eyes from wandering, he glimpsed at the brown legs so near to him. He looked up to find Tototli looking back at him, his eyes dark and warm. Something shifted in his loincloth, swelled. He shook away the impulse and unfolded the cloth. "Not this one, you stupid fish. Where did you find this?"

"From the stack in the far room," Tototli answered.

"You should know that these are for trading."

"I thought you'd want a fresh one for the games."

"These are for trading, I said. Just pass me one from my chest."

"Sorry. I was distracted. I know the games are of import." Tototli kept his head bowed, still looking tenderly at Metzín, as if yearning.

"Yes," Metzín responded pensively, running his eyes over Tototli again. "This day a decision will be made."

NOT FAR from the Great Temple of the Sun in Teopán, the quartile of the gods, with the grand homes of the nobles situated on one side and the imperial palace on another, sat the sacred *tlachtli* court. A representation of the universe itself, the games could mean life or death, fortune or misery, liberty or servitude. Like the gods on high who batted the stars between them in the night, so would the players juggle the ball using their skills and wit. In the middle of two great walls were two carved stone rings placed along the path of Uitzilopochtli, who passed overhead each day. Only divinity could carry the ball through either of the two carved stone rings. This day would determine the fate of many—to battle in the far left of the world—to glory, to death and peace, to triumph and ascension—or to patient waiting. *Come now, gods, grant us your presence, your stealth, and your will, that Motecuhzoma might realize your volition. Great is the Aztec Empire, great you have made it, and greater still, on your command.*

To Metzín, it appeared like the market of Tlatelolco, where throngs of people of all ages and classes walked to and fro. They were filled with quiet excitement and they gathered close to the court to watch and to wager. Cotton and colored stones, livestock, and slaves would change hands. More importantly, this tournament could trigger war.

Like so many, Metzín attended the event for answers. For him, there were two wars. An external war—would he again travel the distance to the left side of the world, to lift his shield and wield his sword against a faraway people in a jungle canyon? And an internal war—would he raise his sword against Tototli to draw the poisonous water from inside him? Or was this affliction, in some mysterious way, part of a purposeful plan of the gods? Was their embrace, their copulation in the darkness, an unseen, unknown flower—a favor? Could there be rightness in something so degraded? In the act it did not feel wrong. It was woeful torment, with the two sides as separate as the rings of the tlachtli court, and the ball, the moon's earthly manifestation, bouncing and rebounding between the two.

A group of the emperor's guards caught the collective attention of the crowd as they dispersed from near the court a number of vendors of honey-corn cakes and citrus water. The people divided, opening a wide path in the direction of the temple. They could hear the sound of conches and beating drums in the distance. An awed hush came over the crowd as the first wave of dancers approached.

They wore the paint of warriors on their faces and chests and the gloves and padded aprons of the tlachtli players. Each of them had an arrangement of feathers in his hair or on a half mask or on his clothing. With rattles of hollowed seeds strapped on their calves, they performed a mock tlachtli game, kicking a crimson leather ball between them while they spun and jumped and skipped from side to side, shrieking and screaming throughout.

Behind them, musicians of all sorts—drummers, percussionists, flutists, players of seashell bells, gongs, and wooden trumpets—filled the air with a captivating melody. They were followed by administrators and nobles in long, colorful cloaks and sandals whose straps nearly reached their knees. Then came priests, with their flamboyant adornment and body piercings. Some walked with staffs, others with lit incense in bowls held in their hands or smoking from dangling pots.

Finally, preceded by a cadre of gigantic spear-bearing guards, in a headdress of long, spotted feathers, and wearing a cloak encrusted with jade and gold, the Emperor Motecuhzoma entered, a god embodied. The citizens knelt before him, raising their heads to watch him in awe as he passed, though never looking directly in his eyes. A couple of advisors walked beside him. Many others were a step or two behind. And yellowed women with reddened teeth, intricate loops and braids in their hair, and elaborate jewelry, followed behind them. After they passed, the crowd filled in the path and watched as the entire party of nobles, administrators, priests, the emperor, and all of his women, climbed the steps on either side of the walls. They perched themselves atop the stone barriers to view the forthcoming tournament and to see destiny played out before them.

From the top of the walls, conches sounded, one and another and another, until many giant shells harmonized throughout Tenochtitlán, calling the players to the court. From the far side of the court, the first team entered—noblemen's sons, roughly of Metzín's age, bedecked in aprons, kneepads, gloves, and padding. A few wore partial masks on their faces to protect their chins and cheeks. Each of the four had a stark red feather or two entwined in his hair or along the strap of his apron. One stood out from the rest for his gigantic size, both in height and width, a player bestowed with powerful muscles and tremendous physique, and this one churned Metzín's stomach for whom the player reminded him of. The conches continued to bellow as they lined up along one of the walls, awaiting their opponents. From the grassy, I-shaped floor, they jumped up onto one of two stone ramps, about waist high, adjacent to the walls that completed the four sides of the court. The team raised their arms to the cheers of the crowd and trotted in place with prebattle jitters.

The second team ran out much like the first, except their feet were in lockstep, their coordination impressing the crowd. Their feathers were of brilliant blue. Inside, Metzín had chosen this team, even before he noticed the one particularly dark-skinned, lithe young player, whose lean back tapered to a narrow waist, reminding him of the man for whom, in Metzín's universe, this game would be played. They lined up along the opposite ramp and, bringing their hands to their mouths in unison, chanted a verse to the gods they were honoring.

With the players waiting in the court below, priests on top of the walls invoked the deities with mumbled prayers to the rhythm of handheld drums, rattles, and shakers. Afterward Motecuhzoma spoke of the heavy burden of his obligation to safeguard the honor of the Aztec empire, protect the many people beneath his vast shade, and defend and justly maintain such a great realm. He spoke at length of the necessity of virtue, integrity, and courage. He reminded men to be sincerely humble and said, "For the gods see what is in our hearts. They know all secret things." At times the people in the crowd let out dull murmurs as they concurred with his message, admonished children, and thanked the gods for their mercifulness and gifts. Finally, he produced a crimson ball, which he cupped in one hand. He raised it high for all to see. "Now we gather as servants for the greater good, and as witnesses, like an image in a pool brought to the surface from the depths below. Oh, we who can see only the surface of life's pool, let us perceive today the steps we will take tomorrow."

He held the ball in his outstretched hand. The players shifted to ready stances. He released the ball to the middle of the court. The game had begun.

The red-feathered team, bigger men from Teopán, received the ball first. They moved around their side of the court, batting the ball between bounces with swings from their hips. A pair remained high upon a ramp, obviously intending to win swiftly by getting the ball through a ring. It proved a difficult feat. Their teammates batted the ball up the ramp easily, but the bigger men could not adjust quickly enough to receive it. For a successful triple pass without a bounce, a priest indicated an awarded point. But after the ball bounced three times between hits, the point was lost, and the ball was ceded to the blue team of Cuepopán, the place of the blossoming flowers.

The strategy of the blue team involved slower, more careful maneuvers—keeping the ball on their side through controlled bounces and constant passing. On its first bounce, the heavy ball reached barely above the players' knees, so they had to move quickly before the ball bounced three times. After the blue team scored two points for handling, the ball took an awkward bounce and flew over the top of the ramp. Once they recovered it, they had to bowl the ball to the other team.

The most muscular red player took a position on the far side of the ramp, closest to the ring high overhead on the wall. Again the red team sought a quick win, and again despite the giant throwing himself on the ground to save the play, they lost control of the ball. It spun to the blue team's side.

Thus the game played on, and the spectators watched as the ball bounced and ricocheted from one player to the other and from side to side. The red team had shifted tactics, attempting to win by points instead of making a ring. Points were scored and points were deducted. Despite the size difference between the teams' players, the tally remained almost even. One team raised the score by a point, and then the other pulled ahead.

Suddenly silence fell over the excited crowd as two players, one red and one blue, crashed into one another high on the stone ramp.

The red player fell with his feet toward the lower end of the ramp, but the blue player fell so that he tumbled down the ramp and dropped heavily to the ground, beside the still ball. The red player got up slowly and shook off the effects of his fall. The blue player did not get up. His teammates ran to him, but were unable to revive him. At the direction of the presiding priest, they dragged him off the field and were left with three players against four.

With the advantage in players, the red team pulled ahead. Looking tired from the constant running, they abandoned their attempt at the ring and began to rack up points in their favor as the blue team lost most of those they had accumulated. The eventual winners were apparent. The crowd could not know the meaning of a red win, but Metzín knew what it meant for him. He watched as he stood alone, trying to comprehend the intentions of the gods. But men were not meant to understand, only to obey.

A conch sounded twice. The game neared its end. The blue players tried desperately to catch up while triumphant smiles appeared on the scoffing faces of the red team. Metzín suddenly thought of Tototli. The conch sounded once. The red team possessed the ball. They batted it softly between them, waiting for the final gong. The giant laughed and raised his arms in victory. The ball came his way and took a third bounce before he bumped it. He looked up, awaiting the gong from the suspended disc, but the sound did not yet come.

The ball would be rolled to the blue team once more. It went toward the slender man, and rolled flush along the grass, but it hit a divot in the sod, and bounced up to the player's clenched shoulder as the blue captain ran up the ramp as fast as a jaguar. The slender one knocked the ball into the air beside him. *Tototli, Tototli.* As the ball came down, he took a few giant steps and batted the ball with all his might up to the captain at the top of the ramp. The captain leapt off the edge to a perfect pass, intercepting the ball with an upward stroke of his thigh. The crowd held a collective breath as the ball hit the wall at an angle and bounced through the carved ring.

A massive gong sounded. The game was over. The crowd erupted. And the red players fell to the ground in defeat. The two blue players on the grass ran to their captain and lifted him from where he had fallen. Triumph! The captain limped and grabbed tightly to the shoulders of the other two players.

In a moment priests surrounded the players, offering their forearms in congratulations. The group followed Motecuhzoma and his cadre of advisors to the top of the temple behind the court. The throng of onlookers gathered at the steps of the temple.

"For your courageous play and sacrifice, you will forever be remembered," Motecuhzoma said to the captain who knelt in front of him. "Your likeness will be etched into this very temple." The emperor turned to a priest beside him and received a long necklace of jewels and stones. This he placed around the captain's neck to the roars of people below. "And your family will be honored with nobility and gifts as you travel the path of Uitzilopochtli for eternity!"

The priests took the captain's arms from around the shoulders of his teammates and slowly led him to a round stone at the top of the stairs. The victorious captain first sat down on the stone and then, with the assistance of the priests, lay back, clutching the forearm of the presiding shaman.

The emperor and his entourage followed them. Now, he stood before the crowd. "For your brave effort, the Aztec empire praises you," the emperor shouted. "A player of fortune and godlike prowess, you have shown us the way. To war!"

The crowd erupted again.

"You honed your skills and demonstrated your stealth. And now you so willingly give your valiant water. Let all citizens aspire to your greatness!"

A black-faced priest produced an obsidian knife of awful length. While looking into the eyes of the glorified captain, he dug the knife deeply into the man's chest. The captain's body writhed. Blood gushed and spouted. Uitzilopochtli drank of the hero's blood. The priest pulled the knife out and the captain turned his head toward the crowd, precious water spurting from his mouth, his dazed eyes blinking their last time in the hardened world before beginning his blessed trip to the sky. The priest raised the knife in a two-handed clutch and brought it down on the captain's neck. But the captain's head did not come off immediately, so the priest sawed upon his throat and pushed down hard against the bone, until the head fell into the waiting hands of another priest.

He raised the head high, the way Motecuhzoma had done with the ball before the game. The crowd wondered at the amazing sight—the passing of a great warrior to a different and better realm.

After being lost in the bedazzling spectacle, Metzín returned to his senses. Tototli reentered his mind, as did his own knife. The same knife that he'd thrust into his own leg to shed his own blood would soon cut into Tototli. *To war!* The emperor's words echoed in his head. Metzín thought of Tototli and then the black knife in his wicker chest, and he begged for courage. The outcome of the game frightened him, not because of the prospect of war, but because of the private act he had been charged with carrying out.

Chapter Twenty-One

DIEGO HAD previously spent many hours each day in the temple. Now he spent the majority of his time at the gravesite. Though he trusted Gerardo and his team to competently complete the dig, he had begun to feel a deep connection to the entire project, as if Jade and Handy were his kindred spirits. Their bone surfaces were entirely exposed now, except for the tatters of their clothing and the places where they contacted the soil below them. The team had found minimal artifacts in the immediate vicinity, and he had instructed them to focus entirely on cleaning the soot from the skeletons and preparing them for removal from the site.

The team slowly inserted planks, one by one into the soil beneath the bodies, until a complete wood floor had been created, like the beginnings of a posthumous coffin. It reminded Diego of the painstaking work of so many demolition men in Mexico City or gravediggers who, without the luxury of power tools and heavy machinery, still worked with chisels, hammers, and shovels. The team had spent all day Friday preparing the bodies. On Saturday morning they lifted the skeletons into the cushioned bed of a pickup truck for transport to the university.

They watched in silence as the truck drove away—a melancholy, unceremonious moment. Diego supposed that many of them wondered what they would do after the project was over. He had almost every reason to believe that he would see the bodies again in the laboratory, but given the political climate, a part of him remained doubtful.

As they stood around the flat bed of earth where Jade and Handy had rested undisturbed for hundreds of years, a moral debate arose in Diego—the same one he had pondered so often in his own studies and brought up in all of his courses: Did the furthering of education or the quenching of curiosity justify such an abrupt upheaval? Who was he to remove these two from their grave? He'd long rationalized the practice—after all, the people were dead. If he didn't remove them in the name of science, then someone else would in the name of greed.

Though no one's intentions could be left unquestioned—sometimes the best thing was the lesser of two evils—at least science was intended to benefit the greater good.

His team looked somber. A pair of them tearfully made eye contact with the others, as if hoping for consolation. The others stood in silence, but their sadness was surely shared. Mostly they gazed at the ground. Diego finally darted a glance at Gerardo. "Well, let's check the earth here. You never know what we might find beneath them." He cleared his throat. "I guess I'll go finish a report." He moseyed away without looking back.

"So, WHAT about your family. Won't they miss you over the holidays?"

Diego looked at Gerardo's mother, her combative mood clear from the stern tone of her voice. He supposed the chile sauce would be particularly spicy too. Everyone knew that overly spicy salsa meant an angry cook. But given the departure of Jade and Handy, and the sense of mourning he and his team felt, Diego was in no mood to battle wits with her or exert the energy that constant politeness required.

"They're all up north," he answered. "We hardly speak at all."

"Not even phone calls? What about your mother?"

He looked at her blankly. "We talk as much as we need to."

"Don't you ever go visit them?"

He sighed and twisted his tongue at her interrogations, wondering why Eunice had sought him out in the yard and sat right beside him on the rickety bench. "I have little interest, Señora, in traveling to the north. They decided to leave the city some time ago, and I don't feel the need to go chasing after them. If they would like to find me, they know where and how."

"I see," she said. She dropped her nearly assaultive posture and leaned back on the bench. "How sad."

"I'm not sad about it. Besides, I have too much work to do. I don't have the time to travel during the holidays. I'll be writing a research article, preparing for classes, advising students, and looking for grant money—"

"What about your personal life?" she asked.

"What about it?"

"I mean, friends, family. Don't you need to socialize?"

Diego strained a smile. "Here I am with you dear folks."

"I mean, *we* could hardly live without being close to one another."

"Yes, I've seen that." He wished someone would call her to tend to a boiling pot of stew or a bleeding grandchild.

"It's important to be close to people," she said.

"Yes. I guess I meet most of my needs by socializing with the people with whom I work," Diego explained.

"That can't be enough."

He raised his brow. "I'm not complaining. I've always been more on the introverted side."

"But no wife, or at least a girlfriend?"

He cocked his head and looked at her penetrating eyes. He clenched his jaw slightly in an attempt to slow his rising heart rate.

"Don't you plan on getting married?" she asked.

"I haven't thought of it," he muttered.

"Or a *sex* life?"

"Excuse me?" he asked, batting his eyes.

"Professor, we're both adults here. We both know that a person's sex life is important. I'm simply trying to get to know you."

"I can see that."

"And I only mean to make a point that, in the absence of your own mother, perhaps few of your colleagues would dare to point things out. Don't you think an intimate relationship is important? You've studied people enough to know that."

"Of course it's important. But, Señora, it's a very personal question."

"Yes, it's a personal question. But you've been visiting us for several months. Aren't you part of the family now? Can't I ask a personal question?"

Diego started to wonder what Gerardo was doing. Chatting it up with his siblings? Talking over some soccer game, beer in hand? Diego had walked out to the patio to get a little space from all the people, and he found himself being interrogated by this outspoken woman. What was she looking for, he wondered. Given his present mood, he was quite capable of giving it to her. He tried to restrain himself, because he'd made a promise to Gerardo to keep things private.

"After all, you do want children, don't you?" she continued badgering.

He bit his bottom lip.

"Or will you just be a single old university professor down the road? You do like women, don't you? I can't imagine that you're—"

"I'm gay." To hell with restraint. To hell with privacy. Coming out to her did not break his promise to Gerardo.

A quiet pause ensued as the two regarded each other.

She put her palm to her chest. "I don't know what to say."

"There is nothing to say."

"And that's why your mother...."

He shook his head. "That's got nothing to do with it."

"But don't you know what the Bible says about—"

"I'm not religious like that," he said matter-of-factly.

"And, and... does Gerardo know this? Because I'm sure he—"

"I can't speak for Gerardo."

"I just don't think that—I mean, I don't believe you should or...." She turned her head away.

"Baa-aa-aa." Barbie shared her thoughts from where she was tied near the back wall of the patio.

Gerardo's mother stood up and turned toward Diego. "It's not a choice we condone here. It's not something God condones."

He stood up beside her. "You've said enough, Eunice."

"I just—"

"Thank you for your hospitality. I think it's time for me to go. If you'll permit me, I'll just step inside and let Gerardo know that I *choose* to be on my way."

"I'm not trying to say you should leave," Eunice said.

"It's what you said to your daughter Ruth, wasn't it? Apparently that message remains the same."

"It's not my message. It's God's."

"God gave you the power to think for yourself," Diego retorted, shaking his head as he began to walk away from her.

"People can change, you know?" she shouted behind him.

He turned back toward her. "Really? Show me."

He looked at her—a middle-aged woman with desperation in her face, trying hard to cling to her beliefs and simultaneously keep her family together. They were her only connection to order and rightness. He took a mental snapshot of her—the way her apron was tied so tautly around her waist, the way her stringy hairdo tried unsuccessfully to keep its round shape, the way her face was finally giving way to wrinkles and bags beneath her eyes despite the creams and treatments he knew she employed. He felt sorry for her in that moment. What would she be without her children? What would she believe if she forsook the interpretation of the Bible that had been fed to her?

"Good-bye," he said.

As he had imagined, he found Gerardo inside by the television, which blared a match between the American and the Xolo soccer teams. A few of his brothers stood while Gerardo and a couple of other guys sat on the couch, munching on spicy fried peanuts from a bowl on the coffee table. All had beers in their hands and were glued to the game. Gerardo looked so much like his siblings. He was neither the shortest nor the tallest, the fattest nor the skinniest. In so many ways, he was exactly in the middle of them all. They all had something in common—a smile, a cowlick, an Aztec nose, a characteristic gesture, a glint in the eyes.

Diego had felt sorry for their mother. But now as he took them all in, he saw something decent, respectable, and so enviable. Guilt entered him like a shot of dizzying adrenaline. He was only a few steps away from Gerardo, but he could hardly imagine the sentence he might compose. How could he say good-bye without forcing Gerardo to make a choice? And if he did, how could he not choose his family?

Diego stopped in his tracks. It made no difference now, he thought. The project was nearly over. The subjects of the study had been removed, and the money had dried up. Gerardo would continue to live the life his family required of him—or at least make it seem that way and continue his other life privately. Diego would return to the city, get lost again in his work, and hide away in the safety of his cramped office. What else might he have hoped for? To be buried for eternity with his lover, holding hands beneath the surface? *Ridiculous.* He reversed his course and went back out the way he had come in, fumbling with his keys inside his pocket.

Gerardo would find his own way back to the site. He'd find his own way in the world, for that matter. And so much for the barbacoa.

When he walked outside, he saw Gerardo's mother standing where he had left her. He got into his car, closed the door, revved it up, and began pulling away.

He heard banging on the roof of his car before he'd even driven ten meters toward the gate. He hadn't looked in his rearview mirror, but thought Gerardo's mother might somehow have caught up to him. Maybe she'd like to make herself feel better by apologizing for their difference in views. Maybe she'd like to wish him a happy Christmas as a subtle reminder for him not to return. Or maybe he'd simply forgotten something.

He pushed down on the brake and unrolled his window.

"Where are you going? We haven't even eaten yet." It was Gerardo, his expression a mixture of irritation and concern.

"Sorry," Diego said. "I didn't want to disturb you, but I have to go."

"What do you mean? Is something the matter?"

Diego checked his mirror, which caused Gerardo to look to where his mother stood.

"Oh. Did something happen? Did she say something to you?"

"It's nothing. I just have to go. I'll explain later."

Gerardo stepped back and looked at him, then toward his mother and the house. Diego regretted the situation. He knew he should have kept his mouth shut. Worse, though he had known whom Gerardo would choose, he still preferred leaving room for a tiny doubt. Some hypotheses were better left untested.

Diego had the impulse to simply drive away, but he couldn't leave Gerardo standing in the dust like that. Gerardo shifted his glance between his house and Diego. *Why was love so complicated?* Diego braced for the blow.

"Wait for me," Gerardo said. "I've got to get my stuff."

"No. You stay here with your family."

"I'm going with you. You're my supervisor."

Ouch. The momentary happiness inside instantly deflated.

"I didn't mean that. You're my lover. Just wait for me. I'll get my bag." He sprinted into the house, leaving Diego alone in the driver's seat. He leaned forward, rested his head on the steering wheel, and thought of his family and the distance between them. He imagined Ruth also far from her roots. And he pictured the pride he had seen on Gerardo's face whenever he spoke of his family. He knew he had no right to pull Gerardo away from them. Besides, he knew he probably had little to offer. Gerardo's mother was right. He'd end up an old man—single and lonely. He had no relationship skills. It could only end in disaster. It would be unthinkable to destroy Gerardo's relationship with his family and then fall short as a partner. He sat up in his seat, shifted into first gear, and drove away.

Chapter Twenty-Two

THE MOOD in the telpochcalli was of anxious excitement. As the young warriors sharpened their weapons and debarked sticks for arrows, their shaky hands contradicted the determination and valor brewing in their eyes. They all hoped for a live capture or two. They all professed the desire to die in battle and join the great god of the sun. But with the exception of boastful Peo, they spoke little.

Metzín wondered if he were the only one who pondered his own existence. If he were to die, what would become of his mother? She would miss him immensely and mourn at length. How would she get over the loss? What would the house be like without him? Who might he have become? And what of Tototli? He put his hand on his thigh, which was still sore from his bloodletting, but finally beginning to heal. He wished he'd let Tototli tend his wounds. The servant-slave's sensitive touch would surely have found a way to mend the skin and take away the pain.

No. He mustn't think of Tototli now. He must focus on the task of preparation for war. He must leave with a clean spirit. Yet a thought burning inside him—the thought of Tototli and the act he had to commit—called him homeward. He chipped away at his black knife of stone, his eyes as intent on the weapon as on avoiding the gaze of the others. They might see his thoughts and read his guilt.

They took a quiet meal and were dismissed for the day to spend time with their families and make peace in their souls. When he stepped outside, Metzín noticed that the entire city seemed to be under a cloud of solemnity. The normal whispers and muffled laughs of women were absent. Even babies in the arms of their mothers and children at their sides seemed respectfully quiet. The movements of the populace seemed hurried, but it was not cheerful as on days of celebration. Rather, there was the dutiful swiftness of tending to the needs of a loved one who might never be seen again.

He hoped for tranquility at home—a moment of solitude so that he might find a private place with Tototli and carry out his task. Ideally he would have taken him to the little cave in the canyon over the causeway and do it in the darkness, where no one would be startled or frightened. There was no time for that now. Perhaps in the garden, in the patio near the canal, or in the temazcalli. Indoors he would surely call the attention of others.

The sound of children playing inside the house dispelled his hope. As he entered their voices became hushed. He saw his sisters sitting in the front room with his mother, and they looked at him with affection, standing to receive him as if they'd been waiting for him to arrive. Tototli came in from the patio with a jug, but he stopped in place when he saw Metzín, as if uncertain of how to behave. He swallowed nervously, set the jug down, and exited to the back patio.

The women approached with proud smiles on their faces. His mother stood in front of him and put her hands on his shoulders while his sisters gathered around.

"Mother had a vision," his eldest sister said.

"Yes, son," said his mother as she gazed into his eyes. "You will make captures and return a *tequiua*. You will soon wear a bird on your lip and jade on your neck. Your ears will be adorned with pendants. You will be a respected man and claim a share of the tribute. Men and children will learn from you."

He returned her gaze and listened without responding.

"He is anxious," his sister said.

"He is eager," said another.

"He will bring honor to us," his mother said. "For now he must purify himself, and we must allow him some time while we prepare the food for him."

She continued to look into his eyes with wonder, amazing Metzín with what seemed to him her ability to see inside him and understand him. She lowered her brow and her voice. "We have a surprise. The temazcalli has been prepared for you." Metzín looked to where Tototli had disappeared. He envisioned the fruition of his plan. She shook her head. "You must put away boyish thoughts. Your wedding has been arranged." Her voice became still softer. "And I have arranged for her, a beautiful and important girl, to come here and be with you before your journey on the morrow. She awaits you in the temazcalli… and no one must know this but us. I must not even tell you her name. So, purify yourself and let this be a beginning where impulse becomes control, desire becomes sacrifice, and your destiny becomes fulfilled."

Metzín was stunned and methodically obeyed his mother, who could so easily make him feel vulnerable and as naked as the day he was born. There was an unspoken confidence between a mother and her son, and she wielded incredible power over him because of it.

As Metzín dropped his cloak outside the steam bath, he watched Tototli, who knelt by the water, vigorously scrubbing a clay pot. Tototli stole a few glances while he worked, a serious, almost resentful look in his eyes. Metzín knew that his mother was right. He had to resist temptation and embrace the responsibilities of manhood. Yet he could not help but continue to watch the young man, wishing that Tototli could be entirely extinguished from his life on the one hand, and wanting to be inside the temazcalli with him on the other. Metzín got on his knees and crawled into the dark, steamy chamber.

"Will you like a massage?" he heard from a delicate voice. He imagined Tototli.

"Yes." He lay down, too bashful to remove his loincloth. He immediately felt a light hand on his back, which startled him.

"Are you okay?" she asked.

"Yes."

She began to rub her hands slowly up and down his back, as skillfully as Tototli. Her small hands had strength. She worked up to his shoulders, kneaded his neck, and moved down his spine. He closed his eyes, delighting in the illusion for a moment. Her hand neared his buttocks, and his loins swelled as they should, though the image of Tototli had not left him. Then she touched his leg near the wound on his thigh, and a pain shot through him. How the gods toyed with and baffled him!

By the time he exited the brick temazcalli, the rest of his family had arrived at the house. All of his brothers were pochteca, merchants like their father, and they all talked incessantly of faraway regions and unusual peoples. They spoke of numbers and units of cotton cloths and cacao beans, gems and stones, livestock and dried fish, sacks of herbs and spices. Halfway through their meal, their father stopped the conversation, set his food down, and stood up to address Metzín and the family.

"The boy-child of two worlds," he began. The many family members stopped eating to listen, as they all enjoyed hearing the slow speeches and wisdom of their father. "Like each of us, who has come into this world a mere minion of the gods' will, the tiniest leaf in the wind or upon the current of the river, my youngest son will follow the way prepared for him. And as each learns to behold his own insignificance, so each will find a reason for being, each will carve a shape from a stone. Our boy-child of two worlds, march forward and do not look back. Do not wonder at what is behind you or what lies on the path far ahead. You may never get there, and you may never return. Instead, confront that which is at hand. The tlachtli player does not contemplate the ball before it arrives. He adjusts to its every bounce." His father moved his hips for effect as his adult children nodded their heads. "He swings his hips, he whips his legs, he jumps high, and crouches low. We never know in what moment the ball will arrive or what direction it will take when it approaches. But we will be ready, stealthy, and intelligent, to meet it with power and effectiveness. We know it is a challenge of the gods and we will take it such that we might be with them, soaring above the hard earth and extolling their greatness with brightness and beauty."

As his father went on, Metzín's gaze met his mother's. His father had played an important, official part in his life—guiding him with his words, reminding him of his duties, and punishing him for his infractions. Metzín respected his father and knew that his was the final word. His mother watched him with her dark eyes. Perhaps his father had the final word, but she often had the first word and determined the direction of his path from the first step. Her voice had been a private one, as powerful as her husband's. He respected the voice of an authority figure, like Motecuhzoma or the master warrior who relayed the Aztec dogma. But her voice was a personal one that penetrated and reflected him. Like a sacrificial knife, she could dig into his chest and pull out his raw, thumping heart.

The evening before his departure, his family honored him, bestowed on him their words of wisdom, and blessed him. More than anything he knew that after this journey, things would never be the same. As a warrior he would seek respect and status, or the glory of a battlefield death. As a man he would seek to fulfill his duties, produce a fine family, and provide for his wife and children. Inside was his painful and pressing secret. He yearned for Tototli. He would not satisfy this yearning before he left at the morning's first light.

The drink of octli his father had given him made his sleep restless and his dreams disturbing. He awoke a few times during the night, looked at the ceiling, wondered about Tototli, and imagined him asleep. With his knife beside the bed, it occurred to Metzín to find Tototli and complete the act dictated to him by the tlachtli game. His brothers lay all around him, and the house was full, so he could not risk making a scene. Surely they would not approve. They would not understand why he had to do it, especially with all of his siblings there. Besides, he knew that the trip would be a long one and that he needed as much rest as he could get. He anticipated the sound of the conches awaking a thousand warriors across Tenochtitlán before the first light. He drifted to sleep again and dreamt of singing birds.

It was not conches, but his mother's stern voice down the hall that woke him. "What are you doing with that? Why are you here? Give it to me."

Metzín got up quickly to see her with Tototli. He was handing her the little flute as she reprimanded him. "You must see to your duties and let the people sleep."

"The conches will sound soon," he answered timidly.

"What did you say? Do you dare answer me?" She put the flute on the ground and raised her foot to crush it.

"No, Mother." Metzín put a hand on her shoulder. She set her foot down in place. "Do not destroy the few possessions he has." He stooped to pick up the flute. "Please. Let him be."

"It's because I could not sleep," Tototli said. "The birds visited me in my dreams and told me to play."

"Nonsense," Metzín said, supposedly to Tototli, while looking at his mother. He gave the flute back to him. "You mustn't play while others sleep."

"I am sorry."

"It is forgotten." Metzín gazed at Tototli and felt far more than he could say. "Go now and busy yourself. All will be up soon."

Tototli nodded and went away. The woman had turned her focus to Metzín.

"Why are you so harsh with him?" he asked in a low voice.

"He is distractible."

"I am distractible. You are not harsh with me."

"He… he is strange. I do not trust his intentions. He is like octli—tempting—and he can still make *one*…." She raised and lowered her brow quickly and looked into Metzín's eyes when she said, "…carry himself beyond normal teachings."

He put his hand on her shoulder. "Mother, I am leaving this morning. I am ready to step into the destiny the gods have planned for me. Did you not say I would return tequiua, with jade on my neck? Do you not remember that my marriage has been approved?"

"Yes, I remember." She began to rub his hand with her cheek.

"Easy, Mother. I am prepared to step into my destiny. I do not pretend to see the future, but I believe that, one way or another, all will change."

B-ROOOM. B-ROOOM. The conches began to resonate across the city. Metzín dropped his hand from her shoulder. Both of their faces brightened.

"Yes," she said. "You go off to war now, my son of two worlds. Then come back to me. And all will change."

Chapter Twenty-Three

THE SITE seemed abandoned. Most of the young interns had Sunday as their only day off, and Gerardo had not yet returned. The spot of the burial, aside from footprints, stakes, and markers, was barren. Even the skeletons had looked livelier than the empty rectangular dirt bed. Birds barely seemed to chirp in the late autumn afternoon. And aside from a few silent ants, even the insects seemed to have gone away with the rest of the living.

Diego sat in the middle of the plot. He had brought his excavating kit down from his temple office. Not knowing when he might be out in the field next, he decided to get his hands dirty while he still could. Most of the work had been done, but he had little else to do and he found solace in the manual task.

First he prodded the soil centimeter by centimeter with a wooden dowel to test for anything big or hard. Then he removed a layer of soil with a shovel so tiny it looked like a spoon. He stopped intermittently to examine discolored particles in the soil—perhaps remnants of pots or clay instruments or tools. It was easy to get lost in the repetitiveness and the constant need to focus.

Or at least it used to. He couldn't keep his mind from returning to the gate at Gerardo's house, and the way the opening had appeared to expand as he had approached it with a firm foot on the gas pedal, as if driving straight out the portal of hell... or into it. He'd felt so resolute in the moment, so sure that he had left Gerardo behind for his own good. Now self-doubt and guilt crept in. How could he have done such a thing? How could he have just left him there without a single word, especially when Gerardo had told him to wait, to let him go get his things? What an imbecile. He had never had luck with relationships, and at this rate, he never would. Of course he knew that every relationship had its problems, but he wondered if it was all worth it.

Prick! A shooting pain ran through his finger. He jerked his hand back and immediately thought he'd been bitten by an ant. It wouldn't be the first time—more than one aggressive soldier ant had gotten the best of him before. He looked at his bleeding finger. It was not the typical wound from an ant bite or a centipede sting, but rather, a cut.

He looked at the soil and saw a black point protruding from the ground. Forgetting his wound, he surveyed the area and made quick mental measurements. He was digging exactly where Handy had been lying. He crouched down to get a better view and felt around his knees for the magnifying glass he had left there. His heart started to pound. Could it be? Or was it just a stray piece of glass that had found its way to his dig?

With his tiny shovel, he cleared the dirt from around the black point. Little by little it began to take form—the blade of an obsidian knife, the telltale edge sharpened by chipping. He started to move the tiny shovel faster, as if cutting away the meat of a top-notch rib eye from its bone. He admonished himself to relax, as though he were one of his students. Too often artifacts had been ruined, not by time, but by carelessness. Yet giddiness and joy were feelings he hadn't felt for as long as he could remember, and he sat up to look for Gerardo or another teammate with whom to share the find. No one.

He continued to uncover it—a nearly perfect specimen and still sharp. He couldn't believe it. He had told his students that one could never be sure, that there could always be one more thing, but he hadn't really thought there was anything left at this site. And he hadn't thought he'd be the one to find anything if it were. The youngsters had spent all the time on the dig while he had toiled away on his laptop.

After two hours of debris removal, he finally uncovered the entire object. It was a beautiful specimen with a pair of encrusted amethysts and a greenish stone, once polished but now dulled with time. A leather cover on the handle had disintegrated, leaving only a few remnants stuck to the hilt. But otherwise the piece was spectacular. Although he had reprimanded his interns countless times for handling ancient items, he couldn't help himself.

He grasped the knife as if ready to slash at the enemy, and he imagined the fiery eyes of Handy, the warrior, headed to battle with knife in hand. *Come on!* he'd beckon. *Come one, come all. Let me introduce you to the unfriendly side of my companion. He'll show you the way to the path of Uitzilopochtli!*

Then Diego heard a car door slam. He stood up and considered taking the knife with him, but thought better of the idea. He set it down and ran toward the noise.

A couple hundred meters from the site, halfway between the dig and the highway, he ran into Gerardo walking up the road. He'd never felt so happy to see his face, and he all but disregarded the sternness of it.

"Darling," he said, out of breath. "You've got to come see. You're not going to believe what I found."

"*Darling*?" Gerardo answered scornfully. "You have got to be kidding me. First, you break a promise. Then you leave me stranded. Now you call me *darling*. I don't think so. I've just come for the rest of my gear and I am out of here."

"No. Listen. I didn't mean to... I wasn't sure what to do. I thought it would be best, but—"

"Maybe you were right about that. I've got to hurry. My brother is waiting for me." He lifted his pack onto his shoulder. "And I'm not the type to leave someone hanging."

"Really? You're just leaving?" He watched as Gerardo walked up the road. "And you expect me to give you a letter of recommendation like that?" he shouted.

Gerardo turned around, smiling. "Excuse me? Are you threatening me? Give me a break. You can take your letter and shove it up your ass. You'll need something up there."

Diego stood, his mouth agape. He wanted to shout "Fuck you." He thought of the obsidian knife and the way he had clutched it, ready for war. He imagined that same knife stuck in Gerardo's chest. But he held himself back. Gerardo was right. He shook away his villainous thoughts. The knife. The knife. He had to show him the knife. And without thinking, he started running after Gerardo, who was nearly up to the clearing.

"Gerardo, wait!" Gerardo didn't stop. But when Diego caught up to him, he grabbed his shoulder and pulled him around. "Please, stop. You're right. I shouldn't have left you there. I'm... I'm—"

"What? An idiot? An asshole?"

"No. I'm sorry."

Gerardo's shoulders fell. He looked away and shook his head. "What do you want me to say? You practically told my family about us, about me. I mean, how stupid do you think they are?"

"I know. It's that your mother—she was pushing and pushing, pressing and pressing. What else was I supposed to do?"

"I don't know. Honor your promise, perhaps."

"I guess I should have found another way. I hope I didn't do too much damage."

"Well, she expects me to go right back and stay at home, nice and far away from a misfit like you."

"So that's what you're going to do?"

Gerardo shrugged his shoulders. "After what you did, leaving me there and all, I didn't see many other choices. It was humiliating."

"*Please* stay. Let's go and tell your brother you've changed your mind. Tell him I offered you a big bonus or something."

"Yeah, right." Gerardo frowned.

"But get rid of him so I can show you what I just dug up."

"Alright," Gerardo said, as if giving in to Diego's apology and politeness. "I'll be right back."

"Wait," Diego said. "I'll hold your bag for you."

"Why? So you can be sure I'll come back?"

Diego pulled the strap off of his shoulder. "Maybe."

When Gerardo returned, Diego's serious countenance had changed to one of relief.

"Done?" Diego asked.

"Yeah. He's gone," Gerardo answered.

"What did he say?"

"That my mother was going to be upset."

"Sorry about that."

Gerardo shrugged. "Not much I can do about it right now. So, what's this fantastic find you have to show me?"

Diego led Gerardo back to the dig, where the knife sat exactly where he had left it. Diego pointed toward the ground. "Right before our eyes."

Gerardo knelt beside it and seemed afraid to touch it. He seemed to have stopped breathing for a moment. Finally he said, "But we'd been through the soil. The crew's been digging for days."

"It's like writing a manuscript. Seems you never find all the errors. They just appear."

Gerardo tenderly slid his fingers beneath it and lifted it. "This is no error," he said.

"That's not what I meant. I meant that—"

"I know what you meant. I was just kidding," Gerardo said. He held the knife up close to his face, seemingly mystified. "It's beautiful." He turned it slowly and gingerly in all directions. "What will we do with it?"

"You know the protocol," Diego reminded him.

"Well, we've already picked it up. Did we even get photos of its positioning?"

"No. But I remember exactly how it sat."

"Doctors are always the worst patients."

"Well, we'll still include it in the report. I can approximate its placement, and we can take all the measurements. Then we'll enter it into the inventory list."

"Fine," Gerardo said. "Let's take it up to your office and mass it. Um, does anyone else know about it?"

"I haven't seen a soul all day."

"This will be a great surprise for them."

"Right. I have half a mind to rebury it so they can find it themselves. They could use a little morale boost."

"Protocol, Professor. Anyhow, I think you needed a morale boost too." He stood face-to-face with Diego, looking him in the eyes. He smiled bashfully.

"Are we good, then?" Diego asked.

Gerardo closed his eyes and puckered his lips.

"Someone will see us. The crew might arrive any moment."

Gerardo didn't flinch. He didn't even open his eyes. Diego smiled bashfully, leaned in, and let his lips meet his lover's. A peck turned into a wet and sloppy, full-on kiss. Gerardo pulled back to speak. "I've already lost my family today. The project's practically over. What more do I have to lose?"

Diego cocked his elbow and held it out to him. "To my office, monsieur?"

Gerardo grabbed his arm. "Oui, oui, monsieur. To your office."

Chapter Twenty-Four

AFTER ONLY a few days of traveling, everything was strangely different. Because Metzín had been there not so long ago, he recognized the jungle and the various Aztec towns they had passed on this side of the world. But his previous journey had been with his father, siblings, and a merchant party. With hundreds of painted warriors surrounding him, all anxious at the prospect of war, it felt as if he were in some different place.

He marched on, chanting along with the others, as if separated from his body. He heard the songs and the drumbeats, heard his own voice, and even felt the occasional slaps on his shoulder and back from his comrades. But inside he was not among them. He was alone with his thoughts, present yet hidden, like the birds flitting in the trees overhead. Also like the birds, whose song had been cheerful on his previous trip, his mood had changed to one of alarm. They did not sing. They shrieked calls of warning that echoed through the greenery, from one tree to the next, as group upon group of soldiers filled the woods and trails beneath them.

Metzín thought of his mother and the chants she had recited the morning he left. Since all of his siblings had taken up new homes, her attention had been focused on him. In truth, even when his siblings still lived in the family home, she had subtly doted on him. The embroidery on his cloaks was a bit more detailed, his sweet corn cakes a smidgen bigger, and his citrus fruits a little riper. As long as he could remember, she had enjoyed combing his hair or running her fingers along his scalp. He had sensed her fear as he left for war, and the sadness of his eventual, inevitable departure for death or marriage. And now she had found a bride for him in her own likeness.

He also thought of his father, the master warrior, his brothers and sisters, and all those who had raised him in one way or another, taught him the skills he now possessed, and shared their wisdom with him. There were many people to be thankful for—many people to never let down. He suddenly looked around him at the tall trees and the mountains and was conscious that he had been utterly absent, as if flying in the sky. He would need to be focused on the day of battle. Very soon the time allotted this distant tribe would expire, and the Aztec warriors would pounce on them like a hungry black jaguar. Yes. He would need his focus, for he was a claw of that jaguar.

But more than all the images and thoughts in his mind, which were more numerous than all of the glyphs on the great temple of the sun, a single bird occupied the most space. The bird was a mystery to Metzín, who could not understand why the gods had placed Tototli in his path, or let him penetrate his entire being so deeply. Surely it was not natural or normal. No other boy could have ached for another boy as he had. So, why? What was the meaning of it? What was the purpose? And why had he not been allowed to complete the act upon Tototli that he had been charged with? What if he were to die and Tototli were to live? What then of destiny?

The warriors made camp along a river. Hundreds of men were scattered among boulders. Many sat around fires, the smoke their only relief from annoying mosquitoes. A crew of cooks prepared venison and corn cakes, and group captains admonished their respective squads with lengthy sermons reminding each to honor the gods, to honor Motecuhzoma, and to honor their families.

After eating and chanting, pairs and triads sparred along the riverbank. Some practiced roping and knotting techniques. Still others sharpened obsidian swords and daggers, or tightened the fixtures of arrowheads to shafts.

"I will soar like an eagle and rip out throats with my mighty talons!" Peo appeared from somewhere up the river, his broad chest painted with white dots.

"There are no wings big enough to keep you flying," someone retorted.

The big man ran to him, toting his sword at the ready. "Do you challenge me, you useless grub?"

The other, a soldier not as tall or as young as Peo, but more lean and muscular, stood up. "I need not challenge the skills of a boar, one supposed to be a comrade."

Peo raised a finger to his face. "Then sit down or I shall sit you down."

"Nor have I the need to take his orders. You have burdened us with your foul breath and simpleminded banter for all these many years. Will you never learn that greatness never needs to identify itself? A fire need not call itself bright. And we can all see which fire here burns the dimmest."

The warriors in the vicinity laughed, inciting Peo, who rushed the muscular man. But the man moved with agility, and Peo's momentum carried him past. Peo charged again, and a quick dodge and a single push in the back from his adversary caused Peo to fall forward toward Metzín. He stumbled and landed on top of him before Metzín could react. The big man awkwardly tried to get up, pausing on all fours in a doglike pose over him.

"You," he shouted. "What is a dung beetle doing here among the scorpions?"

"Speak for yourself," someone said.

Peo stood up. "Don't get excited," he said to Metzín. "I only copulate with women."

Metzín, who had been nothing more than an observer of the entire spat until now, remained seated and dumbfounded.

"Sure," another man said. "You only copulate with women when you can afford to pay them." By this time, four men had formed a semicircle around him. "Now go on. Find someone else to pick a fight with. Unlike you, *we* know whom the battle is with."

Peo glared at them all and finally fixed his gaze on Metzín. "This is not over. You'll see." He hit himself in the chest with his fist, screaming as he walked away, "I am an eagle. I rip out throats with my talons." Within a few moments, the warriors returned to what they had been doing, and Peo's ridiculous behavior was all but forgotten.

Metzín returned to his own preparations. Though the wounds on his legs had mostly healed, a sharp pain occasionally shot through his body from the center of his thigh. He also felt sore from so many days of hiking. And in the nighttime, he ritually cut his arms to pay tribute to the gods and ask for their guidance. He searched his dreams, the trees, and everything else around him for answers but, as always, they remained elusive.

As the entire party got closer to their destination, the mood became more serious and united. Minor squabbles between individuals began to lose importance—except for Peo, who curled his lip or growled or put out his elbow to push him or hit him, whenever he happened to pass by Metzín.

Metzín did his best to ignore him, knowing that this journey, whatever the outcome, would decide his destiny. His path was like a causeway to an uncertain gate. He walked it with care. Peo was merely a nuisance to be avoided.

Finally they arrived at a site Metzín recognized as the place where he had slept with his family on a previous trip to this region. Word spread that they would set up a camp there, send a negotiation party to the tribe, and wait the final few days for the tribe's decision. Aztec custom dictated that any tribe be allowed three months to decide—sixty days to realize that resisting the will of the gods was futile. On occasion the tribes understood and succumbed. But in truth no young warrior, after having traveled so far, hoped the tribe would surrender. A battle would be their chance to gain respect, ascend in rank, or earn a place behind Uitzilopochtli. The gods needed blood, and the Aztecs were charged with giving it to them. They would wait the remainder of the sixty days, but they wanted war.

Chapter Twenty-Five

MID-DECEMBER TRAFFIC in Mexico City was heavy. Between shifting gears, Diego rested his hand on Gerardo's thigh. They drove down one of the ten lanes of Paseo de la Reforma and waited at traffic lights where street performers blew fire or juggled on stilts, and vendors sold cell-phone chargers, rubber-banded bunches of asparagus, or packs of Chiclets they would set on the driver's side window sill of every waiting car and scurry to pick up before the light turned green. A part of Diego had missed the city and the sense that he lived and worked in the very heart of the country. It was the pace-setting mecca of Latin America and the biggest metropolis in the western hemisphere. Another part of him was melancholy, for the project would soon be over, and the temporary feeling of newness in the city would soon give way to drear.

Multifloor chain stores had erected gaudy plastic Christmas decorations, reminding Diego of the holidays to come, his lonely existence in the capital, and his now-doubtful invitation to Gerardo's family celebration. The stop-and-go traffic had exhausted the other topics of conversation—the character nuances of each member of the project team—most of whom had already left the job site because their contracts had expired—speculations about the dig, and superficial childhood and college stories. They had reached an awkward silence, and Diego approached the question that had been burning in him since they began their trip to the university.

"So, have you heard anything?" Diego asked.

"About what?"

"You know. Have you talked to your mother, your family at all?"

"No. Don't you think I would have told you?" Gerardo said.

"Well, I just—I mean, of course. I guess so."

"No, I haven't."

"You didn't call or anything?"

"No. In fact, I admit I've been avoiding them—her—a bit. I've kept my phone off for the last couple of days."

"Oh. You don't want to talk to her?" Diego said.

"I don't know. I guess I've been as afraid that my mother *won't* call as that she will."

"In the end you stayed with them at the house, right? What's the big deal?"

"Come on, Professor. It was only because you left me there. My mother could have had no doubt. She was watching the whole thing. She saw me come back out with my bag and then stand there in the dust."

"I said I was sorry."

"I'm just saying that I may as well have left. Not only does she probably feel slighted by me, disappointed that I'm hanging out so much with a gay—and so maybe I am too—but she also has ammunition against you, since you left me like that." Gerardo shook his head hopelessly.

"What can I say?"

"Nothing."

"But it doesn't mean that she's disowned you either. Don't you think you should talk to her?"

"Look who's telling me to talk to my mother."

"You don't have to turn the table. Our situations are totally different."

"I know." Gerardo paused. He shifted his hand from beneath Diego's to clutch his other hand between his legs. He looked out the window, away from Diego. "I'm just a little scared to face her, I guess... to face them all."

Diego reached between Gerardo's legs and pulled his hand back to where it had been. "It will be alright. We can blame it all on me if you want to."

"Let me do it in my own way, in my own time."

"Fair enough."

The rest of the ride to the university was pretty quiet, except for the radio Diego had turned up.

They passed the security gate and turned into the staff parking lot, which was mostly empty due to the coming holidays. Indeed the entire university seemed all but abandoned, the corridors desolate, the doors closed, and the classroom lights off. But in the basement lab, the fluorescent lights illuminated the long, narrow room where the technician, Luis, sat in front of a computer screen.

"Hey, Professor. I thought you'd never make it," the tech said cheerfully.

"Traffic. It's easy to forget how congested the city is."

Luis got up from his stool, shook hands with the two of them, and led them to a microscope in the corner. "We've been doing some dating on the bones and artifacts. It's really an incredible find."

"I know. We're ecstatic. But we can't believe they're pulling the plug."

"Did you get any official word?" Luis asked.

"No, but knowing Dr. Pedraja, I know that no news is *not* good news. If things were looking hopeful, or if he had found another funding source, he would have called me right away."

"Politics. Money."

"That's redundant."

Luis shook his head. "I know. Rest assured your find is in good hands now. We'll do everything possible while we can. Right now we're waiting our turn on the MRI. It's scheduled for late January."

"*January?*" Diego asked.

"I'm telling you. We don't carry much weight around here. The medics think it's theirs. Maybe we'll be able to push it up a bit. They overbook and then cancel all the time."

"So, what did you ask me to come for, then?"

"Oh. I was going to send you a picture, but I thought you might want to see this for yourself. It's one chance in a million. I found it myself," Luis said proudly.

"Let's see it."

Luis led them to a microscope on a crowded counter in the corner of the lab. "Where'd I put it? Oh, here it is." Luis pulled out a Petri dish from a lab shelf and put in under the viewer. He squinted into the lenses and turned the knobs to focus. "Okay. Check it out."

Diego looked at the rough edge of a black mineral. He stepped back to give Gerardo a turn. "Nice. What is it?"

"Take a guess," Luis said.

"I have no idea… a piece of bat shit? Don't toy with me, just lay it out."

"Okay." Luis turned back to the counter and produced a pair of photos. Diego recognized the first as a picture of the mineral he had just seen in the microscope. "Look. See the irregularity in the edge?"

"Yes," Diego said. Gerardo stood beside Diego and nodded.

"Well, I pulled this little piece, a triangular shape about one millimeter across at the widest point, from the right femur of the specimen you call Handy."

"Okay. Tell us more."

"So, I noticed a tiny scar on the bone when I was brushing it. The bone had healed over this piece, so it was premortem."

"Interesting."

"Obsidian, I presume," said Gerardo.

"Affirmative," answered Luis. "But that's not it. Look at the other photo." The second image was a larger piece of a similar black substance. "Check out the edge."

Diego held the photos together. The edge on the second image was the obvious opposite, like a matching puzzle piece of the first. "Don't tell me."

"Yes. It's the point of the knife you sent in."

"No shit. He was stabbed in the leg by that same knife"

"Not only that. My guess, judging by the depth and angle of entry, plus indications of his right-handedness, is that the wound was self-inflicted."

"He stabbed himself in the leg?" Diego said.

"He stabbed himself in the leg with *that* knife," Luis clarified.

"Well, we know the Aztecs practiced regular bloodletting in tribute."

"True. But usually flesh wounds, right? I mean, why would a warrior stab himself in the leg, piercing his own bone, if he knew he was going to fight? Sacrifice is one thing. This may be another," Luis explained.

"As if he had mutilated himself," Gerardo suggested.

"That's my guess. I mean, can you think of any other explanation?"

"I guess they had their problems too," Gerardo added.

"Without a doubt," Diego said.

"But that's not the cause of death, right?"

"A little wound like that, already healed? No, I don't think so. Of course, he could have become infected from the wound, but it appeared to have been pretty well grown over. I'm telling you, it was a lucky find, a tiny anomaly in the bone."

"Okay, okay. You're the greatest technician. Is that what you want to hear?" Diego held up his hands in praise.

"Maybe," Luis smiled.

"It would have shown up in the MRI, wouldn't it?" Gerardo asked.

Luis frowned at him.

"Never mind," Gerardo said.

"Well, you've certainly made the trip worth it. I was worried for a second you had me looking at bat guano," Diego said.

"I wouldn't ask you to come out here for nothing. Give me some credit."

"You're desperate for credit these days, aren't you?" Diego patted Luis's shoulder.

"Hey, I've learned to toot my own horn. Us lab techs don't get much human contact, and even less consideration when it comes to job security. Money's tight everywhere."

"I'll be sure to include your name in my report."

"Thank you, Professor."

Diego held out his hand. "Keep up the good work."

"You watch my back; I'll watch yours."

"SO, WHAT do you think?" Gerardo asked, sitting across a dinner table in a restaurant in La Condesa, a bohemian Mexico City neighborhood.

"Wow, now I really don't want to speculate!"

"Wait till Brother Shoemacher gets word of this."

"Don't even remind me of him. Can't I just enjoy a nice dinner for a while?" Diego pleaded.

"Well, what could he say?"

"He'd play it off, of course, thinking all the while exactly what you and I were thinking."

"In all fairness, we can't pretend to know for sure," Gerardo said.

"I know. For that reason, I'll never speak it aloud. But, maybe inside at least, I *can* pretend to know. This seems so far beyond any typical archaeological dig."

"Don't they all become part of you like this?"

"Of course they do, but not so personally as this one, you know?"

"I don't really know. I haven't been in the field long enough. But I can imagine. And I can take your word for it."

"Thanks for making me feel like an old man."

"I didn't mean that, just more experienced."

"Perhaps, but not in all the ways that count."

"Maybe old, but never too old to learn."

"True. Never too old to learn," Diego said.

They held up their glasses to each other and took sips of their wine.

Chapter Twenty-Six

THE FIRST day was spent in organizing the camp. Though their stay would be relatively brief, they would wait at least the remaining days until the expiration of the final month. Metzín realized it was still long enough to require the arrangement of hunting and gathering duties, washing and food preparation areas, a place for prayer and tribute, and designated places for bodily functions—especially considering the large size of the Aztec party.

After he had completed his delegated duties, Metzín spent the first night with his warrior group from the telpochcalli, playing the patolli dice game by the light of a small fire. The fire served to keep some of the mosquitoes away. They were dreadful in this part of the world and, even with the fire, left him full of itchy welts. When he slept, he covered himself with his cloak to keep them from his face and ears.

On the second day, his group was tasked with surveillance—to scout out the plateau above the canyon. All indications suggested an attack was imminent, so they'd need to plan a way in and be aware of any lookouts the tribe had in place. On their previous visit, they had seen none, but these jungle people likely had clever ways of blending into the trees and greenery. However, given their resistance to the Aztec dominion, their intelligence was certainly in question.

Metzín led his team of six far down the canyon, which was like a spearhead-shaped cutout from the side of the mountain—as if a god had struck the mountain with a mighty blow and left a sliced wound in its side. The tribe had chosen to dwell in the depths of the canyon, an advantageous place for the shelter of the sheer cliffs, the naturally trickling fresh water, and the protection on three sides from foes.

The team followed a thin trail as far as they could, until it turned downward. Then they made their way through the thick jungle on the far side of the canyon. They used hand signals to communicate, never knowing where or when a savage might be lurking in the greens. But they often lost sight of one another, so they resorted to the clicks and whistles that they had refined and practiced in Tenochtitlán. In any case one could not wander far from the others, as he might be lost forever. The slopes and trees, which all seemed alike, were readily disorienting.

He had appointed ropers, swordsmen, and bowmen among his team, but they all served as scouts that day. Along the way one scaled a papaya tree to bring down a quick meal, while another dug up mushrooms they knew were edible because they recognized them from the market of Tlatelolco. They progressed slowly through the thick jungle, moving quietly, so they didn't reach the ledge of the canyon until Uitzilopochtli had passed overhead and begun its descent. There were no signs of any savage lookouts.

They peered down from the ledge, and Metzín could see some of the huts of the village between the trees on the floor of the canyon. He could not make out a temple or pyramid of any sort. A few yellow fires burned, and some villagers walked to and fro. All life seemed normal, as if the Aztec empire had never set foot on their soil or explained to them the gods' will that they accept Aztec rule. They would soon see.

Metzín visually measured the face of the cliff, a wall of jagged, gray rock, five times taller than any tree he had ever seen. It was strewn with tree roots and vines and it glistened with moisture. Metzín could imagine how slippery it would be. A fall from the cliff would mean certain death, and descending it by bare hand would take an entire morning. By the time an attack party reached the bottom, if they could, the battle would already be over. He had questioned the wisdom of the village's location, but could see now that the cliff provided ample protection. The only logical entrance point would be the mouth of the canyon. In any case the small village could not compete with the number of Aztec warriors at hand.

He directed his team along the canyon until they reached the point of the giant spearhead, where a creek turned into a waterfall that tumbled down the rocky face. Spongy green plants clung to jutting rocks where they could, and clear water became a white splendor of splashes between them. Metzín dunked his head in the pool at the top of the waterfall and felt the water's current tug him toward the plunge. If only they could grow wings like a bird or scales like a fish and soar to the bottom unscathed. The sun drew close to the horizon. Uitzilopochtli would disappear soon and make his way to the other side of the world. They would not make it back to camp by the light of the stars and the moon. They would have to stay in the jungle for the evening.

After a meal of coconuts and corn cakes, the small group of young men huddled together, covering themselves with their cloaks, unwilling to build a fire lest they call the attention of any lookouts. Each of them took a shift during the night to watch for any danger. By the time Metzín was awoken for the third shift, the jungle was eerily black despite the white light of the half moon that glimmered through the trees overhead.

While the others slept, he lay back, listening for any movement in the bush. Night birds flew across the sky and danced silently in the light of the moon. They reminded him of Tototli, and he imagined a fluted song drifting from the beaks of the birds to the ears of the rabbit in the sky—whose face was shaded on one side as if he were hiding, or shy. At once he felt guilt for thinking of Tototli again, though he could fathom little harm in his thoughts of a boy who would be sleeping so far away from him. Besides, he did not create the thoughts. Rather they seemed to arrive in him the way the songs of the birds arrived at the ears of the moon. And in the darkness, who but him would know of his pondering, of his dreams? He shook himself awake, realizing that he had begun to drift off, and he sat up to deter the sleepiness.

A noise in the black woods startled him. He could hear the falling water not far from them, but this noise came from the opposite side. Something might have fallen from the trees—a branch or a nut. He heard another noise, then another, like careful footsteps. He stretched his hand out to where he had placed his sword. He considered waking the others, still unconvinced. Perhaps it was nothing more than a deer passing through. Then again it could be a jaguar, a boar, or a savage. When a whispered voice cut through the air, he knew it was no animal. The savages were upon them.

He shook the comrade beside him. The young man did not wake. Instead he began to moan. Metzín stopped moving him, afraid to call the attention of those in the wood. Metzín and his party had not been authorized to attack or fight, only scout. None would want the retribution of the gods.

The footsteps approached. They seemed close. But then they moved past them and toward the ridge of the canyon. They had not been detected. It was only a chance near encounter. And it was a confirmation that the savages did not leave the plateau unpatrolled.

After a few more moments, he was convinced they had gone on their way. He lay back again, certain that drowsiness would not overcome him. The moon hid behind the leaves of the trees, outlining vines, long and thick, that hung in abundance from the boughs. They had not brought sufficient fiber rope from Tenochtitlán to lower themselves into the canyon, but around them he saw all the naturally growing rope they could ever desire. For now he would let his team sleep.

At the first light, he woke his team with quiet whispers and shakes. Having heard the voices of the savages in the dark of the night, he knew that they could pass through at any moment or be watching from hidden nests. Aztec law dictated the etiquette of war, the proper allowance of time, due warning, and the conquest of the enemy temple as the objective. But though the conches would sound, and the screeches of the Aztec soldier would be heard from all around, nothing prohibited a certain element of surprise.

Metzín climbed a tree and was amazed by droves and droves of ants that he met along the way. As far as he could see, the little creatures marched up and down in straight lines, bearing green shapes carefully cut from leaves somewhere high in the branches. Each individual seemed to haul an immense piece compared to his tiny size. Intermittent ant warriors with bulbous heads and spiky jaws patrolled the marching lines, and as he climbed, he did all he could to avoid them. He had seen the painful welts the ants could inflict.

The task had seemed a simple one, and he had imagined enough vines for each of his team to descend into the canyon in a single wave. When he reached the first mighty bough, shimmied out on its length by straddling the thick wood, and began to cut the first vine that he gauged would support their weight, he discovered that cutting through them would be no easy chore. And some that had appeared as flexible as cotton fiber were actually rigid little trunks themselves, covered with bark—like posts that had grown to support the heavy branches.

As he sawed away at one vine, an amber-colored, striped insect crawled up between his legs. Metzín had been leaning over the branch and all but shrieked when he saw a pointy sort of beak on its head. He lost his balance and nearly fell to the ground. His comrades below only snickered.

When the first vine fell, colorful birds in the vicinity began to make a ruckus. Metzín looked all around the thick of the jungle, trying to see where all the noise had come from. He spotted an inquisitive toucan just above him that must have felt safe, given its distance and Metzín's obvious lack of wings and apparent lack of coordination. It stared at him as if trying to determine the goals of his actions.

Then he heard buzzing about him that shifted from one side to the other. He watched as a tiny hummingbird inserted its skinny curved beak into the red cones of a nearby flower. The one seemed perfectly suited to the other. He wondered if the bird was a warrior from a past battle in a past time that had come to visit, and then his mind wandered again to Tototli and his little bird flute.

"Hurry up!" they whispered loudly from below. "You're going to alarm the entire village."

"Get into the trees yourselves," he retorted. "I can't do this by myself."

By the time the sun passed overhead, they had managed to cut and splice only two lengths that appeared both long enough to reach the bottom of the canyon, and flexible enough to be wielded efficiently. On the one hand, Metzín knew they could not take the chance of making them too short, lest they make themselves easy targets halfway up the canyon wall. On the other hand, they didn't dare measure them out, for they could arouse the lookouts or even the villagers below.

A third concern was about worrying the Aztec leaders at the camp. If they did not return for a second night, the leaders would send a search party, increasing the chances that the enemy would see them. Instead of being recognized for ingenuity or resourcefulness, he would be reprimanded for stupidity and perhaps replaced as leader of his team. A pair of vines would have to suffice. They hid the two enormous coils of vine, attached on one end to a solid tree trunk, and began their trek back to the main camp—but not before dousing themselves once again in the cool, clear water above the cascade.

Chapter Twenty-Seven

DIEGO SHOOK his head as he looked at his cell phone.

Continued funding doubtful. Sorry. Dr. P.

All but two of the interns had left the excavation site. Diego would have a lot of letters to write, returning the favor of cheap labor and poor living conditions with the promise of better employment, or at least another short-term project. Most aspiring archaeologists subsisted on meager wages from projects in undesirable places until they bolstered their resumes or their contact lists enough to land a job on a high profile site or get a teaching gig someplace. The letters could wait until after the holiday, because even archaeologists tended to put aside their exploring, writing, and project administration during the Christmas season. There would likely be few opportunities for the bulk of the interns and recent grads until late January.

The gray day brought a cool breeze from the east, and Diego wanted to spend his time out in the dirt. The only hope of keeping the current project alive seemed to be some great new find. Given the tepid reception of the obsidian knife by everyone but the lab technician, Luis, he'd have to find the Holy Grail. Diego and his few helpers had been over and over the site with shovels, probes, and brushes. Nothing else turned up.

They removed the stakes from the burial site, knowing that the grave, so singularly important to someone at one point in history, would now become little more than a patch of dirt. It would be described in his writings, global-positioning coordinates specified, and fixed in the memory of a handful of young archaeologists, half of whom would likely return to their hometowns and eventually find jobs outside the field anyway. Diego mourned the second death of Handy and Jade. Their concrete existence—their final resting place—might soon be reduced to a journal article, a batch of pictures, and the worst kind of phobic expression. The one that pushes a truth into the shadows where it will never be witnessed by anyone.

"Are you hungry?" Gerardo asked. "We still have some machaca in the food storage."

"No," Diego answered. "I don't have much of an appetite."

"What's going on? Why so quiet?"

"I hate leaving a site under these circumstances."

"I know. I wish there was something I could say or do."

"Maybe just change the topic." Diego sighed.

"Okay. What do you want to talk about?"

"I don't know." With Gerardo at his side, Diego walked aimlessly around the site, looking into the sky, at the ground, or at the horizon. "Tell me about your mother."

"Ha. From one despotic situation to another." Gerardo chuckled.

"Well, you don't have to talk about her if you don't want to. Forget it."

"Whoa. Take it easy. I was just thinking you'd want to hear a pleasant topic."

"You mean your mother is not a pleasant topic?" Diego asked.

"Of course she is. Just, considering all that's happened. That's not resolved yet."

"It will certainly serve to get my mind off this cursed project."

"Where do I start? I mean, you know her already. What else can I tell you?"

"I don't know. What's her big problem? You can start with that."

Now Gerardo let out a sigh. "Her big problem. I guess she's just stuck on having things her way."

"A matriarch."

"Yeah."

"And your father?"

"You have seen him too. I guess he figured out a long time ago that he had two choices—either be quiet and let her dictate, or get the hell out of there. Of course by the time he'd figured that out, they already had a bunch of kids, so there really was only one choice."

"And you think it's okay?"

"What?"

"That your mother makes all the decisions like that."

"I never said that."

"You implied it." Diego stopped and touched his shoulder. "I've seen it myself. He mostly hangs out watching football with the guys and a beer, waiting to be called in for dinner, called on for a chore, or called out for screwing something up."

"I know that's how it looks. But we all know that things are not always as they appear."

"Really? Do expound."

"My father may seem like an easygoing caballero, and generally he is. But there are certain things he won't accept. Like this one time that they were fighting, God knows about what, and he decides to hop in his truck to head out to the cathedral, or the bar for all we know, and standing at the porch, she hurls a tomato directly at him.

"As soon as he looked up, the tomato hit him square in the face. It splattered on him, leaving his face as red as the tomato, but not because of the juice. I happened to be outside and saw the whole thing.

"He stood there, glaring at her. She was horrified at what she had done, never imagining, I suppose, that the tomato would actually hit him! He wiped his face with his sleeve and drove off."

"Horrifying." Diego sucked in a deep breath. "You're not convincing me that he's making the decisions."

"I'm not done yet. See, after he left, she went crazy, like a lost child. She didn't know what to do. She made one of my brothers drive all over town and to all the neighbors' houses to look for him. They never found him.

"He returned home late that night, completely sober, and never did tell her where he had gone off to. They shared quiet words behind a closed door and she changed, at least for a while."

"She changed?" Diego asked.

"Yeah, well, she respected people more. She listened a little more. She doted on him."

"Was this before or after Ruth left?"

"Before. The whole Ruth incident was a different story."

"And what did he think about that?"

"Honestly, I think he blames my mother," Gerardo said.

"So, what did he do about it?"

"They've tried to get her to come back, especially after she had her children and all. At that point, Ruth was more fed up than he was. There wasn't much they could do."

"He did nothing, then?" Diego said.

"What was he supposed to do?" Gerardo answered. "I'm telling you, we never know what's going on behind the closed door. See, he's a smart man—much smarter than he might appear—and he has a lot of faith and a lot of patience. Hell, he's seen all of his kids grow up. He's put up with an awful lot."

"But don't you ask him? Don't you say, 'Hey, where's Ruth? Let's go get her back!'?"

Gerardo nodded. "I've asked him. He kind of shrugs it off."

"He doesn't say anything."

"He's efficient with his words."

"*Efficient*?"

"A word is worth a thousand words."

Diego was losing his patience with the conversation. "Sounds like a lot of denial to me."

"Things aren't perfect, but I think he has a better grasp of what's going on than you think."

"This coming from a guy who turns off his phone to avoid talking to his own family."

"What would you have me do? Go there and beg for their acceptance? Beg to be told that everything is okay?"

"It's basically what you've been doing all your life, isn't it?"

Anger seemed to overcome Gerardo. "Huh. This coming from a guy who doesn't even talk to his family. Please. I thought you wanted to change the topic to get your mind off of things, not find a punching bag to let out your frustration out on."

Diego put a hand on Gerardo's shoulder, which was briskly swatted away. Diego stood in shock, realizing he had crossed a line. "You're right. I'm sorry. I had no business saying that."

Gerardo stuffed his hands in his front pockets. "See why I'm like my father—not always communicative—because I open my mouth and get tomatoes thrown at me."

"I'm sorry. Am I being like your mother, then?"

Gerardo ignored Diego's attempt at a joke. "But like him I also have faith and patience. People come around. Sometimes they do it faster if you let them be, instead of prodding them all the time."

"Point well taken."

"Now, can we make something to eat?"

Chapter Twenty-Eight

"SWINGING LIKE monkeys? Sounds about as stupid as one. All they'll need is a couple of darts and they'll drop you down like easy hunting."

"Are you sure they didn't spot you?" asked the master warrior. "You said you heard them walking in the night. They must have a few eyes up there."

"We were as quiet as we could be," answered Metzín, disregarding the scowl of Peo, whose comments Metzín also tried to ignore. "I don't think they saw us."

"It may be worth a try. What have you got to lose?"

"Besides being crushed on the rocks below?" Peo balked.

"And you?" the master warrior said to Peo. "What ideas have you attempted? How do you intend to bring honor to the empire?"

"I am ready," he answered, leveling his sword to Metzín's face.

In the blink of an eye, the master warrior stood up, grasped Peo's sword hand by the thumb, and twisted his wrist so the sword came flying out. "Your words are tiresome, your readiness doubtful. Go. Continue your sparring. If you die in battle of incompetence, don't expect to be honored in the wake of Uitzilopochtli."

Peo indignantly picked up his sword, snarled at Metzín, and turned to walk away.

"And Peo," said the master warrior, waiting for the big man to turn around. "You will keep your tongue behind your teeth, or I will top my corn cake with it."

For the next few days, the warriors waited, filling the time with prayers, chants, and sparring. Envoys were sent to the village every second day to give the savages ample opportunity to bend to the will of the gods. At this late time, their chief's heart would be a required tribute, but was he so blind that he could not see? And did he not comprehend the great honor it was to be laid upon the sacrificial stone? Many would gladly trade places with him for the promise of eternal tranquility in the path of Uitzilopochtli. Metzín realized that if this savage chief could understand the clarity of this reasoning, he would not be savage at all. Indeed he would already be a leader of a small village of the Aztec empire. The days passed slowly, but the warriors would wait them out and ready their swords, spears, and shields for the gods' final judgment.

THE FAMILIAR sound of conches woke Metzín from a deep slumber. He opened his eyes to the strange appearance overhead of one tree twisted upon another, its branches wrapping around the thicker trunk at even intervals. The small one had small, canoe-shaped leaves that contrasted with the large ovals of its host. He had made his bed beneath the coupling for the last few days, and the wait was a true test of patience and endurance. He had unexpectedly begun to feel lethargic and lazy.

He sat up. The sun had barely risen. He remembered the many restless nights since the scouting party, which explained his sleepiness. He recalled his dreams of the vines and the birds and his many thoughts of Tototli. The conches had blown. The time had come for his destiny to turn in one direction or the other.

Many warriors scurried around him, putting a final detail on body paint, tucking in a weapon, or tightening a piece of clothing. Those few who had earned the honor bore the jaguar suit, a spotted affair of black or yellow. Their faces would occupy the mouth cavity, surrounded by its ferocious teeth poised for the hunt. Fewer still wore the greatly admired eagle suit. It boasted a grand, beaked eagle head of feathers and fiery eyes atop its headpiece. Only those who had taken five captives were given the title of *quachic*, soldier of the sun. Only they were allowed to wear jade in their ears and lips. All aspired to such a rank.

At the other extreme was stagnation. Those who failed to increase in rank were soon relegated to work the chinampas at Tenochtitlán. Those men would never be entitled to a share of the tribute or have the right to wear jade or embroidered cotton.

Metzín stood up and wiped the sleepiness from his face. He looked at himself in a pool of water and painted the eyes of the moon on one cheek. On the other he drew a hummingbird to conjure those great warriors from battles of old. He gathered his battle group together and they awaited the final order. The conches had blown. The savages would not capitulate. Their blood would be spilled. The god of the sun would rise again.

The teams dispersed to their assigned positions. Metzín hurried his troop because theirs was one of the farthest. They'd have to make it in time for the second sounding of the conches, when the fury of the Aztec empire would fall upon the village. Without further ceremony, they readied their weapons and shields and headed to the canyon.

As if he had done it every day of his life, Metzín scurried through the jungle, a savage himself. His heart beat fast, and his focus was suddenly uncanny. He reveled in the sensation, darting like a fox with no thoughts but the hunt. He had to stop regularly to allow his team to catch up.

"Move," he told them. "We are jaguars running. We are eagles flying." And he proceeded to glide between the trees.

He reached the coiled vines before the others. They were exactly as they had left them days before. Metzín noticed that they had stiffened somewhat, but he decided they would still serve their intended purpose.

He heard footsteps again and kneeled down with his sword at the ready. It was only his team members, their pace slowed to a near walk, each one panting.

"Get down," he whispered. "We may not be alone. Rest while you can."

They crawled to the ledge of the canyon and peered at the village below. As before, a few fires could be seen through the trees, but none of the villagers were visible. Metzín could not distinguish any obvious preparations for the impending attack, so he could only imagine they had made plans in secret. It mattered little because the fate of each warrior was now in the hands of the gods.

With the sun high overhead, birds flittering in the trees, and the sound of water trickling and splashing at the nearby waterfall, the conches echoed through the canyon. The first conch sounded, and then a second, third, and fourth began to blow. For a moment it seemed as if the jungle froze, the birds silenced, and even the sound of the water paused. The screams of the Aztec warriors followed—shrill calls as wild as those of the most incited monkeys—and Aztec warriors in bright colors appeared below and up on the ridge. The attack had begun.

Without hesitation Metzín and his team threw the pair of coils over the side. Down they fell, reaching the bottom as hoped. A few extra coils bunched up on the ground below. They clutched hands in a gesture of camaraderie, and Metzín grabbed the vine closest to him and directed a warrior toward the other. When he looked up, he saw the eager eyes of the youngest of the group, and Metzín allowed the boy to descend first.

"May the gods bless you," the man-boy said, and disappeared below the rock.

The others lay on top of the ridge, watching as the two lowered themselves down the vine, their shoulders and arms flexing, their feet feeling the wall for holds. Below, Aztec men swarmed into the valley, their wails carrying to the top of the canyon as if they stood only a short distance away. The savages did not immediately appear. Then suddenly he heard the thud of falling coconuts. Across the canyon, savage men and even women came out from hidden nooks in the wall. They hurled rocks, not coconuts. The warriors scrambled to dodge the stones that came down incessantly. Some of the wails became cries of pain from those who fell victim to the projectiles.

Metzín surveyed the entire canyon and ordered the second pair of warriors down the vines. Then, not far from where they were, a group of savages emerged from similar hiding places on the side of the canyon below him. *How could we have missed this? How could we have underestimated them?* They must have been hiding there since late in the night or early in the morning, awaiting the impending attack. The same weakness he had seen in the savages' defense was now being used against the Aztec army.

"To them. To them!" Metzín called to his warriors below, pointing at the savages not far away. They attempted to swing the vine in the direction of their enemies but the vines were weighted down by the first two warriors who had descended. He and two others remained atop the ledge. They looked for projectiles to throw and wondered what other surprises the savages had in store.

Metzín and his two warriors returned to the ledge with small stones and branches. Though not enough to inflict real damage, they might at least scare the savages back into their holes. Metzín could see numerous Aztec warriors climbing up the walls across the way to neutralize the stone throwers.

He called for the four men still on the vine to let go of it and climb toward the savages, who were about halfway up the cliff wall. Metzín and the other two pulled the vines closer to where the savages were, and he directed his men to overtake them. He wondered if they could, fearful they might plunge to their deaths. Let the gods decide. He would join them down the vines and share the same fate.

He secured his weapon in a sling, turned around so that his backside faced the open canyon, and knelt to grab the vine. The foliage near him rustled. He looked to one side of him, then the other, and realized he was on the ledge of the canyon completely alone.

He could hear a scrimmage below. His soldiers had reached the savage fighters. He could not risk another downward glance because the rustling near him was getting closer and closer. Two savages appeared from the thick of the jungle, spears raised overhead and ferocity raging in their eyes. In an instant he realized how vulnerable he was; a simple push could knock him off the ledge.

The face of the master warrior flashed in his mind, then the frightened image of his mother. Finally, Tototli appeared with the rapid wings and the silent flight of a hummingbird. He hovered near Metzín's head one moment, and in the next, he dove toward one side. Metzín resisted his first impulse to draw his sword. Instead he dove for the ground in the same direction as the hummingbird had gone, landing first on his side and then rolling onto his back.

The first savage jabbed his spear at him and nearly staked him to the rock floor. The tip of the spear grazed Metzín's ribs and wedged in the crack of a rock. The savage spread his feet to work the spear out, blocking the man behind him from attacking, but the tip of the spear snapped off.

Metzín hooked his arm around the savage's foot. He realized that, though his balance was already compromised, with but half a roll of his body, the savage would topple. He pushed on the rock with his back foot and the man fell flat on his back against the stone. This was both good and bad for Metzín. He had temporarily disabled the first threat, but he provided a clear path for the second.

The other man, a dark one with white painted stripes all over his body and a headdress of black and white fur, threw his spear. Metzín had rolled and exposed more of his body. As quickly as he could, he reversed such that his body was flat against the rock again. The spear flew over his chest and landed on the rock beside him.

Not knowing where his sword was or how it had fallen, he reached with his right arm to retrieve the spear the savage had just thrown. But the man wielded a club in his other hand. He lifted it high as Metzín took hold of the spear and swung it in the man's direction. The length of the spear beat the reach of the man with his club, and the tip punctured the man's midsection. He released the club and grabbed the spear, which was now lodged deep in his gut.

The other attacker managed to regain a standing position, as did Metzín. The wounded savage flailed about and his comrade picked up the fallen club. When the wounded man spun around, Metzín managed to catch the throwing end of the spear. He clutched it firmly and yanked it from the man's gut, which released an explosion of blood in his direction. The man staggered and dropped to his knees, but the man with the club lunged at Metzín.

Metzín held the spear horizontally over his head to stifle the strike of the club. It smacked hard against the wooden handle. The man raised the club again and struck down a second time, snapping the spear in two. He raised it a third time and held out his free hand to block the thrust of the spear that Metzín jabbed in his direction. The spearhead sliced his hand open but he brought the club down hard against Metzín's shoulder.

The savage stepped toward Metzín, squeezed him hard in a violent hug, and forced him toward the precipice of the cliff. Metzín pushed against the ground with his feet but was unable to stop the momentum. Instead he pulled his knees up and fell to the ground, flat on his buttocks. The savage nearly straddled him. Metzín jerked his head back and landed a stiff blow to the man's groin. He fell backward, giving Metzín time to right himself. Metzín dropped the blunt half of the spear and placed the long spearhead on the other half directly on the sternum of the savage. The man stopped struggling as his hands massaged his injured crotch. The other man lay facedown. A small pool of blood formed on the gray rock beneath him. In the melee, Metzín's sword had fallen from its sling. He pulled the rope sling from his throbbing shoulder, cut it in two, and bound the hands of the savage behind his back. Then he turned the bleeding savage over. The wounded man's breathing was labored, but the pupils of his eyes did not look hazy or large. The man would live long enough to make it to the sacrificial stone. After a few moments, soreness and exhaustion entered Metzín's body. He sat down on the rock beside the two savages he had captured.

He recalled the rest of his team and looked at the ledge of the cliff where the vines disappeared. What had become of them? Before he could lean over to check, he saw the vine moving and heard the grunts of someone ascending. Metzín went for his sword, unsure who might be coming up to join them. He took a stance over the vine to either help a friend or meet a foe with a heavy stroke to the face, whichever the case may be.

The head finally appeared. "Help me up," Metzín heard. He stood as if paralyzed by the distasteful face of the last person he had expected to see. Peo.

Chapter Twenty-Nine

"WHEN ARE you leaving?"

Gerardo asked Diego the question that had been on Diego's mind for days. He'd been skirting around the issue, afraid to approach the topic, afraid to know the disappointing answer.

"I'm the captain of the ship. I'll be the last one out of here." His voice sounded confident, but inside he was anything but. *Is now the time to ask the question? Am I sure I'm ready to invite him to Mexico City to live with me? Dear God,* live *with me?* Even in his thoughts, the word nearly made him choke. *Then again what if the answer is no?*

"What about you?" Diego finally asked. "Are you leaving soon?"

Gerardo smiled awkwardly. "Well, I'm the first mate. I guess I'll leave with the captain."

"Okay," Diego answered simply as he tried to decipher the precise meaning of Gerardo's answer. *Did he mean leave at the same time as the captain or go wherever the captain was going?* He felt embarrassed, as if he should understand the answer without asking. He despised the meticulousness of relationships and having to piece together the clues.

He imagined his apartment back in the city, and the way he had left it—stacks of books, file folders, and papers on the particleboard desk, the small couch with flat cushions, and the coffee table that came with the discount living room set. The kitchen had a single set of boxed dishes he'd bought at Walmart on which he mostly ate takeout food or meals he heated from cans. Had he left the dishes out? The bedroom was as austere as the rest of the apartment. He really only thought of it as a place to sleep and work, though he had tried to liven it up with potted plants and a couple of trees. He wondered if they were still alive.

He tried to imagine Gerardo there with him. They wouldn't have enough space. They'd have to find a new place. Gerardo would have his own things and expect Diego to keep the place neat. They'd need new furniture because what he had was only sufficient for a single person. Gerardo would have to find a job. What if he didn't? Who would support him, then? Would he think he could finish his degree at Diego's expense? They'd fight over all these things. It was all a bad idea. What was he even thinking?

He shook away his negativity and thought about the security, pleasure, and intimacy they'd shared during this project. Though they'd already had a few ups and downs, they had also come to know each other far better than Diego had ever imagined. They'd developed little routines, discovered nuances in personality, and enjoyed sex together. Every relationship would have its obstacles, and though the entire proposition terrified him, he could not imagine going on alone forever. If any relationship ever had promise for him, it was this one.

He looked into Gerardo's eyes and found comfort and safety. He noticed a tiny mole on his eyelid, nestled between the black eyelashes, and wondered how he had never seen it before. Surely, there would be plenty more to learn about this man—every day something new. It would be an adventure, and he loved adventures. He had gotten into archaeology for the prospect of discovery, for the promise of learning new things and seeing new places. In his career he never knew what was around the corner. He had only to transfer his sense of adventure to his personal life.

How had he become such a frightened hermit crab? No more. He prepared himself to make a direct proposal. *Come with me to Mexico City and let's build a life together.*

"Well, Capitán, I guess I'll go see what loose ends need to be tied up." Gerardo put his hands in his pockets and turned away.

"Wait." Gerardo turned around, which made Diego swallow nervously.

"Yes?"

"Um… are you expecting someone?"

They both turned toward the entrance road and tried to see who was walking up the dirt road. When the man came into view, Gerardo spoke first. "It's my brother, Julian. What is he doing here?" He waved his arm to signal him over.

Julian walked over and greeted them both with a handshake and a one-armed hug. "Is this where you guys have been hiding?"

"Hiding? We haven't been hiding," Gerardo answered.

Julian looked around the site and shrugged. "Looks like you're all alone out here to me."

"It's just that we're closing down, not hiding."

"We haven't seen you at the house."

"We didn't leave under the most pleasant circumstances last time."

"So, what? We're family. You know how our mother is. She'll get over it."

"Perhaps I should leave you two alone," Diego interjected.

"No," Julian said, "there's no need. I just came to make sure you—both of you—are going to be at the barbacoa. The whole family is going to be there."

"The *whole* family?" Gerardo asked.

"As a matter of fact, yes. We just heard from Ruth. She said she'll be there."

"Really?" Gerardo said.

Julian nodded.

"That's an interesting development."

Julian shrugged.

"And so you came as a liaison to make sure I'd go?"

"Bro, don't make such a big deal out of it," Julian said. "Just tell me you're going to be there."

"Who put you up to this? Did Mother send you?"

"Let's just say that Christmastime is important to us all. It's a time to have the family together, you know that, and to celebrate our unity, not our differences."

"What a philosopher."

"Listen, little shit," Julian said. "I'm gonna kick your ass if you don't go. Got it?" He held up his fists, waving them around like Julio César Chávez before a fight.

"Right. Why should this year be any different?"

"So you'll be there?"

"If God so wills," Gerardo answered.

"We'll have a Styrofoam plate for you." He turned to Diego. "And you too, Professor."

"Thank you. I'll check my calendar," Diego responded.

Gerardo, whose face had become more cheery, rolled his eyes. "Okay. You can tell her *we* will be there."

"Good enough, bro." They slapped each other's hand. "I can see you don't have any food around here, and probably no beer either," Julian said.

"You are correct about that."

"Then I gotta go. I'll see you guys. Don't be strangers."

As Julian walked away, Diego watched Gerardo and was touched by the satisfied, glowing expression on his face. A few minutes before, Diego had hoped to see that expression when he asked Gerardo to move to Mexico City with him. Now he doubted if he could ever fill Gerardo like his family did, if he could ever compete.

When Julian was out of earshot, Gerardo patted Diego's shoulder. "Can you believe it? Can you believe she sent him?" he asked with a smile. "Wow. And Ruth is going. Incredible."

"Not at all what I expected."

"And at least now we won't have to figure out what to do for Christmas, right? Find some lonely restaurant that's open on the holidays, and sulk?"

"I don't think I would have been sulking—not if you were there with me."

Diego's comment didn't seem to register with Gerardo. "You're gonna love it. The barbacoa is delicious. And you'll get along great with Ruth. Wow. I haven't seen her for… a long time."

"I'm happy for you."

"Hey, this is for both of us."

Diego tried to emulate Gerardo's glee, but he wasn't in complete agreement.

"And you have to 'check your calendar.' Please."

Diego attempted to laugh it off. "Well, not everyone needs to know that I have no friends."

"Oh, stop feeling sorry for yourself. This is a time to celebrate," Gerardo said. "I mean, I was more worried about how things were going to be at home than I let on—"

"I suspected."

"But now I can see things won't be so awkward after all."

"You must be very relieved."

"Yes, I am." Gerardo put his hands in his pockets, pulled them out again, patted his hips, and smiled. "Okay, focus. I guess I have some things to do. Oh, you were about to ask me something, weren't you?"

"What?" Diego asked.

"Before my brother got here. You were going to ask me something."

"Oh, no, I was just going to ask if you could help me close out an expense report."

"Always thinking about work, aren't you?"

"Captain goes down with the ship," Diego said.

"Do you still need help?"

"No. I can do it on my own. Just take care of your own affairs."

"Two weeks till Christmas."

"Then get a move on."

Chapter Thirty

"WHAT DO you have here?" Peo asked Metzín, nearly straddling the captive who sat on the rock. The other lay beside him, moaning, a small pool of blood gathering beneath him.

"A couple of savages who came out from somewhere in the jungle."

"Could be their lookouts."

"That's what I figure," Metzín said, noting the normal tone in Peo's voice. If Peo wasn't using his weight advantage to push people around, it was unusual that his tone would be anything but arrogant or sarcastic. "What's going on down below?"

"It's over already. We conquered the temple and subdued their warriors. The chief is in our hands."

"I couldn't see anything from up here."

"And my pathetic team was as useless as arrows without arrowheads. I sent them up the cliff and they froze in place for the falling stones."

"So you came up here?"

"Well, your team handled this side of the cliffs, so I came up to see if I could cover the peak. I see you managed by yourself."

"I guess I had Uitzilopochtli behind me."

Peo looked at the two captives, slanting his eyes diabolically. "Yes. You've got enough there to become a jaguar knight."

"Yes," Metzín smiled with relief. "And they almost got the better of me." He held up his hand to show Peo the cut.

Peo stepped close to Metzín, and suddenly took a threatening stance. The bigger man forcefully grabbed Metzín's upper arm. He lowered his voice and spoke through his clenched teeth. "These captives will earn *my* jaguar suit for me. Do you understand?"

"What are you talking about?"

"You cannot act away your immorality now." He squeezed Metzín's arm harder. "I have kept your little secret—you there in your little cave. I know your darkness. I know about the heat in the earth with your slave toy. Did you think I had forgotten?"

"Have you no honor? You cannot ascend rank on the captives of others."

"I told you my team was useless, so I came up here to rescue you. I captured these savages, who were about to slay you."

"You speak of morality. Have you none?"

"Do you want to face an execution? How would you like your insides pulled out of you? How would you like to see your slave boy pulled to pieces? Morality? You have committed the vilest act. You disgust me. You deserve a worse death than these savages. You believe Uitzilopochtli is behind you. You will never fly with him. You are nothing but a stinkbug."

"You cannot take them from me."

"Then we both lose." Peo pushed him down to the ground and pointed at him. "I take them now, and we never speak of your depravation again. Your deeds will be forgiven and forgotten. You may think me a brute"—he turned his finger to his chest—"but I do know honor. I will keep my word. I am helping you to become a better man."

Metzín turned over and hid his face in his elbow. "Then they are yours," he said. "Take them away. Do not let me see them again."

"If that is your wish, then you go away."

Defeated and infuriated, Metzín gathered his things, strapped them to his body, and descended the vines to find the rest of his team.

THE LEADERS of the Aztec war party held a ceremony to accept the savages' acceptance of their blind error. The Aztec priests directed the rebuilding of the temple top, which would emphasize a new shrine to Uitzilopochtli, though the Aztecs also adopted a number of deities known to and worshipped by the savages—the newest Aztec children.

The priests ordered the leader tied, along with those captured warriors whose precious water would soon be offered to ensure the rising of the sun. But they left a hearty group of savage men to protect the new children of the sun. As the branches of the empire spread, so would Motecuhzoma provide for his dominion.

An entourage of the Aztec party, headed by a priest and the master warrior, was left to guide the ignorant people. They would need war training, religious schooling, and moral discipline. As Metzín began the journey back to Tenochtitlán, he held the master warrior in his mind, feeling as he had when they had left the homeland, as if he were leaving his family behind.

He clutched the forearm of the mighty man. "I will stay with you, Father," Metzín said. He found some allure in remaining in the safe shadow of the master warrior to begin anew, or at least postpone the life rapidly approaching him.

"No," the master warrior responded. "Your destiny is not here with me. Return to your blood father and your blood family. You will have a woman soon and your own children to provide for."

Metzín listened to the calm, unwavering voice of the master warrior, already missing the solace he had always found in his presence. He was partly relieved at the master's rejection. Yes, he had a different future to attend to, one not found in the jungle among a strange people. As the last of the captives had his back loaded with goods from the village, Metzín said his final good-bye and joined the return party.

WEARY, HUNGRY, and riddled with bug bites after a long, uneventful journey home, the Aztec party arrived at the mountainous rim of the Lake of Texcoco. Most viewed the vast panorama—the promised land, the heart of the Aztec empire—as a happy return to a well-known bosom. Metzín, however, could not shake the anxiety that had been growing in him with every step closer. The leaders decided to push on and make it home before nightfall. Metzín fidgeted nervously with the handle of his dagger.

As darkness fell, Metzín, exhausted, entered the front door of his house. It seemed strangely empty. His mother came from the hallway and rushed to him.

"You are home, my son. Tell me how you fought with valor. Tell me how you brought honor to us and to your new wife. I have foreseen it. Will you be granted a parcel in the Quartile of the Blossoming Flower, or the Heron?"

"I am tired, Mother. I do not wish to speak now." Metzín recognized his coldness, a stark contrast to the fervent warmth with which his mother spoke. Had he detected an unusual nervousness in her? Did she not seem overly emphatic? Was something the matter?

"Come. Sit down. We must get you something to eat. Let me call a servant-slave."

"Tototli? Call Tototli to me."

"No, son. I have acquired a girl-slave to help with preparation of the food. She will serve you. And soon your wife will bring your food to you."

"I am not hungry. Can you not have him prepare the temazcalli for me? I am filthy and must carry a dreadful stench."

"Listen," she said. "The conches are sounding. You must return to the telpochcalli. They will be expecting you. They will celebrate your victory, grant awards, and recognize the valiant. You will eat and drink there, and they will praise your greatness."

"I said I am not hungry. I am filthy."

"Son, bathe yourself rapidly in the canal. The moon is out tonight. It is watching. Fly by the moonlight to your reward."

"But I shall not be rewarded. I did not fight."

She approached him and touched his face tenderly as she had countless times before. "You are a modest man, which only increases your greatness. Now go. The signal has been sent."

Of course, she was right. The conches had sounded. He could not ignore their call. He scrambled to his room, where all seemed to remain as he had left it. As he passed the front room, he noticed that the stack of cotton cloths had been greatly reduced in size. What once symbolized a mountain of wealth, stretching nearly to his shoulders, now would barely reach his knees.

He thought of what his mother had said—a girl-slave—and imagined she had purchased the girl with the cotton. But he had no time to wonder about such things. He'd have to hurry before the awards began.

He approached the canal, ready to submerge himself, and recalled the wide face of Peo—his snarl and the spit that spewed from between his malformed teeth when he spoke. He imagined his gloating face as he accepted his jaguar skin prize. How Metzín desired to alter the destined meeting of his knife. How satisfying it would be to thrust the sharp stone in the bulbous gut and watch the big man writhe. Would the oaf never pay for his crimes of selfishness, arrogance, and dishonor? It did not matter now. And perhaps as loathsome was the knowledge that Peo had not been incorrect. Metzín had his own disgrace to remember—which reminded him that he had still not seen Tototli.

The telpochcalli was filled with all those comrades Metzín had left not long before. All night celebrations were a part of the Aztec tradition. Though they looked tired, each seemed to have conjured a new burst of energy. Their faces showed that they were content to be once again in a familiar setting. Refreshed from the water, Metzín did his best to feign excitement—his team had achieved their task—but his guts roiled with anger and acidity. An urgency to see Tototli and complete his pending task overcame him. Yet he knew he'd have to see the smug face of Peo and endure his ascension instead.

Musicians had been summoned, and a great feast had been prepared. Drummers and percussionists set a happy, fast-paced rhythm. Boys and women gyrated. Small vessels of octli were passed around—a rare and normally prohibited intoxicator—which Metzín gulped down liberally. He imagined he'd fall to the ground soon. The prospect did not entirely bother him. Anything would be better than to hear lauding words about Peo.

After a lengthy round of food and song, a stout, elder warrior stood in the center of the room, holding his hands high over his head until the music stopped. The entire room fell absolutely silent as Ciuacoatl, the woman-serpent, entered. On several occasions high ranks of priests and military leaders had visited the telpochcalli. Metzín had never seen the vice-emperor himself make an appearance. The supreme judge of martial and criminal law had the broadest powers over the very life and death of all Aztecs. His black and white cloak was second only to the blue-green cloak of Motecuhzoma. An entourage of tall guards and painted women took places around the entire hall, and all of the warriors dropped immediately to the floor when they saw him.

"Ciuacoatl," said the elder warrior. "Great woman-serpent, son of Uitzilopochtli, purveyor of blessings, wisest judge, merciful and powerful leader, we are humble servants before you, mere fingers of the mighty Aztec hand." The warrior's words of praise went on—all of the Aztec empire appreciated lengthy addresses and sagacious sermons—until he concluded by thanking the woman-serpent for hearing the great acts of heroism and expressions of continued Aztec potency. "Your presence is a gift, and we delight in the generous awards you bestow upon our most earnest fighters."

Ignoring the speeches of great leaders was an atrocious offense, but Metzín could not find it within him to care, especially under the influence of the octli. Worse, as he had presumed and feared, Peo was called among the first awardees to accept his prize—a spotted jaguar suit. The elder warrior, who hadn't even accompanied the war party, shared the account of Peo's fearlessness during a perilous situation, and the manner in which he single-handedly overcame two attackers. Inside Metzín chuckled as the bigheaded man struggled to squeeze into the uniform.

Others were called and recognized, promised a share of the tribute, and granted a home in the Heron Quartile. Had Metzín paid more attention, he might have become nauseated. But instead he was spinning inside his head—so much so that he had to be nudged when his own name was called.

"What?" he said to the young comrade nearest him.

"Go. You've been summoned."

"For what?" he slurred.

"Idiot," the man whispered. "You do not ask when Ciuacoatl calls for you. Go up. They await you."

In his drunken state, Metzín could not piece together the trick the gods were playing on him. He did his best to walk without staggering, then listened to the elder warrior, who stood beside Ciuacoatl, discussing the leadership skills of Metzín and the way he had trained his warriors to use innovation to stop an unexpected onslaught. Luckily, tradition would have him only bow his head and accept the award quietly.

Ciuacoatl raised his arms over his head and placed a necklace around his head. Metzín fixed on the small jade pendant that sat at the center of his chest. Jade could only be worn by the most exalted warriors. It was no jaguar suit, though. And when the flutes began to play, the thought of birds came to his head, and then the thought of Tototli. Metzín clutched the pendant in his fist, knowing to whom the award truly belonged. He returned to his seat and allowed himself to drift to the music and await the morning, when he could return home and fulfill his promise.

He awoke in the morning, lying beside a host of snoring comrades, and nowhere near where he had been sitting. His head still spun, but now it pulsed also. He quickly washed his face, left the telpochcalli, and walked at a quick pace toward home. He thought about the disappointment his mother might feel for his meager award and his failure to earn a share of the tribute, much less a home. But his thoughts returned to the stronger current that flowed inside him. He clutched the pendant with one hand, and with the other his knife. He had to find Tototli. He had to see him.

When he entered the house, it was again eerily empty. He searched the entire place and found nobody, though some clothes were left at the edge of the canal, partially washed, and a melon was left halfway through the process of cutting. Once inside his sleeping room, weariness overcame him again, and he collapsed on his mat.

He awoke later to sounds of chatter in the road, and then footsteps inside the house. He went to the door to see who was outside. Citizens in droves walked to the city center.

He turned in the doorway. His mother stood behind him, as if she had been waiting for him. "Mother, where is Tototli?" he asked.

She did not answer. She averted her gaze, as if ashamed, and fixed her eyes on the doorframe beside him. He looked over. His heart nearly stopped when he saw beside him the ominous blue stain of a hand. He had not seen it there before.

"Mother, where is Tototli?" His voice became slightly whiny, like that of a frightened, yearning child.

She looked away. Finally she met his gaze. Tears of pain welled up in her eyes, belying what had looked like confidence, near defiance, only a moment before. "Enough! Your wedding is arranged! This is a time for celebration. No longer concern yourself with the fate of a servant-slave."

"Where is he?"

"I did for you what you could not," she muttered before she walked away.

Chapter Thirty-One

"I WILL see you there," Diego said, desperately wishing to kiss Gerardo one last time. Not with his brother waiting in the car, of course. Despite their last couple of days alone at the site, spending more time all over each other than on any archaeological tasks, Gerardo still hadn't come out directly to his family. And Diego felt reticent about any displays of affection in front of anyone.

The past days had been dreamlike. They had taken nighttime walks, holding hands in the great outdoors. They had prepared the last of the food together, feeding each other at times like silly newlyweds. They had romped on the temple top and then cuddled together until the light of dawn. With every romantic moment, Diego visualized a life with Gerardo as his partner in all senses of the word. More and more each day, he was convinced they could build a strong, lifelong relationship.

The idea sat on the tip of his tongue during all those days, but he never conjured the courage to bring it up. He found it hard to believe that fear could still keep him silent. In his defense, however, it often seemed that Gerardo would interject some comment about his family just as Diego was preparing to make a proposition. Was he doing that on purpose? Was it a subconscious way of avoiding the topic or dodging a commitment? Didn't he feel the same as Diego? In either case, he accepted Gerardo's comments as a forewarning, a way of answering Diego's pending question without it ever being asked. It was a way that Gerardo spared Diego's feelings, and a way of letting him know that Diego couldn't or wouldn't take priority over his family. Shouldn't they talk about it?

"Okay. We'll be waiting," Gerardo answered. Diego thought he saw a look of regret in Gerardo's eyes, but he couldn't be sure. As many days as they'd had to discuss any future steps, Gerardo had never brought it up. Perhaps he was content to end it, or just satisfied with Diego's visits to his family home. And Diego couldn't empathize with Gerardo's need to be so closely bonded to his family. But that only made him doubt himself even more and wonder if the absence of family had so seriously screwed him up that he could never successfully navigate a relationship with anyone. He remembered his plants. He couldn't even take care of them.

Gerardo unceremoniously got in his brother's car and closed the door. They were off. Diego watched as the car got smaller and smaller and disappeared behind a curve in the road. Was that it, the end of a short-term romance? Would it ever be the same? In his fantasy the car came speeding back, and Gerardo rushed into his arms. Nothing.

He sighed. Then a wave of sadness came over him, and he cursed himself for being such a weakling. He knew he was getting what he deserved. The barbacoa was only a few days away. He imagined the continued disappointment he'd find there, watching Gerardo happy with his family, and he thought it might be best to not even go. A clean break would be better than prolonging this state of turmoil.

WHO WAS he kidding? After three days alone on the site, all Diego could think about was Gerardo. Of course he'd be going to the barbacoa. Besides, he had no other place to go, no particular friends to meet, and he hadn't spoken with his family in the longest. He wouldn't even have a class to teach for several weeks, and the entire department would be on Christmas break.

Something inside him had changed. He no longer wished to be alone.

He decided to take Gerardo up on his offer to spend Christmas night and return home the following morning. There was no sense in making too many trips, especially as Gerardo's house was closer to the city, and he'd heard that alcoholmeters were being set up around the city and would slow traffic.

As he packed the last of his bags into the trunk of his car, he wondered why he hadn't accepted Gerardo's offer to stay even longer. Some remnant of pride persisted in him—some strange need to one-up him, or to retain his sense of independence. Not enough, apparently, to simply return to Mexico City without some closure. He had promised to go, and he kept his promises.

He turned back a final time to view the site. He thought he'd feel more sentimental about leaving. But now he was alone, with an unknown future in front of him, and the circumstances of the project shutdown had left a bitter taste in his mouth. Rain began to fall. He flipped on his windshield wipers. They clicked and clunked, removing only some of the water on the window and smearing the dirt in streaks of mud across the glass. He revved up the engine. It was time to go.

When he arrived at Gerardo's home, he was surprised by all the cars in front of the house. They were parked in all directions, an obvious sign that people weren't concerned about leaving immediately. He wondered if one of the cars belonged to Ruth. Farther back on the lot, he saw the rope still tied to the tree where Barbie used to stand and stare. The end of the rope lay in the mud.

He left his things in the trunk and walked to the door, wondering if he should knock or just walk right in. Though they had said he was part of the family, he hadn't left on the best terms last time he was there. He heard a lot of music and talking inside and decided to try the doorknob. As he walked in, one of Gerardo's sisters immediately recognized him. Diego could not recall her name. "Come on in, Professor. Everyone is in the living room."

A Christmas tree had been erected in one corner of the living room. People stood everywhere, most holding a beer or a Coke, presumably with rum in it. A few held glasses filled with yellow *rompope* and were sipping the egg-based alcoholic drink so common at the holidays. Diego recognized the cinnamon smell of the fruit-filled alcoholic punch called *ponche*. Children squeezed between adults, chasing their cousins, and the television blared with yet another soccer game.

As he walked into the living room, the men reached out to shake hands with the newest arrival, and the women presented their cheeks for an air-kiss. Though he had feared their disapproval, he noticed none. But he still felt apprehensive about seeing Eunice.

When Diego had greeted everyone, he began to look for Gerardo, who eventually appeared from the back of the house, dragging two young nephews at his feet.

"You made it," Gerardo said, lifting with exaggerated strain each foot that had a giggling child sitting on it. "Okay, kids. I've got to introduce your uncle to your mother. Where is she?" The little ones got up, shrugged, and ran off.

"*Uncle?*"

"The more, the merrier," Gerardo said, leaning over for a quick, masculine hug. "It seems like it's been forever, Professor."

"I thought for a minute you'd completely forgotten about me."

"Your insecurities do die hard, don't they?" Gerardo chuckled.

Diego answered with a grin.

"Come on, let's go find Ruth."

The kitchen was a factory at full tilt. All the burners on the stove were occupied with huge pots, which were tended by one aunt. The blender whirled, women chopped at cutting boards, and another woman stood at the double sink, washing the dishes as they piled up. A pair of older ladies hovered over a table where they pressed out tortillas from a huge mixing bowl of corn masa. At the far end, Eunice, on top of a stepping stool in front of a cupboard, handed plates down to a short-haired woman who was unfamiliar to Diego. She stacked the mismatched plates and bowls on the counter. Diego sensed an awkward tension between them. They didn't share the easy chatter and comfortable smiles of the other workers.

"How's the barbacoa coming?" Gerardo asked as he approached his mother.

"It's ready. Right there on the stove." She pointed with a nod to an aluminum pot the size of a laundry basket.

"You pulled it from the underground pit already? I didn't even notice."

"You can't even blink your eyes around here," she said. "Or else you'll miss what's going on."

"Oh, excuse me," Gerardo said, putting his hand on Diego's shoulder. "Diego, this is my sister, Ruth," he said, indicating the woman who had been receiving the dishes from Eunice.

"Ah, I've heard so much about you," she said, stepping over to him. They shook hands and gave each other a cheek kiss. "So nice to finally meet you."

"Likewise," Diego said. "It's wonderful that you're here after all this time."

"You know, I couldn't keep the children away from the family forever. I wanted them to meet their grandparents."

"Of course."

Eunice stopped pulling the dishes and turned around on the stepping stool with one hand on her hip. "And it is nice to have her back. You did meet that *nice* husband of hers, didn't you?"

"I'm not sure. There were so many people out there," Diego answered. He noticed that Ruth flexed her jaw slightly and that Eunice hadn't formally greeted him. "Señora," he said, and waited for her to respond.

"Yes?"

"Merry Christmas. Thank you for the invitation."

"Oh. Yes, of course. I wasn't sure if you'd be here, but we do get all sorts at Christmastime."

Ruth turned to Diego and rolled her eyes.

"Mother," Gerardo scolded.

"I'm just saying that a lot of people come at Christmas. What did I say wrong? Look at how filled the house is." She turned back to the cupboard. "Well, that looks like all of them." She closed the cupboard door but did not step down. "And it's wonderful to have the entire family together, to see my children and their spouses, and to see the grandchildren." She stepped down a single step, still one step above the rest. "And let's admit it, Ruth. Your husband is a sweet man, so much nicer than that girl you were hanging around with."

Ruth opened her mouth wide and put her hand to her chest. "Oh my God," she shouted. Silence fell on the kitchen. "You'll just never change, will you?"

"Can't I say that I appreciate your husband?"

"For your information, *that girl* broke up with me. And in part because of all the stress and drama you constantly caused us!" Ruth pushed past Gerardo and stormed out of the kitchen.

"A mother knows what's best for her children," Eunice answered behind her.

"Mother, you've got to stop," Gerardo said to her.

"Why? Can't I have my own opinions? Am I supposed to stop being your mother?"

"It's not like a mother to drive her children away."

"It's not like a mother to watch her children go to hell either!" She looked sternly at Gerardo and then at Diego.

"Perhaps this was a bad idea," Diego said calmly and followed Ruth to the living room.

A few minutes later, Ruth had gathered her family and things together. Gerardo caught up with them. "I'm sorry," she said to Gerardo and all those who were listening. "Enjoy your Christmas. We can buy barbacoa on any street corner in the city and not have to tolerate this. We don't need to be here, and we can't be here if we're constantly judged."

"If you go, we go," Gerardo said.

"You have to make your own decisions."

"Enough is enough," Gerardo said. "We can put together our own Christmas party. Diego, let's get out of here. Let me get my things— but don't leave here without me this time."

Eunice stood in the kitchen doorway as she watched them walk out.

Within a few minutes, Ruth and her family, Gerardo, and Diego all stood outside in the drizzle and mud. Eunice had stayed in the kitchen. Diego imagined her coming out to stop them, but no one came.

"Well, it was worth a try," Ruth said. "It was nice to see you guys anyway."

"Don't you think we should celebrate in some other place?" Gerardo said.

Ruth looked at her husband, who seemed content to conform to her wishes. "I think I've had enough for now." She handed him a card from her purse. "Why don't you give me a call, and we can get together under better circumstances in Mexico City. What do you think?"

Gerardo looked at Diego. "Yes. I might just be spending a little more time in Mexico City from now on."

Diego beamed. Though he would never have wished for the awful events that had transpired, he felt like he had received a wonderful

Christmas present. When they got in the car, he asked, "Are you sure you want to do this?"

"No," Gerardo answered. "But I am sure that I can't accept my mother still treating my sister like that. She came all the way out here, just to get practically driven out again."

"It's your call."

Diego started up the engine, threw the car into gear, and headed out the front gate behind Ruth's minivan.

Chapter Thirty-Two

METZÍN WAS afraid to understand his mother. He knew what the blue handprint meant, but he wanted to deny that knowledge. He wanted to chase after her and make her say that she had traded Tototli, set him free, or even punished him—anything but the stark blue print. He could shake it out of her or make her change the story, but nothing would undo the fact that Tototli was gone. He looked up, hoping to find an answer to the riddle, a way to take back mistakes. It was as impossible as unbreathing air or unslaying an enemy. The ceiling was as blank as his mother's face.

He wanted to yell, cry, reprimand his mother, and curse the deities. None of those things could bring Tototli to him. He thought of all the comrades he had left at the telpochcalli. Most had been asleep when he left them. There could still be a chance. He ran to his room to fetch his sword and dashed out the door, headed for the tlachtli court.

Droves of citizens were walking toward the city center. They surely had the same destination in mind as Metzín. They would gather to celebrate the glory of the Aztec empire and the return of the fighting men, and to witness the spectacle of the sacrifices to the god of the sun. Metzín, on the other hand, cared nothing about his duty to praise his leaders, to worship the gods, or even to bring honor to his family. They had all forsaken him. He was driven now by a single, burning concern.

He pushed his way through the flux of people and searched the crowd for any sign that might lead to the war captives or the blue-stained slaves. He saw none. And so he reached the tlachtli court with no direction, one more citizen among the countless Aztecs who had come.

The sun would be directly overhead soon. Uitzilopochtli was strong, doubtless intent on receiving the tribute to be offered soon. Metzín pushed through the droves of people who were taking places close to the field where there would be carnage to watch. Metzín could not wipe the image of the blue handprint from his mind. He waited for the priests to arrive with the captives—a sight that he needed to be present for but that he also feared.

I did for you what you could not. Wicked woman. How dare she? How could she? Yet for all the anger that swelled within him, a part of him knew that she was right. He knew why she did it. For all the time that he had been away, hoping for a new start, he had returned to the same city, the same home, with only one driving desire—Tototli. What could he do now that everything had been turned against him, even his own mother?

As the sun made its way toward its pinnacle, conches began to blow and drums began to beat. Metzín became so focused on his objective that he was oblivious to the sounds, to all the people around him, and to the procession of caped priests. He did not hear their words or even attempt to mutter the chants—while everyone around him sang praises to their life-giving god. To keep that life-giving force in balance, many had to sacrifice and be sacrificed.

Like an eagle on its prey, Metzín fixed his eyes on a group of men who were brought forth. Each of their hands was as blue as the feathers of a parrot. Some were older, some were younger, and each bore the nervous look of one about to meet his destiny. They wore simple loincloths. Each of them appeared the same, and Metzín did not immediately locate Tototli. Perhaps he had made a mistake. Perhaps he had misunderstood. There might be hope.

Then the slender brown form appeared from behind the others. He had a rope around his neck and was being led by a warrior clad in full battle garb. Tototli looked around like a lost child, the fear so obvious in the others somehow absent in him. Rather it seemed as if he were in a dreamlike trance, unsure if what he was seeing was real.

Metzín watched him from afar, though he felt close to him, as if he could reach out and bring him home where he belonged. He wanted to clarify the mistake, cut the rope, and walk with him to the market for a turkey, or dash away with him to the cave. He wanted to touch his smooth skin again, run his hands down the slim ridges of his back, or feel Tototli's hands rub him in the temazcalli. He wanted to see him smile and hear the sweet sound of his flute, as he flew away with little songbirds. He wanted to hold his brother of flesh one last time and look into his dark eyes—for there were no words for such feelings.

Instead, he stood helplessly as Tototli was pulled toward the center of the tlachtli court, along with the other slaves. They were all tethered to separate stone hoops like supper dogs being prepared for slaughter. The warriors handed them each a wooden sword and left them. Metzín stared at the skinny figure of Tototli, who seemed to have no awareness of the situation, nor even that Metzín was watching him. A pain came to Metzín's heart. For the first time, he saw the cruelty in it all. Offering death to the giver of life was as much of a contrast as the blunt sword in the hands of an untrained boy. And all the citizens who gathered to praise Uitzilopochtli seemed more interested in the slaughter, the spectacle of doom, and the happy knowledge that they had been spared... this time.

A priest stood on top of the great rock wall, delivering a sermon to the spectators. Metzín registered only a few words—the greatness of the gods and the Aztec empire, the constant need to give lifeblood, and the first act of honor for the newly ascended.

The drums beat in unison, making a penetrating sound that seemed to follow the pace of the spectators' heartbeats. All eyes turned when a squadron of warriors jogged into the court. They were bedecked in ceremonial battle gear. The eagle knights wore great capes of feathers and headdresses constructed of birds of prey with sharp talons hanging near their ears or foreheads. The jaguar knights bore jaguar skins, some black, others spotted. The toothed heads of the wild feline made a frightening mask with the warrior's face in its very bite. They came with ceremonial weapons—swords with their hilts wrapped in colored leather that dangled in long streamers, bows adorned with feathers, and shields freshly painted with symbols of the sun, ferocious animals, birds, or flowers.

Metzín watched Tototli, who held up the sword as if it were a broom, his feet together, his other hand at his side. Clearly, none of the slaves would be a match for the trained and virile warriors, especially with wooden swords against obsidian, and bare skin against shields and armor. The Aztecs had always said that if the gods willed victory for a slave, the wooden sword would suffice. But as many times as Metzín had seen these proceedings, the gods had never had such a will. His heart pounded at what would surely be the last time he'd ever see Tototli alive—and wailed at his inability to do anything to save him.

The group of warriors separated so there were two or three against each of the slaves. They immediately began to swing their weapons and strike blows, though some of them seemed to toy with their prey for the entertainment of the audience.

Metzín watched in horror, his stomach twisting, as one slave and then another fell. Limbs were severed, blood splattered, and one was decapitated by a screaming eagle. Tototli had not yet had his turn. The thin man held up the sword now, as if ready to defend himself, but he could do nothing against the bowman who knelt several paces from him, an arrow readied in the taut bowstring. Metzín clutched his sword, as if from a distance he could possibly defend his young soul mate.

The bowman released the arrow, which flew directly toward Tototli's chest. He twisted in time. The arrow missed and ricocheted against the rock behind him. The crowd made a collective *ooo* sound. The bowman did not look away from his target. He nocked another arrow. Tototli strained against the tether, trying to escape. A second arrow flew, lower this time, and struck directly in his thigh. He let out a yelp and released the sword to hold his leg. "Ah." The crowd was delighted.

Tototli limped a few times in place before he fell to his knees. Metzín wanted to run to him, hold him, and take him away to a safe place. Tears of fury slid down his cheeks and his knuckles were white from the strength with which he clutched his sword. Still, he could only watch.

The slaves were nearly all dead. Tototli and a couple others were writhing from their wounds. The warriors regrouped calmly, apparently to discuss their final acts. A couple of warriors approached the wounded slaves, hoisting weapons to make the kill. But the largest jaguar knight put his arms out to detain his comrades. He pointed at Tototli, as if staking a claim. Metzín, suddenly recognizing Peo, could no longer control himself. Let Tototli die, if he must. Offer his blood to the sun. Send the servant-slave to the sky. Grant him wings. By anyone's hand but Peo's. Metzín pushed through the crowd toward his lover-brother and toward his greatest foe.

The sacrifices of the slaves were nearly complete and the line of guards at the edge of the crowd had relaxed. They would be focused next on the temple where the captives of war would be offered to the gods. Metzín quickly slipped through and ran toward Tototli. The rules now were of no value to him, the consequences of no import.

The remaining warriors stood to one side. They flinched, obviously confused by Metzín, because he was wearing jade and so was also a brother in arms. Metzín moved too quickly for their actions to matter. Within moments he arrived between Tototli and Peo—just in time to block the mighty blow that he intended for the young man.

Peo's eyes lit up with rage. He made a powerful backswing and the side of his sword struck Metzín, knocking him toward the rock wall without cutting him. Metzín watched as Tototli stole the moment to thrust his wooden sword at the gut of Peo. The sword penetrated the big man's belly, surprising them all. But it was too late. Peo had already landed another heavy blow. The sword struck Tototli on the side of his head, opening a bloody gash and throwing him to the ground. Then Peo dropped his weapon and wrapped both hands around the wooden sword that had stuck him like a wild boar.

Metzín did not hesitate. As Peo bent over in response to the pain, Metzín raised his sword and swung it downward. With a loud crack, it cut through the jaguar skin and met the base of Peo's skull, partially severing it. Peo plunged to the earth with Metzín's sword wedged in the nape of his neck.

Without any other thought, Metzín knelt to the ground and took Tototli in his arms. "I have you here at last," he said.

Tototli struggled to breathe. The side of his head was a bloody tangle of hair and skin. His eyes rolled as he tried to maintain his consciousness. "You came to me?" he managed.

"Yes. I was waiting to return to you to deliver a message."

Tototli gurgled and choked. "What? What is it?"

"That you are my brother in blood, my second-world partner, and we are one in flesh."

"I know." He spat up blood. "But now I go."

Metzín looked at the other warriors who were approaching them. "Quickly. I must take your hand and do this." He did not wait for Tototli to concede, but reached for his hand. He pulled his dagger from the tie in his cloak and sliced a cut along the palm of Tototli's hand, then made a matching cut in his own. Tototli lay nearly unconscious, not even wincing at the pain. Metzín pressed their palms together, wrapping his lover-brother with his other arm. He embraced him tightly and pressed his lips against his head. Blood streamed down from their hands.

"I… I am yours," Tototli gasped. He blinked rapidly, his eyes glossy and teary. The young man took a last breath, and the struggle left his eyes. His body, tense for a brief moment, fell limp.

A couple of warriors arrived behind Metzín and attempted to pull him away, but not before he took the dagger again and made a deep, determined cut in his wrist. His blood spurt in pulses. "Do not bother," he said to them, clutching Tototli as long as his muscles would allow. "I am leaving with him."

Chapter Thirty-Three

BEFORE DIEGO made it out the gate, he felt something pound the car. He cringed, fearing he'd hit one of the parked cars. He pressed hard on the brakes and looked behind him. It was Diego's father, who stood at the driver's side window with his index finger up.

"Do not go anywhere," the man shouted. "Just wait a minute." Diego watched as he ran through the mud in his leather boots to stop the minivan in front of them. Diego had never seen him move so fast. He slapped the back of the car until Ruth's brake lights came on. Then he stood at the driver's window, as he had with Diego, reasoning with Ruth, his hands moving emphatically.

She backed the car up and parked again, then slowly got out with her entire family. Her father beckoned for Diego and Gerardo to get out of the car too. They formed a circle to listen to the unequivocal words of a normally docile man. "I won't lose any of my children again," he said. He brought his arms up, wrapped them around the shoulders of first Ruth and then Diego, and pulled them close to him. "This is no time for family fights."

"But Papá, you did not hear what mother said. I don't think we're really welcome."

"Oh? Says who? Don't you pay any attention to her. Now come back inside and make yourselves at home. You *are* at home." He walked back to the doorway and signaled for the rest of the party to follow them in. They silently obeyed.

He led them into the living room, where the crowd stood watching with apparent shock. He signaled to the people—a few adults and kids—on the couch and loveseat. "Get off the seats for a minute. Let's make some room for these… our guests of honor." He spoke with a stronger, more serious voice than Diego had ever heard from him. "We should all be ashamed to ever let our own family members think they're not welcome here."

"Ashamed?" came Eunice's voice from the doorway of the kitchen. All other noise suddenly dissipated. "Should we talk about shame right now? Should we accept any and all behavior, fearful that one might leave us? Don't we have morals to uphold? Do we go to church and pray to God, only to ignore his teachings? No. We should show tough love and expectations. Of course the door is open for all who make good choices."

He turned toward her. "You are wrong. What teachings of the Bible are we missing here?"

"If there is a man who lies with a male as those who lie with a woman, both of them have committed a detestable act; they shall be put to death," she recited loudly.

"*Put to death,* Eunice?" her husband said. "What has happened to you? Is this the woman I married?"

"Brought up with Catholic principles, married in a Catholic church, to someone of opposite gender. Yes, I am the *woman* you married."

"And since when do you memorize the Bible, only to use it as a weapon to attack your own family?"

"Perhaps it is you who has strayed."

"No, Eunice. I have not memorized the Bible, and perhaps I don't read it like I once did, but I know enough to guide me. For starters, I know it says, somewhere in there, 'thou shalt love one another,' and that's enough for me. God knows I've committed as many sins as the next person, and I am not one to throw stones.

"Once I left this house because of you and your stubborn ways. I will not leave again." He pointed at Gerardo and Ruth, who sat on the couch listening. "If anyone is leaving, it won't be me, and it won't be them. It will be you."

"How dare you?" she said.

"How dare I not? I have loved you through all these years, your flaws and all, but do not make me choose between you and my children. I am too old to tolerate your… intolerance. If there is but one thing I would like to see before I die, it is that each of my children is happy in the lives they've chosen for themselves."

Diego was as petrified as the rest of the family seemed. He supposed by their awe that they hadn't heard him or anyone speak to her like that in a very long time—except maybe, Ruth. The Christmas get-together had become a spectacle. He worried for Gerardo. Although things had swung in his favor, Diego could hardly imagine an outcome that would be positive for everybody.

Eunice said nothing more. With the entire family as an audience, she removed her apron. "I can see how you feel about this," she said to no one in particular, or everyone. "And I hope you have a very happy Christmas. You seem more than content to fend for yourselves, and I'm sure you'll figure out how to cook without me. God knows you can all eat without me." She threw her apron on the floor, stomped off, and disappeared down the hall.

"Papá," someone said. "I didn't know you had it in you."

"Don't you think we should go after her?" another said.

"She'll be fine," he assured them. "Leave her be." He looked at his adult daughters. "Now, I think you'll be able to put the finishing touches on the barbacoa, won't you?"

One of the women picked up the apron and marched into the kitchen. Then someone turned the volume on the television back up. Surprisingly, things started to return to the holiday ambiance that had been there twenty minutes before.

Soon they began passing around full plates of food. Diego took in the aroma of the gamey, succulent meat that was so tender it flaked off the bone. The meat was slathered with dark red chile sauce, chopped onions, and fresh cilantro. On the side were served his favorite— frijoles churros made with whole beans in a thick sauce of diced onions, peppers, and big chunks of bacon. Beside them, cooked romeritos, a spinach-like vegetable customary at Christmastime, provided yet another festive flavor and smell. People passed homemade tortillas around the living room and dining room in cloth-lined baskets.

Finally, they turned off the television in favor of Christmas music from the radio, and the large group enjoyed the sumptuous meal together. Eunice had still not reappeared.

As the evening wore on and the last drops of the third bottle of tequila were served in a shot glass, the conversation became easy and lighthearted. The children opened a few presents—puzzles, Barbie dolls, wooden clicking noisemakers called matracas, soccer balls, coloring books with color pencils, crayons, markers, and candy of all sorts. Soon after, firecrackers and giant sparklers were lit in the cold, dark night. The children ran around in dizzying circles, unaware of the nippy weather, the mud caked on their shoes, or the absence of their grandmother.

At various times late in the night, or early in the morning, most of those who lived nearby got their sleepy children and their things together, said good-bye, and drove off. Diego considered taking the long drive to Mexico City but, as a guest of honor, he had been served a number of tequila shots. He knew that driving in his condition would be ill-advised. Moreover, Gerardo's many suggestions that he spend the night, that there was plenty of room in his bed, became harder and harder to refuse, especially considering his drowsiness and dizziness. Not long before the break of dawn, he crashed on one side of Gerardo's twin bed.

THE SOUND of clanking dishes woke him. He opened his eyes and squinted at the light piercing through the sash curtains. He could hardly believe the sun had come out after such an overcast Christmas Day. He had no idea what time it was either, and was afraid it was closer to noon than his usual early rise. He hadn't stayed awake until such a late hour since his childhood with his own family.

His sense of surprise shifted from the weather and the hour to the arm around his chest. He recalled noticing in his trancelike sleep that he hadn't had any space in the tiny bed. He turned over to see Gerardo nudged up against him—in his mother's house. He looked around the room and was startled by the other few people, one of Gerardo's sisters and her family, lying on the bedroom floor. He nearly gasped when her eyes met his—she was wide-awake and looking at him, and he had Gerardo's arm around him. Inside he jumped and wondered how he could discreetly remove the arm. But there was no way without being obvious.

"Good morning," she said.

"Um, good morning," he returned. He'd forgotten her name— there were so many of them—and he expected to see Eunice's scowling look of disapproval in her face. There was none, though. Instead her tone seemed genuine and normal.

"Did you sleep well?"

"Dead. I can't even remember going to bed," he answered awkwardly as Gerardo squirmed beside him.

She took in a deep breath. "Me too. And I've got a splitting headache." She put her hand on her forehead. "Anyhow, I think my mother's downstairs cleaning. I can tell by the ruckus in the kitchen. Who knows where she disappeared to last night?" She folded the blanket down and stood up to stretch her arms and back.

Diego asked hesitantly, "And do you think she's upset?"

"I have no idea," she answered. "I've never seen her walk off like that." She looked back at the bedding on the floor. "Gee, I haven't slept on the floor in ages. I'm definitely getting too old for it."

"I'm sorry. I would have gladly given you the bed had I been aware."

"No, no. You're more a guest than me. Anyhow, you look quite comfy where you are. I'm just not as young as I used to be."

"You and me both."

"Well, get my brother up to help, would you?" She straightened out her clothes and left the bedroom.

Diego lay in shock, staring at the ceiling.

"Are you going downstairs with me?" Gerardo asked in a low tone.

"Are you awake?" Diego whispered. There were still other people asleep on the floor.

"Yup."

"You mean you heard all that?" Diego asked.

"Yup."

"Why didn't you say anything?"

"I don't know. Tired. And I wanted to hear what she'd say to you," Gerardo answered.

"You rat."

"Debra seemed unfazed."

"Yes, she did, didn't, um… Debra?"

"And I guess my mother has come out of whatever alcove she crawled into last night."

"What do you think she's going to say?" Diego said.

"Another reason why I'd rather be sleeping. I'm not sure I'm ready to see her." He sighed like his sister and started to get up.

"You're going down there to face her?"

"Are you kidding?" Gerardo answered. "It's going to be way worse if she ends up cleaning up all by herself, especially considering she wasn't even with us last night."

"Where do you think she was?"

"In her room, I guess. She doesn't really like to drive. Anyhow, she's most comfortable at home. To be honest with you, nothing like that had ever happened before. My parents' *discussions* always took place behind closed doors."

"Thank goodness for your father," Diego said.

"Yup. Who'd have thought? I guess people always have the power to surprise."

Before Diego knew it, Gerardo got up and left the bedroom. Diego listened intently for any screaming or arguing. He heard nothing but the continued sound of clanking dishes and running water. After a few minutes with no clues, he couldn't stand his curiosity anymore and went into the kitchen.

He found Gerardo and Debra washing dishes. Eunice was sweeping in the dining room.

"Well?" Diego signaled with his shoulders when Gerardo looked at him.

Gerardo only shrugged back. "Nothing," he lipped.

"Good morning," Diego said in the direction of Eunice.

She stopped sweeping for a moment and looked at him. "Good morning," she said cordially. There was no bitterness in her tone, but perhaps there was defeat.

"Is there something I can help with?"

"Of course not," she answered. "You are a guest in our house."

He took a place beside Gerardo and began to rinse the clean dishes while the sound of the sweeping broom gathered fury. He opened his senses, fixating on the dishes, but alert to any shift in the awkwardness. Eunice worked her way down the hallway and back. The sweeping stopped.

"I only have one thing to say and then I don't want to speak of it again," she said, entering the kitchen. The three of them froze in place, all ears. "You might think I'm just a cold and inflexible person—"

"No, Mother. Nobody ever said that."

"Let me finish."

Gerardo obediently stopped talking.

"But I do care about doing the right thing." She paused, seeming to struggle to get her words out. "I don't know if… what I mean is that maybe your father was right. Last night, I realized that *I* had been rejected, sent away for my way of being or believing."

Gerardo's mouth moved as if he wanted to respond but didn't know what to say.

"And I realized that wasn't right. There are a lot of us, and we're all so very different. I guess I was brought up in a certain way, but maybe it's not always the best way. I don't want you ever to feel unwelcome or that I don't love you, because I do. I guess I'll just have to take you the way you are. And I had to miss a whole Christmas to figure it out."

"Oh, Mother," Gerardo said, rushing to her and hugging her. "I don't know what to say. I think what you just said was the best Christmas present anyone could ask for."

Debra followed behind Gerardo and hugged her. "Don't worry, Mother. There is enough barbacoa left over. We can make another Christmas tonight."

She pulled away and smiled remorsefully at them. "I am sorry. And I know I've got some making up to do with Ruth as well."

"Stop, Mother. There is nothing to be sorry for."

She turned to Diego. "I'm sorry, Professor, if I've made you feel uncomfortable."

"No apologies, Señora. I'm just glad to be a part of it."

"I hope you'll come and visit often, even though your project is over."

"*We'll* come to visit," Gerardo corrected. He turned to Diego. "I've decided to go to Mexico City with Diego. He's been trying to ask me for some time. I'll have a better chance of finding a job there and will see what I can do about finishing my degree."

Diego couldn't believe his ears.

"Besides," Gerardo said, facing his mother. "It's not just for job opportunities and education. It's because—"

"I know," Eunice said. "I can't say I totally understand. It is hard for me. But you have to do what is in your heart. And you better both take care of each other and visit often. Now, let's get this place cleaned up so we can dirty it all again tonight."

Chapter Thirty-Four

QUETZAZOZTLI HAD paid a fortune in cotton to reclaim the bodies. Although the administrators knew the high cost of corruption—public execution—she would not stop until she had her son and Tototli back. She had spent the entire evening preparing them—cleaning their wounds and saying prayers—and now drifted down a canal before dawn to get far enough away that they might be laid in eternal peace.

Metzín's father was at a meeting of dignitaries. Supposedly responsible for his son's upbringing, he had seemed aloof throughout the boy's suffering, even unaware of his death. The pochteca cared little for games or gambling, only their merchant business. They were separate from the common Aztec life.

But she had known. She had seen the looks her son had given the servant-slave, and she had heard the abundant interest in his voice. Their sessions in the steam baths had been lengthy. Their frequent whimsical trips to the market had seemed strategically planned. His father had no clue. Did men ever really know what was happening with their children? Could men ever put aside regiment or custom for parenting? She knew. She had witnessed their deaths. And she could make any sacrifice to mother her son this final morning.

The boatman poled the canoe along in the darkness. The only sound was the water dripping into the river and the subtle swish of the canoe along the smooth surface of the water. The moon had traveled beyond the horizon. They traveled by the scant starlight reflecting on the black water.

At her feet, two young men, mere boys in her eyes, lay lifeless. So much had she planned and hoped for him. So much had she feared for him. She saw now the futility of her planning and fear. The gods had their own plans. She was powerless to change destiny. She had tried, and she had lost everything.

Another hired man sat in the front of the canoe. Perhaps he had misgivings about the task at hand, but she did not care about his feelings or the consequences. She even considered sacrificing herself and following in the steps of her youngest son somewhere in the big sky. But this was the death of a child, not the birth of one, and a woman could never join a warrior in these circumstances. The only thing she could do was attempt to set things back on the path that had been created for him even before the hollow day on which he had been born.

They drifted on, past the edge of Tenochtitlán, past the rows of chinampas, toward the far shore of Lake Texcoco. By the time they reached it, yellow light had appeared beyond the mountain peaks. The burial would be Uitzilopochtli's first sight.

"Stop here," she said somberly, eyeing the black outline of a decrepit temple. It was a remnant of a bygone people, yet still the sacred ground of a god who certainly remained. They turned toward the shore and the boat bumped gently against soft clay. She stepped out of the canoe, and her feet sank into the muddy shore. She walked a few steps up from the water. An invisible bird flew overhead. Its flapping wings made a clapping sound. She closed her eyes and mumbled a chant. "Here," she ordered. "Dig here."

She watched and waited as the men dug with gravity and liquidity working against them. At the bottom of the pit, a shallow pool formed, and the workers waded ankle-deep.

"Stop now," she told them, signaling them out of the grave.

She pulled Metzín's dagger from her tunic and grasped it tight, feeling the energy of her son's hand where hers was. Then she threw the knife into the bottom of the pit, as if to measure its depth. "Okay. Bring them."

She stared into the grave as the men pulled Tototli from the canoe. They carried his body easily but carefully between them, like a bunch of cut flowers brought to market.

"Lay him down." There would be no cremation for these two. The gods would know where to direct their spirits even if she did not. Metzín, her child of two worlds, would remain on this plane too, ever close to her, and ever close to him.

They set the bodies in the hole. "We cover them now?" the man said.

"Wait," she said. She lowered herself into the grave with them and put her hand on Metzín's forehead, then on his cheek and on his cold neck. She recalled his round black eyes and the way he had looked at her on the first day of his life. Her boy of two worlds. With her fingers, she found the clasp of the necklace behind his head. She unclasped his necklace, brought it over to Tototli, and fastened it on his neck. "Whoever you are, for whatever magic you carried over my son, he would give this to you."

She turned again to Metzín, who was wearing the cloak she'd made for him with such attention to detail, so much more than she had exerted for his siblings. She lifted his soiled hand to her lips one last time and rubbed her thumb against the sliced skin of his palm. She then put her hand on Tototli's face and slid it down over his eyes and lips. She touched his chest and then his hand with the matching cut. "My children, be together for eternity, if that is the path meant for you." She put their hands together, and laced their fingers together.

Finally, she stepped to the side of the grave and waited for the boatman to help her out. At the edge of the pit, she looked at the little temple not far from them and then down at the pair. She sang a quiet song.

> *I sing here*
> *To call on the sunrise*
> *And life like purest jade*
>
> *I sing here*
> *Where you are now*
> *Where your parents live in toil*
>
> *I sing here*
> *Not knowing your destiny*
> *Not knowing your fate*
> *Lamenting your passing*

"Now cover them, and forget you ever saw this place or these boys. They are beyond us. Do as I say and be blessed, or betray yourselves to cursedness," she said to the waiting men.

The tip of the sun shone over the high mountains as the canoe returned to Tenochtitlán. She would not see her son again, she knew, nor would she ever speak of him again. Even if her husband were to ask about him, she would not say. She had to make up for the desperate error she had made. She had to let him be in peace where no one would ever know about their secret, or their gift. No, she would never see him again, but she would look for him in the freshness of the flowers, in the flight of the hummingbird, in the whistle of the songbird, in the savory flavor of his favorite dish, in the brightness of the sun, and in the quiet face of the moon.

Chapter Thirty-Five

DIEGO HAD left an envelope from the archaeology foundation on a corner of his office desk for over a week. "Official Business" was boldly stamped on it. He had no interest in opening it, but he figured he'd put it off long enough. He peeled it open and read the header: "Notice of Termination of Project Funding." Then he read the first lines, "Dear Professor Alvarado, We regret to inform you...." He scrolled down to the signature: "Brother Shoemacher, Biblical Archaeologist, Catholic Archdiocese of Mexico." He signed his name in tight block letters with a little cross above the last letter.

He began to crinkle the letter in his hand but regained control of himself as another thought occurred to him. He set the letter down without even showing it to Gerardo, who was his new teaching assistant. Instead, he said to him, "Come downstairs with me."

They went directly to the lab and found Jade and Handy right away. Luis looked on apparently chagrined.

"Why the hell were they separated?" Diego asked furiously, looking at the two individual skeletons on the stainless steel table.

"They had to be," Luis responded timidly. "Direct orders from the dean. Besides, Professor, they wouldn't have fit in the MRI machine. We're due early next week." He rubbed his chin. "If it's any consolation, we've got plenty of pictures."

"*Pictures*? I've got pictures. Do you realize what you've done?"

"I have to follow the directives I'm given, Professor. You know how it works. We're passing the baton to the forensics guys now."

Diego clenched his teeth. "Fucking bastards," he said under his breath. "Could you at least leave us a few minutes by ourselves with them? We spent enough time with them in the field and I fear this may be the last time we'll see them. Funny, I've been asked for the report by this Friday, *before* the MRI is scheduled, and I've been assigned an extra pair of introductory classes."

"Of course, Professor. I was just about to take a break anyway. Take your time."

He went to Gerardo, who stood over Jade. At least no one had the power to alter the free-hiring practice of teacher assistants or the course-load-to-assistant ratio. They both looked down at the familiar body and shook their heads at the stupidity. Everything about the skeleton was familiar to him from the countless hours he'd spent with it. But he knew it would just be another skeleton in the annals of history—one more set of Aztec bones. They were all important in their own way, but the fact that they'd been carefully connected at the hands had made the find distinct. Surely there were other ways to scan them.

He walked to Handy and looked at his face. He was immediately aware that science was meeting subjectivity, because he saw a more sullen expression in his sockets, as if they were deeper, sadder, or lonelier. Diego had traveled back in time with him and tried to piece together his story, his plight, and all the highs and lows he had lived that brought him to such an unusual resting place. Because of politics or phobia, it seemed impossible to keep them from ending up as nothing more than two skeletons in separate wooden crates stored in a warehouse someplace.

"Oh my God, you're not going to believe this," Gerardo said, his hands beneath the remnants of loincloth at Jade's hips.

"What is it?" Diego asked, stepping over quickly. His first impulse was to reprimand Gerardo for digging in so forcefully with his fingers, but he was already too angry to care.

"I don't know, something wedged in the hip, between the bones in the obturator foramen."

Diego would have expected nothing but sediment between the bones. They had been so careful to preserve the remaining cloth that they could have missed something beneath it. The fluorescent bulbs in the laboratory certainly provided more light to work with than the varying shades of gray and yellow in the outdoors.

"Hurry it up, then," Diego said, glancing at the door.

Finally, Gerardo pulled a round chunk of dirt about the size of a plum from the lower cavity of the pelvis. He turned it over so Diego could make out a form. He darted to the counter, located a hard brush among the tools, and passed it to his partner. "What is it?" he asked, unable to control his excitement.

Gerardo took the brush and scraped away the soil to reveal a tiny black vessel in the shape of a bird. It still had some of its original painted designs. Four little holes on the top and another on the beak indicated that it was a musical instrument. Diego went back to the workbench to fetch a pick, which Gerardo used to clear the soot from the holes.

"A little flute," he said delightedly. He held it delicately up to his lips by the little wings, watching Diego's reaction, as if waiting for a reprimand. He blew. A single note cut through the air. "Still works," Gerardo said with a satisfied smile.

Diego regarded him lovingly and felt some of his anger disappear.

"Well, Luis will be back any second," Gerardo said, setting the flute on the table. "I guess it's one last thing for the inventory."

Diego picked it up, feeling unusually mischievous. "Keep it," he said, handing the tiny bird to Gerardo. "It's a welcome-home present."

Gerardo put out his hand reluctantly. "Are you serious, Professor? That's totally against protocol."

"Shut up and put it in your pocket before I change my mind."

Gerardo stowed it in the front pocket of his coat as Diego, still standing beside Jade, replaced the loincloth as best as he could.

A minute later Luis returned with a steaming cup of coffee. "Did you have enough time, gentlemen?"

"Yes, Luis. We were just on our way out."

"Don't be a stranger, Professor. We'll get 'em the next time."

Diego positioned himself between Luis and Gerardo. He shook Luis's hand. "Take good care of them, Luis."

"I'll do my best."

"YOU'RE A bit of a rebel, Professor." Gerardo still had the prize in his coat pocket. The two stood on the metro platform, waiting for the next train to appear from the tunnel at the Universidad Station. They had agreed that they could save money and time by taking the metro from

Diego's apartment in the center of the city. Gerardo had few personal belongings, so he adapted easily enough to Diego's apartment. But they aspired to start anew, perhaps even purchase a condo together a little closer to the university, where they would both work while Gerardo studied. Because he was now an employee, his application to reenter the university to complete his degree was a shoo-in.

They made the commute in relative silence. The long orange wagon was packed during the early evening hours. It had taken Gerardo a couple of weeks to become accustomed to a place of such enormity, diversity, and constant movement, but now he seemed to have adjusted to the flow of people in one of the world's busiest public transportation systems. They stood in the aisle of the train, grasping the handrails to maintain their balance against the constant jerks and sways. They stole giddy glances at each other among the horde of people.

Once in the apartment, they inspected the flute again, dusted it carefully, and removed the debris. They talked over where it might have come from—the great market or a faraway city. Gerardo played it for a short while but was afraid of damaging it. Then they each went to their personal routine. Gerardo tended to the potted plants and supper while Diego sat at his laptop to continue his work.

An hour later Gerardo called Diego to the dining room table, and he arrived carrying his laptop. "Will this be a working dinner?" Gerardo asked as he placed a plate of chicken in pipián chile sauce in front of Diego.

"Just putting the last finishing touches on it," Diego answered.

"Finished with the report already?"

"No, not the report, the *article*."

"Article? I thought you were finishing up the report," Gerardo said.

"The report can wait. I think this is more important. Anyway, no one else ever gets their report in on time. And what difference does it make? The project is over."

"What article are you talking about, then?"

Diego turned his laptop so Gerardo could see the title on the screen: "A Homophobic Cover-up in Aztec Archaeology." He scrolled down so Gerardo would see the pictures of the ancient couple, pausing on the close-up that emphasized their joined hands.

Gerardo leaned in and placed his hands on Diego's shoulder. "Seriously? Is that for *The Journal of Archaeology*?"

"No, my dear. This article is for *Muy Interesante*. But I'm not stopping with a Mexican news magazine. I'm sending the article to a translator and to connection of mine at *Time Magazine*. He owes me a favor."

Gerardo let out a triumphant whistle. "I take back what I said, Diego. You're not just 'a bit of a rebel.' You are becoming the definition of one."

"You give me wings," Diego said, tilting his head back for a kiss.

"Well, how about we celebrate with a beer downtown?"

"Sounds good," Diego answered as he pushed his plate of chicken away. "You know, this looks delicious, but what do you say we save it for tomorrow and go get something to eat? I think I have just the idea for hungry eagles."

"What do you have in mind?"

"Ah, let me take you to one of my favorite taquerías, then, not far from the cantina. You're going to love this place."

"What kind of tacos?"

Diego smiled and winked. "Barbacoa."

Born in San Francisco in 1970, ERIK ORRANTIA studied psychology, determined to become a therapist. When he began working as a school counselor, he found a calling in education and, later, all things Mexican. He studied in Mexico City for a year and decided to live in Tijuana to perfect his Spanish and remain immersed in the Mexican culture. He has lived there since 1998, absorbing more about Mexico every day. He taught middle school for fifteen years in California, and now works in the world of finance.

He has traveled extensively throughout Mexico. One objective of his writing is to share the nuances of Mexican culture unknown to most. In addition to teaching, traveling, and writing, he spends time in the gym, attempting to stay fit. He also enjoys cooking and relaxing with his husband and partner of ten years, Francisco Orrantia. He won the 2010 Lambda Literary Award in the gay romance category.

DAY OF THE DEAD
A Romance

ERIK ORRANTIA

http://www.dreamspinnerpress.com

A TEXAS PINEY WOODS STORY

Glory
LANDS
VASTINE BONDURANT

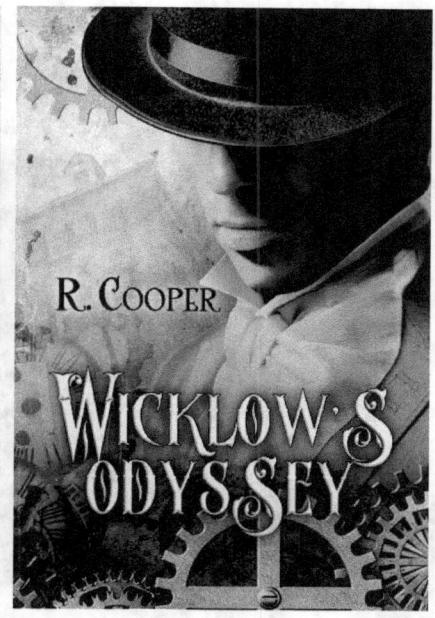

R. COOPER

WICKLOW'S
ODYSSEY

WALLS THAT
DIVIDE
Michael Murphy

Theo Fenraven

Blue
River
A TIME TRAVEL TALE

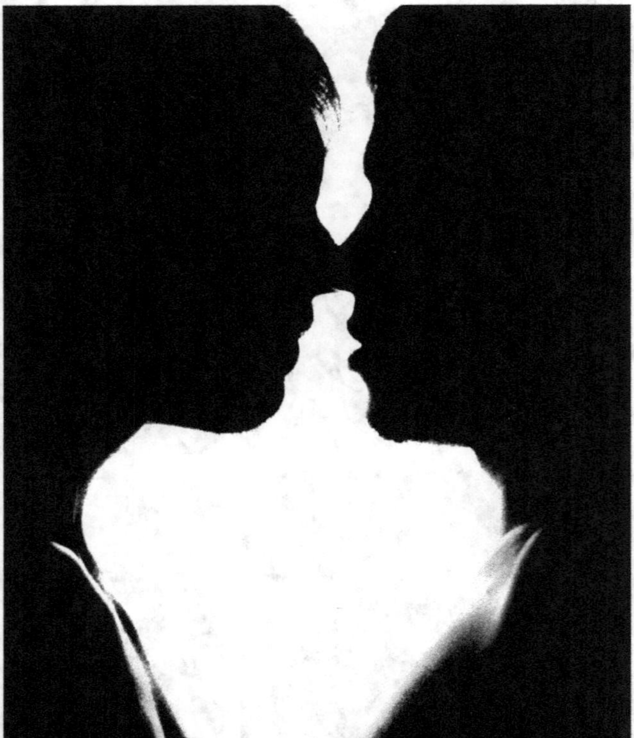